NICCI CLOKE

*Someday Find Me*

FOURTH ESTATE • *London*

First published in Great Britain in 2012 by
Fourth Estate
An imprint of HarperCollins*Publishers*
77–85 Fulham Palace Road
London W6 8JB

1

A catalogue record for this book is
available from the British Library

ISBN 978-0-00-744761-9

FSC™ is a non-profit international organisation established to promote
the responsible management of the world's forests. Products carrying the
FSC label are independently certified to assure consumers that they come
from forests that are managed to meet the social, economic and
ecological needs of present and future generations,
and other controlled sources.

Find out more about HarperCollins and the environment at
www.harpercollins.co.uk/green

*To Mum, Dad and Dan, with love*

*The sun always shines on our house. It shines all day every day, even when it's raining and even when it's dark. We stay up late at night and soak it up, talking for hours and hours about nothing at all. We like to hold hands when we're finally falling asleep, because if we do, we'll be together even in our dreams. When we go out we go to the park and walk in circles with people smiling and the sun shining and the world stretching out around us. We sit in the grass and make chains of flowers and then we lie down and look up at the clouds.*

*People say we're made for each other and maybe they're right. It seems like we've known each other for ever and life before seems dusty and faded, like old memories that belong to other people. Like we only really began when we found each other. We tell each other our secrets and our fears and everything that happens to us each day. When we're at work we're always thinking of each other. We finish each other's sentences and speak each other's thoughts. We're not great minds but we always think alike.*

*We love to go out and catch a high and dance. We like to put the music up loud and dance together until the sun comes up. We dance on the furniture and we find each other's fingers and we hold them tight.*

*We've both been in bad places but we don't look back. Everything in the past has faded far into the shadows and when we think about everything ahead for us together we laugh and dance and sing. And then we look at each other and we smile and it's just the two of us sitting in the sunshine looking forward.*

## (ALL BEGINNINGS HAVE AN END)

There are certain rare moments when it is possible (or so it might seem) to leave your body behind. It might be in a moment of pure joy, with love in your heart or a new life in your arms. Or a moment of desperate sadness, with bad news in your ear or a loss weighing heavy on your soul. A moment of boundless passion, of uncontrollable rage, of icy shock. At these moments in these lives, one thing is true. They are moments when it is suddenly irrevocably clear that things can never be the same again; that a feeling or an action has changed the landscape of everything believed and lived in. It is a window out, but there is no way back in.

I watched myself that day, lying helpless on the bed. I watched them bend and lift me, pulling clothes over my cold body. I watched him watching too, from the corner of the room, a bag of my things in his hand. I watched his eyes meet mine, in a moment that stretched on for ever, in a moment when the light between us flickered and died, and then I watched him turn away, tears falling down his face.

'I'm sorry,' was all he could say.

'Losing'

# FITZ

I still remember the first night I met Saffy clear as day, like it was yesterday. It was at some knobhead's party – someone Alice knew or someone she wanted to shag or someone she had shagged was having a bit of a do and she dragged me along and I said yes even though I really didn't want to. It's not like I don't like parties but I'm not exactly the life and soul and I get a bit weird with new people I don't know and it takes me a few drinks to warm up and have a giggle so it's not exactly my idea of fun, going off to some posh git's Notting Hill pad when I know Al's gonna sack me off the minute this toff's waved his cravat at her. But she really wanted to go and I love her to bits, as a mate I should stress, so I said yeah and I went along and to be fair to her she did buy me a little bottle of voddy as a thanks, and you gotta hand it to her, she knew how to get me out of a funk cos I was made up with that and swigged it all on the way there.

So I was a bit happier when we got to the place, feeling a bit more limber and not like I was going to spend the whole night crouched in corners like a total leper. Anyway, when we got in the house I was buzzing a bit and she slipped me a couple of lines in the downstairs bog, and I was thinking how I'd given her a bit of a rough time, poor old Al, and so I had a little dance with her and then I went and got her a drink out the kitchen, but I was right after all cos when I got back to the lounge with two beers making my hands cold she was nowhere to be found. So I drank both the beers and stood at the side and watched people dance for a bit, and then I realised I still had Al's wrap in my pocket so I did a bit more, knowing she wouldn't mind, and secretly hoping someone would ask for a bit cos bag is quite useful like that in awkward social situations, and then I wondered what to do with myself and I thought I should probably bite the bullet and have a chat to someone instead of standing there like a right plum.

Yeah, that's when I saw Saf the first time. I'd just stood up off my perch on the windowsill and was daddylonglegsing around looking for someone to chat to and not getting far, they were really twatty this lot and I'm easygoing me but even I didn't want to chat to any of them. And there she was, leaning up against a bookcase and sipping at a drink instead of talking, up and down the cup was going to her lips, clink-clink-clink with the ice. And I don't mean it in a wet way or anything but the room did stand still for real, just me and her looking at each other and that was it. We spent the whole night there leant up against the bookshelves, not really saying much just being together being special, her fiddling with the edge of my T-shirt and me twiddling a bit of her lovely yellow hair between my fingers. She was like a cartoon, Saf, big Bambi eyes and loads of big knotted beddish hair all falling down around her. Behind us the rest of the party were yelling out that they were our friends and that we'd never be alone again, and when I looked down at Saffy in her sequinny sparkly top and her little shorts and her biker boots, I did think, You know what, I reckon they might be right. About that last part anyway.

Those days rushed past in a big fizzy blur. I woke up every morning thinking of her little face and the way she laughed, how her eyes creased up and how she held on to her sides with her arms wrapped around herself in a hug, and anyone around would laugh too, because she was catching, she was like happiness in a lovely little bottle, opened up and spilling out. I'd spend all day long wondering if I should call or text her and the best thing was I felt like maybe she was in a room somewhere else in the city, thinking just the exact same thing, just the two of us sat there with our phones in our hands, like the matching bookends my mum had when I was a kid, but with buildings in between us instead of books, just waiting to be stuck back together. I'd go to bed and the last thing I'd think about would be her, and the way her voice would speed up when she was excited, all the words all squeezed together as they flew past you like lovely silver birds. I'd spend all my time thinking about her, and all the time I was with her staring at her, soaking her up and drinking her in and trying to remember exactly how she looked and how she sounded and what she said and the way she stared back at me, because I knew after she left I'd never believe that last bit was true. But it was. She stared at me with her big eyes and I'd feel like I didn't want to breathe or move a single muscle in case the spell was broken and she looked away. Sometimes she'd touch me, really gently, when I was in the middle of saying something stupid or trying and usually failing to be funny: she'd reach out and stroke my hand or touch my knee and it would be like all my fingers and all my toes wiggled and all the hairs on my arms jumped up and did a little dance.

Not long after we met, she had to go away for a week, on holiday with her family; her parents and her three sisters. She didn't like her parents much, you could just tell, not by anything she said but just by the way her face changed the tiniest bit without her meaning it to or even noticing when she talked about them. It's funny the things you see when you're watching someone, really watching them. The smallest silly things that seem like these amazing secrets. Now I know that it's the things you miss that fuck it all up. The big fuck-off-in-your-face things that you just don't notice until it's too late. Seeing is a funny thing like that – it's not straightforward like you think when you're a kid. Sometimes the only things you see are the things you really really want to see.

That week was like the longest week ever invented. Every day seemed like a million days all shoved together and stretching on for ever. We sent messages when we could and I felt like those few words were the only place I could breathe, like I'd open a text on my phone or type one out and send it to her, and I'd take a big gasp of air because that was like popping your head up above the surface when you're swimming deep down in a dark scary sea. I thought to myself that I'd never be without her again if I could help it, and I guess she must've felt the same because the day she came back she asked me to move in with her.

I felt like my head might pop right off with happiness. She said it all shy, like she thought I was going to say no, and in the end I didn't say anything, I just picked her up and swung her round and round and it seemed like by the time we'd stopped spinning I'd packed up all my things and plonked myself right in her life, like I'd always been there.

Life with Saffy was the best thing in the whole world, like living in the kind of picture you drew when you were a kid of a little square house with smoke swirly-whirling out of the chimney and a girl stick-figure and a boy stick-figure holding hands in the garden. Not that we had a garden, or a house, just a basement flat near King's Cross with a strip of concrete at the bottom of the stairs off the pavement, but you get the idea. It was like a made-up happy dream that could never be true, except that the very best thing about it was that it was. She pottered about all day in her pretty dresses and her big fluffy socks, making me tea and big fat sandwiches and sewing things and putting up pictures and pretty paper-chain things around the flat, and she'd do this really cute thing when she was doing the washing-up or putting things on a shelf and she'd blow all the blonde hair out of her eyes and it'd go up *whoosh* and then fall straight back down onto her spiky black lashes.

The whole place was full of things she'd drawn or painted or made and even though I could never let on how properly bowled over by them I was, because she got all embarrassed and shy, I'd sometimes end up just staring at them, just completely done in by them, at how someone I knew and talked to and woke up next to every day could do something so beautiful and special that made you feel something she wanted you to feel, or see a story she wanted to tell you. I didn't know much about art and she tried to explain them to me properly sometimes but even I could see that there was something big behind them, something real.

Al was pretty knowing about all that stuff and once she came round and saw something Saf had left up to dry and she said it was the best thing she'd seen in a long time and Al wasn't really one for false compliments, especially seeing as Saffy wasn't even there to hear her.

And that was how every day was, just chatting and enjoying this tiny space, these three little rooms – bedroom bathroom living room slash kitchen – we lived in and filled up, and forgetting it had ever been any other way. I'd sneak up behind her all the time and give her these big cuddles and growl into her neck even though if I'm honest I'm not really someone who can carry off a growl, and she'd squeal and giggle and it seemed like we were just laughing all the time. I worked the same hours I'd always worked, which was a shedload, but looking back now it pretty much seems like I was never anywhere else, just floating on my Saffy cloud and spending hours and hours cuddling or dancing or chatting or walking through the park or lying in the grass and looking up at the sky.

You can't cuddle in parks for ever and we all know that. Sooner or later it's going to rain or get dark or you're going to sit in dog poo or get stung by a bee. Even when the sun's shining on you you'll get burnt if you try and stay there too long. But with me and Saffy, it seemed like time stopped if we wanted it to, and if we wanted to stay for ever and ever in the park staring up at the sky or lying flat on our backs on the floor in our lounge talking about the silliest things anyone could think of, we could.

I was thinking about those first weeks that night, sitting in my chair with the lappy in front of me, looking at the horses. Lovely smells were coming out of the kitchen, and lovely little Saffy singsong notes as she hummed away at the hob, stirring things and poking things and pouring things. One of her favourite things was cooking, sometimes for the three of us, me and her, and her best mate Quinton, who lived with us too, but most times just the two of us, all special even on weeknights. Quin had gone out, but he was always out, a proper social butterfly was what my mum would've called him.

I could hear her behind me at the counter, cooking away, singing a few lines of a song as she turned off the hob and opened the oven and took down plates and ladled stuff and spooned stuff and sprinkled stuff, and I thought to myself how home wasn't a place, it was a person, and wherever that person was everything could feel okay and warm and magic. In she came then, my little Saffylicious, with a plate as big as her head held out in front of her and a big shiny smile on her lovely face. She shuffled the lappy off to one side and put the plate down and she said, '*Bon appétit*, baby,' because she was good at everything Saffy, even speaking all kinds of languages. Maybe just French and Spanish, thinking about it, but those plus English is three and that's a lot by anyone's standards. And she skipped off to her corner of the sofa because I always sat in my chair to eat and then I'd come over to the sofa and snuggle her up until you could hardly see her for cushions and cuddle.

She turned the volume up on the telly as I got my fork and put a little bit of every yummy thing on the plate all squooshed up on it until it was almost too big to go in my mouth. I hadn't been watching cos I'd been listening to the racing on the laptop and so it had ended up being on the news, which me and Saf always tried to watch because you're meant to when you're a grown-up and living together but we always got bored five minutes in and put cartoons on or whatever girly *Next Best Really Ace Model* and *My Super Amazing Really Expensive Wedding* thing Saffy was into that day. I put the fork in my mouth, and my mouth was so full of food it was hard to chew, but it was so tasty it was okay to just swallow it in big lumps.

The lady on the news had on her serious this-isn't-a-story-about-the-world's-oldest-milkman-or-the-smallest-kittens-in-history kind of face. Saffy didn't turn it over; we both put on our grown-up serious faces too and listened.

> 'A university student has been reported as missing
> in the capital today. Fate Jones, nineteen-year-old
> daughter of businessman Lowen Jones, was last seen
> leaving a pub in the City on Tuesday evening. Police
> are treating the disappearance as suspicious, and
> urge residents who may have any information to come
> forward.'

They showed a picture of her on the screen then, with a police hotline number underneath in bold. We looked at it for a bit without saying anything, and I stopped trying to chew, even though there was mashed potato falling out between my lips, because it seemed rude somehow, a bit like accidentally skipping or whistling when there's a funeral driving past you. She was really pretty, but a different kind of pretty from the kind Saffy was. Saffy made people look at her when she walked in the room and listen to every word she said. Fate was pretty like girls in magazines are pretty, a bit shiny, and hair that you knew would go swish whenever she moved and pink cheeks like she went for lots of walks and played netball and hockey. We waited for her face to go away but it seemed to stay there for ever, so after a minute I slurped the potato off my chin and chomped up my mouthful so I could swallow it, and Saf hopped back in her seat and reached out with the clicker and changed the channel.

'Yay!' she goes. '*Top Idol*'s on!'

A few days after that, I popped into the casino on my way home after work. Fate Jones was still missing and all the way there I saw her shiny hair and pink cheeks on newsstands and tellies and scrunched up between people's fingers in greyish print all framed with shouting headlines.

That year Lucky Chips was my casino of choice because you could be as scruffy as you liked and it was nice and dark and you could gamble with 20ps on some of the tables. It was full of a certain type of people most of the time so it felt a bit like a secret club for hairy and messy people with spare 20ps who smelt a bit of booze, a bit of fags and not a whole lot of soap or showering, generally speaking. The casino was the main bit, with the manky old tables in the middle of the floor and the fruities all lined up along the sides, and then in one corner was the bar, which only had plastic cups and cans of beer and boxes of wine, and then in the other was a Chinese takeaway slash chicken-and-chips shop without much in the way of ventilation so big clouds of greasy smoke tended to hang around in the air the whole time. Around the balcony along the top were three or four karaoke booths, which I'd never been in even though I was partial to a little sing-song now and again, but regardless, I was pretty sure it wasn't just karaoke that went on in them most of the time.

It was just starting to get busy that time of the evening, lots of people in suits who'd popped in on the way home from work for a flutter or a spot of special karaoke if you catch my drift. There were some students piling into one of the booths and I guessed they probably were actually going to do karaoke and soon enough you'd be able to hear them all bouncing up and down on the sofas and singing the words wrong, even though they had them on the screen for you. I went and sat at an empty spot on one of the tables and changed a couple of quid to chips. I watched the cards being turned over and the chips being raked in and it was nice to just watch and listen and not have to think just for a bit. Looking back now it's easy to see I was beginning to have the tickly prickly feeling at the bottom of my belly that things weren't quite how they should be and so maybe that was why I was finding myself in Lucky Chips or on the lappy more and more. I learnt a long time ago that when you're winning or waiting to win – and you can wait for ages and ages but if you still reckon it will happen one day someday then that's still all right – any tickly prickly feelings go away. Because everything can change on a gamble, even if it's made with your feet sticking to the sludgy carpet or with a bloke dribbling on your shoe. Magic's everywhere if you take a chance on it, and only people who live in the too-late hours in the grimmest of gambling joints know this for sure. Your whole life is waiting for you on the stickiest cards or on the last creaky spin of a wheel. And for me it was like Saffy was too, like a tiny Borrower-size Saffy was peeking out from behind the stacks of chips under the dirty glass in front of the croupier, or just perched on the roulette wheel on black number 7 with her little legs crossed under her, grinning up at me with all her long hair whirling up as the wheel spun round and round. And I knew that one day I'd win and I could bundle up my little beauty in money and love and lovely things and we could stay happy for ever and ever. And that for sure was worth a little flutter on.

Thing was, money wasn't exactly lying about ready for fluttering. Saffy was studying for her degree so she got a bit of a loan and she still worked at a clothes shop at weekends and on her days off when she could and I kept taking as many extra shifts in the bar as I could, sometimes splits all week. But with the rent and bills and everything, we didn't have much spare for gambling on dreams. And more and more Saffy was wanting us to use what we had left over to snuffle up our noses. It's not like I didn't enjoy a bit of a buzz every now and again, or all the time when we first got together, when it was all highs and woahs and we could just jabber on at each other for hours and hours and float around on happy wonder. And I felt like a bit of a wet, thinking we should give that a rest, but I was starting to think I'd quite like to snuggle up with her every night and drink big buckets of tea and watch the telly and eat our tea and not wake up with mouths that had been PrittSticked up on the insides and runny noses that hurt your head too much to sniff back up. I just wanted me and Saf to have a real life, you know, something that we could still be doing when we were old and grey and didn't have big enough lungs to snort up a yummy line of gak. But I did want her to have fun and be happy, more than anything ever. And I wanted to have fun with her. Sometimes I just wanted to burst out laughing, right in the middle of us doing the dishes or making the bed, just crack up chuckling, because I was that happy. She just made all the air sing and everyone dance and it was just by being, just by wandering around the world and not even realising how ace she was.

So I guess that's why when she sent me a text a minute later as a nine of clubs and a five of hearts were turned over, asking if I fancied picking up on my way home, it didn't take me long to say yes. And to be fair to her, that's a good hand to twist on.

It only seemed like a bad idea for about five minutes but for those five minutes I sat there all smug and happy with myself, like I was king of the church or head boy. And then I remembered how it felt, just sitting in the same saggy spot of our shit sofa and chatting away to her with all our half-started conversations crashing into each other and carrying on in each other's directions, and deciding to rack up each line and looking at each other with that naughty face and being the first to say, Shall we … and seeing the sun coming up at the top of the concrete wall through the tiny window and looking at each other with that same naughty face and saying, Oops, but just not caring because we were in a tiny bubble of wonder, where you can talk about everything all at once and still have so much more that there just isn't time to say. So even before my chips had run out I'd started standing up off my stool and looking for Alice's number on my phone. Her bloke – who was the same guy she'd sacked me off for on that very first party night, as it goes, so I guess you can't bear a grudge – had started dabbling in dealing, so I sent her a text asking if I could pick up and I got my stuff and shoved the last couple of sticky-chip-fat Lucky Chips chips in my pocket and I walked towards the door.

It's always a bit confusing, seeing that little rectangle of daylight through the glass in Lucky Chips's doors when you feel like it's been nighttime for about a million years, but that's just the magic of casinos – they have all sorts of tricks for you, like having no windows and making the carpets all swirly-whirly so that you can't see your chips if you drop 'em and you can't see the sick you're walking in and so on and so forth. But I blinked my mole eyes at the light and then I made it out and I walked slow waiting for Alice to text me so I could have a little diversion round there to pick up a present for the Safster.

Across the road and down a bit from Lucky Chips was a concrete square with a couple of bus stops around the edges and concrete blocks as benches in the middle and a big screen that showed the news to the pigeons and the crisps packets which were scuttling around and to the two people waiting at opposite stops where I'd never seen a bus stop ever. Up on the screen Fate Jones was having a little flick of her hair and the newsreader was telling us that it was three days now and she was still missing. I felt a bit shit actually, looking up at her and wondering what had happened to her. From what they were saying, her parents were proper nice folks, well off but into charity and all of that, nice little sister and a boyfriend who loved her. I stopped and watched for a bit, waiting for the jumpy buzz of my phone in my pocket. They were doing a video-link interview with a police bloke, who was still asking people who'd been around that night to come forward. She'd been at a pub quiz at her local, the same one she went to each week with the same group of mates, only this time round she'd left early, on her tod, because she was feeling a bit dodgy. Nobody had seen her since. It made you think about how it'd feel to be one of the mates, and whether or not you'd have been different and left with her and got her home okay, or whether you'd have just taken a chance because it was the same place you went every week and things that are the same feel safe.

My phone was buzzing in my pocket and it was time to chip off. I looked up at Fate Jones's fluttery hair and I had a little secret thought, which said, Hope you're all right, chick, and then I scarpered off to Alice's.

It got to Friday, with the happy end-of-the-week feeling bursting out of both of us and we decided to have a couple of people round. We went through phases, me and Saffy, where sometimes we just wanted to live under a duvet for as many hours as we could stretch a weekend into, and sometimes we wanted to let everyone we loved into our little bubble, the more the merrier. So Alice and her bloke came round, and Saffy's friend Delilah and my mate Eddie and his housemate Weird Brian, who wasn't all that weird turns out but it was quite a catchy nickname so it had stuck. We were all standing around the kitchen even though there was the sofa and the chair and Quin's duvet to sit on, because that's always what happens at parties, it's like there's a magical magnet in a kitchen. Although it might be a bit to do with being closer to the booze, thinking about it. I'd set my decks up on the bit of the counter nearest the lounge – and furthest away from the sink and the drinks – and kept going over to have a little fiddle. Weird Brian was licking his lips and looking at Lilah's boobs, which if I'm honest we all were a bit because sometimes you just can't help it when you're trying to talk about *Top Idol* or music or the weather and they're just there all boobylicious. I flicked through some of the plastic wallets of songs I had stacked up and stopped listening to the conversation while I tried to remember what kind of music each person liked best.

Alice came over and started looking through my new records and bopping her head along to the music. She'd tied this spotty scarf round her hair and had big round red earrings in. She was looking really nice and Al always looked nicest when she was happy so I smiled a little smile to myself and gave her a squeeze with one arm. She grinned up at me.

'How's it going, love?'

I changed the song with my other hand and took the headphones off my neck. 'Good, yeah, Al. Everything good with you?'

'Oh, yeah.' She winked over at her bloke and I tried for about the millionth time to remember what his name was. I'd met him loads of times and got on fine with him but his name was one of those things that never stuck in my head, which is a bit like a sieve as my mum used to tell me all the time. She looked back at me and it was like she was going to say something then changed her mind and took a sip of her beer instead. 'Everything all right with Saffy?' she said, as she swallowed.

I looked over at Saf. She had a big pretend daisy tucked behind her ear, and this floaty pink dress on with tiny flowers dancing about all over it. She looked gorgeous-fantastic and she was laughing at something Eddie had said. 'Yeah,' I said. 'Everything's great.'

A bit later we were chomping on the big bag of crisps Al had brought round and talking about whether we'd rather be Richard or Judy. It turned out that on balance both had pros and cons and so it was quite a tough choice. Then there was that little break in the chat that you get sometimes when everyone's just finished laughing and nobody says anything for a minute or two and you all kind of go aaah and look at your feet.

'So,' Weird Brian said after a bit, 'what do we reckon's going to happen with this Fate Jones thing?'

You see what I mean? He was a bit weird. Not really party chat, is it?

'Horrible, it is,' Al said. 'I feel so bad for her parents.'

'Rich though, aren't they?' Eddie said, like that was okay then, because Eddie was a bit like that, always thinking bad about people. 'Must be something to it.'

'Ransom, you mean?' Saffy said, looking all thoughtful and clever like always.

'Yeah, yeah, that's the word,' Eddie said, getting into it then. 'I reckon someone'll send them a note soon, you know, with all the letters cut out of newspapers and magazines and that. And if they pay up, they'll get her back.'

We all thought about that.

'It might be like that girl a few years ago, remember?' Al's bloke said. 'You know, the one who was kept prisoner for years and years and fell in love with the bloke in the end?'

'Stockholm syndrome,' Weird Brian said, and I thought, I bet he watches all those true-crime programmes in the middle of the night, definitely his thing.

'Nah,' Lilah said. 'Cos they're always little girls, aren't they, and then they don't know any different. She's grown-up. I reckon it's just another normal horrible thing, some randomer off the street mugged her or whatever.'

Luckily she didn't go into what 'whatever' meant because, fair enough, news and current affairs and that are party talk if you're that way inclined but as far as I was concerned rape and murder aren't all that suitable for a social atmosphere and I was feeling a bit shifty on my feet with the turn of events. I wanted to ask everyone whether they'd rather be Ant or Dec but now it seemed all inappropriate.

'I mean,' she said, 'I don't really get why it's on the news all the time. It must happen, like, every day to loads of people. What's the fuss?'

'I'm telling you,' Eddie said, even though he hadn't, 'it's cos they're posh and important and la-di-da!'

Lilah took another swig of her wine and nodded a bit too hard. 'AND white.'

There's not much you can say to that without falling into a big hole of awkward and so Al piped up and changed the subject a bit. 'You seen those new billboards everywhere? The moving ones? Must have cost a mint.'

I went and turned up the music a bit and Lilah started dancing. The night turned back into little pockets of chat instead of one big circle, and Al started dancing too, a bottle of wine under one arm and her headscarf coming loose and falling in her eyes when she laughed.

I was halfway in the fridge getting beers out of the back and noticing how mouldy the cheese was when I heard her.

'Dave,' she said, which was Al's bloke's name and Saffy never had a problem remembering it, 'got any bag?'

There was a bit of a pause and my breath puffed out all frosty.

'No, mate,' he said. 'Meant to say – can we settle up tonight?'

'Oh, shit, I forgot all about that! So sorry, hun – I get paid next Thursday, can I drop it round then for you?' Her voice sounded all sweet and singsong, like little birds and bunnies might hop through the door any second and start pouring drinks and emptying ashtrays for her.

'Yeah, sure.'

'Thanks for reminding me – don't let me forget again!'

With that she floated off to dance with Lilah and I came back out, bumping my head on the shelf on the way.

A while later I rolled a ciggie and went out to the front step. It was fine to smoke in the house and we did it all the time, but Lilah's singing was getting a bit much and Weird Brian kept trying to talk to me about the girl who lived across the road from him, but mostly I went out because I thought Saffy was there because she'd disappeared. So I ducked out and found the front door open but out on the concrete no Saffy. I lit my cig and craned my neck to look up at the pavement to see where she'd gone. My heart did a little skippity-skip to the beat, but as my first drag was filling up the last pink bits of my lungs, I heard her tippytoe footsteps along the concrete and then she was at the top of the stairs like a miracle or a dream.

'Hey, beautiful,' she said, and her hair was all lit up from behind by the orange streetlight like an angel's.

'Hello, lovely,' I said, and she skipped down the stairs and hopped off the last one to stand next to me. 'Where you been?'

'To get us a little something,' she said, and she waved a baggy between her tiny fingers, catching the same orange light like it was glowing from inside or on fire.

I was about to ask her where she'd got it and how she'd paid for it and to tell her that everyone was going to make a move soon, but just as I looked down at her smiling face and opened my mouth, the door burst open and Weird Brian came strolling out, followed by Dave carrying Alice in his arms and then Lilah with her arm round Eddie's neck.

'Sorry, guys,' Dave said, hitching up Al's head where it was dangling over his elbow. 'Ally was sick in your sink. Better get her home.'

'No worries.' We both nodded. 'See you, guys.'

They bobbled off up the steps and their chit-chatter faded into the dark as they walked away.

'Oh, well,' Saf said. 'More for me and you, baby.'


Her nails were painted dark dark inky-pen-blue and they drew beautiful patterns all over my arms and round my cheeks and down my neck. 'I love you,' she said, right into the middle of my ear, and the words swirled all round my brain and made everything inside me glowing and bright.

The next day while I was clinking all the empty bottles about in a binbag, I listened to the radio where everyone was still talking about Fate Jones. It had been longer than a week by then and all kinds of characters were sneaking out of the woodwork to talk about her and how sad it was. So far I'd heard from her primary-school teacher, the bloke who drove the bus she got to work, the old girl who lived three doors down from her mum and dad, and the busker who sang Beatles songs outside her university library. It wasn't exactly stirring stuff. Simon Cowell had apparently said that all the *Top Idol* contestants would wear Fate Jones T-shirts on that night's show. Which was nice. Even though it was really bad that she was gone, it kind of made you feel a bit warm in the heart, seeing how everybody wanted to help. Made you feel a bit happier about people, in a funny way, because even though there were baddies who might or mightn't have done something to this blonde clever girl who volunteered at an animal shelter in her spare time and taught little kids ballet, there were a million other people in the world who were good and would look out for her. It somehow made the odds seem a bit fairer.

Once all the bottles were picked up, I put the bag outside the front door and wandered back in. I stood in the doorway to the lounge and looked about for a bit with my hands on my hips like I was about to do something important but I didn't know what it was yet. The radio had started playing music again and it was a bit lonely without all the sad and worried voices chatting out of it, but it was quite dancy music so on the plus side it did make you feel like doing something. Saffy was out at uni in the library and I knew she would be for ages. She was really near the end of her course and so she had loads of work to do that she needed a lot of space for. And that's what made me think.

I went over to the corner where the telly was, and I stood there for a bit with my hands on my hips again. I pulled the telly over to the middle of the wall and scuffed away the dented square on the dodgy carpet. I rolled Quin's duvet up a bit and moved it more behind the sofa. I knew he'd understand, he was just that type of bloke. He hadn't ever complained about having to kip on the floor or about people dancing around him half the time when he was trying to get an early night. He hadn't been about that much of late and I knew Saffy was probably missing him. He'd been there for her through things I didn't really understand, things she'd never told me about, about her illness and the place they'd sent her. For ages and ages it had seemed like it was nothing, just something she occasionally accidentally got close to mentioning and then speedily steered off in another direction so I figured it was just all in the past and didn't matter any more. It had been Quin who sat me down once, when Saf was out at work, and said to me, 'William,' cos he always called me William, just him and my mum really, 'I think you should probably know a bit about Saffy's illness even though she probably won't ever tell you,' and I'd said okay, not sure what to expect, and he'd made me a cup of tea and explained how bad it had got when she was younger and about the place her parents had sent her and how that was why it was really important that we took care of her and kept her out of that dark space she'd been swallowed by before. And I'd nodded and agreed and we never mentioned to her that we'd had the little chat and after a few more months of everything being fine had passed I started forgetting myself because I knew Saffy couldn't go back there now, not when she had me and this little flat of love and light to live in. Regardless, even though that was all in the past and we didn't need to talk about it, having Quin around was important. I knew that and I made a note to myself to organise a night in, just the three of us, when Quin wasn't out at one of his parties or on a date or logged on to Grindr.

I went into our bedroom and I got the little table that was folded up behind the wardrobe and took it back in with me. I set it up and put a folded-up bit of paper under the wobbly leg and gave the dusty top a brush with my sleeve. I'd had this mad idea to set up Saffy a little work station, so she could get all her stuff done properly. She always ended up spread across the floor and never being able to get comfortable and I thought she'd be made up to have her own space. I went back into our room and looked about for her easel, which I eventually found under the bed, which did strike me as a bit odd and I did have to think for quite a long while about when the last time I'd seen her use it was, but I shrugged it off and wandered back out with it and set that up too. Then I went back in to get her work, all the big piles of thick white paper and the sketch books and the giant black folder she carried them around in, which was bigger than her almost.

I didn't mean to look. I was always good at letting Saf get on with things, cos I knew she'd show me when she was ready. I knew I wouldn't like it if she sat listening to me when I was trying to put a mix together because I'd get all flustered and fiddle things about in the wrong way and it wouldn't work. But as I was putting the papers all carefully on the desk, I couldn't help sneaking a peek. No matter how much I got to know her, I never stopped being totally completely blown away by Saffy and how clever and talented she was without even trying. Seeing things she'd made or done made me feel like I was about to zoom through the roof and into upstairs's flat with all the pride and amazement I felt. She'd been working on this project for ages and ages, spending whole weekends in the library and carting all kinds of things back and forth with her and going off into the little dazes she did when she was thinking of an idea and so I knew it was going to be good and meant a lot to her. So I peeked. Just one sheet at first, and then another. And then one more. And then I was looking through them all, through the sketchbooks and the big sheets and the little sheets, feeling confused and a bit like my feet were sinking very very slowly through the floor. There was nothing there. Some of them had sketches that had been scrubbed through with fat black pen, some had words and ideas on them that had been scratched out with a biro. Lots of them had half-started things in faint ghosty pencil, but you could tell they'd never get finished with real lines and colours. All the other pages were empty. There was nothing there.

She was at it again, I knew she was. I tried not to look like I was looking at her, sitting there all bunched up in my massive woolly jumper with just her fingers poking out of the sleeves, pulling at the bit of toast I'd made her that just had a midget nibble out of one corner. But she saw me anyway and she got in a huff, jumping off the sofa with her legs unravelling and speeding off like Fred Flintstone's – you know, when he's pedalling along in his car or just running somewhere really fast and they go round in a little circle and make that twiddly noise. Quinton looked up from behind *Brideshead Revisited*, which was all he ever read, he had a million different copies and DVDs of it, and then looked down all hasty and fiddled with his parting.

It seemed like it had all changed just like that with no warning. There was no sign of lovely pottering Saf any more, there was just sulky-secrets Saf huffing about and pulling at bits of toast. There were dry old lines of coke all over the flat on CD cases, basically my whole last two years' worth of album purchases: Gui Boratto and Bat for Lashes and LCD Soundsystem all sitting there sadly covered with craggy crumbs that had been forgotten about, and the night before I'd caught her about to rack up on a *Brideshead* DVD and it was a good job I did, Quin would've gone flippin' spare if it'd been him that walked in. I sat there staring at a bag of apples, pink ones, her favourites, but you'd never have known it cos they were untouched, just sat there going brown and soggy, and pink apples didn't come cheap, much more pricey than red or green ones and they didn't taste any different to me but then I figured I was no expert. And that had got me a bit wound up because I didn't like money being wasted. When I was in a better mood than then, I sometimes laughed at how we'd both spent too much of our lives thinking of pounds; at how Saffy had spent her past trying to lose pounds off her body and how I spent our present trying not to lose pounds on the tables. It's not so funny now, when I think of what happened next.

There's me looking at these pissing apples and wondering how to turn them and Saf back pink when Quin gets up off his sleeping bag and stands there tweaking at the creases on his trousers and smoothing down his blazer and his parting with his pudgy fingers.

'Shall I have a word, Fitz?' he goes, shuffling from one foot to the other.

'Do what, mate?' I said, still a bit distracted by the apples.

'A word,' he goes again. 'You know, about eating.'

'Oh, right, yeah,' I said, tearing my eyes away from the bag. 'I think so. You know best, Q, but she doesn't seem right.'

'Yeah,' he goes. 'Look, don't worry about it. Sometimes she just forgets. When she's stressed, you know.'

'Okay, thanks, mate.' I had a swig at my can of Coke and sat up a bit. 'You off out tonight?' I asked, because I really wanted to be nice to him all of a sudden because I couldn't help thinking again that it was lucky we had him around.

'Yep,' he goes, big smile, 'I'm off to this thing at Hector's club – it's champagne baths and a pool party. You've met Hector, haven't you?'

I had met Hector as it goes, and it was hard to forget because the bloke was wearing tweed chaps when I'd made his acquaintance. Nice fella actually, bare arse aside. Well, Quin was off then on some spiel and he was rubbing his hands together and then holding them out wide and chortling away to himself, and I was glad I'd tuned out to be honest because who knows what he was describing the length of, you never could be sure with Quin – one minute he'd be telling you he was nipping down the shop for some of the special clove cigarettes he was always puffing, and the next he was on about a party he'd been to where they'd all snorted ket off the host's cock. He was that kind of kid. It might seem strange that the sort of guy who plonked his tubby little bod in Bolly every weekend spent the rest of his time kipping on a My Little Pony duvet in our front room and looking out for Saffy, but underneath all his frilly shirts and dirty stories I was just properly learning that he had the biggest heart going.

So he toddled off out and I got up and had a quick look around for Saf, just in case she'd heard that little conversation cos that'd be the end of it if she thought we were talking about her. She was in the bathroom in the shower, and that wasn't all that surprising cos that was where she always ended up, always in there buffing and scrubbing and rinsing until the cows came home. I even bought her a little shower radio for her birthday the year before, this little blue fish that suckered on there and warbled out tunes right next to your ear. It was like the best present she'd ever had, her eyes went all shiny and she stretched right up on tippytoes and gave me the biggest hug in the world. Shot myself in the foot there really, because there was no getting her out after that, songs tinkling out and pennies trickling away down the drain with the suds and the bubbles and the little grainy things from her scrubby stuff, which incidentally is not suitable for manly bits as I learnt the hard way. But at least it was only pennies not pounds trickling away cos she didn't like her showers too hot like I did, she had them lukewarm so, you know, that was something I guess, if you liked to look for the bright side like I did.

She wouldn't be out for ages so I wandered into the bedroom and had a bit of a half-arsed tidy-up, pulling the duvet up and picking up the glasses Saffy seemed to collect like a little magpie, and the big pot of salt that always wound up floating around out of place because she said that drinking saltwater was really good for you. I wandered back and stuck them in the sink and I was gonna wash them up but then there was no hot water cos Her Highness was still in the shower, so I just stood at the sink and looked up through the tiny jailhouse window at the top of the wall at all the feet and ankles trekking past. It was almost time for me to go to work and I was glad if I'm honest. Right about then the flat was feeling like it was shrinking, like I'd been look-ing at Saf's mardy face and Quin's side parting for too long and maybe the outside world had ended and there was nothing except us left in this flat and outside there was just people's zombie legs wandering around, just stubs that ended at the knee marching around with bloody chips of bone sticking out the top and nowhere to go. I grabbed my work shirt off the radiator where it was steaming away happily next to a row of crispy socks and pants and shoved it on over my T-shirt and grabbed my bag off the side.

''Bye, Saf,' I yelled, as I was opening the front door, and the bathroom door opened and she stuck her little blonde head out rubbing at it with a flannel.

'Off to work,' I said at normal volume. 'See you later.'

'Okay, lovepuff,' she sang, and she blew me a kiss with her lovely pink lips. 'Ooh, Fitz,' she said, hurrying out after me.

'Yes, babe,' I said, turning back with one foot up the steps to the pavement. She was standing on the doorstep in her big beach towel hopping from one foot to the other on the cold concrete. 'It's Alice's party tonight, isn't it?' she said. 'Have you forgotten?'

''Course not,' I said. 'I'll come after work but you go ahead with Lilah if you want, hun, cos I might be a bit late if it's busy.'

'Okay.' She smiled, giving me a little curtsy in her beach-scene beach towel. 'See you there then, sexpants.'

'You will,' I said, skipping up the steps two at a time, and I turned near the top to blow her a kiss but the front door was already shutting.

Work was pants but then it was never exactly my highlight of the day. In general it wasn't all that bad to be truthful – Cadbury, my boss, was pretty decent and it was usually busy enough that the time whizzed by, and even though it was stressful when you were in the thick of it, it was always nice when you suddenly realised your shift was over just like that. Much better than just sitting there watching the clock, which was what I was doing that day, just watching the hands tick tick round slow as you like while the only two lunchers we had were sat there sliding down the plasticky sofas and staring at the last half of the last bottle of wine they'd ordered. The pub next door was heaving but that was because it was a blokey pub and football was on. I just stood there with an order pad and sketched out some set lists. There's something lovely about set lists – it's like maths and art all swirled into one because the timings have to fit and you feel dead clever when you work out how to make two songs go together, when you crack the code and slip the two beats together – like the two bits on a zip – whoosh. And when people tell you something was good you feel like it's a compliment just to you yourself and nothing to do with the songs at all. Not that many people got to hear my mixes, just sometimes at parties if I managed to shuffle my way behind the deck at the late hours when everyone starts to fidget and stare at the ceiling and think about their real lives and get restless and worried and pick at their faces and wonder how they're going to get home, and nobody's really listening then anyway. But I did still carry on doing them, and I'd play them to Saf sometimes, in the middle of the night when we were both magically awake, and she'd listen, lying in bed on her front, wiggling her feet with her face propped on her hands, all blue from the glow off the laptop screen and it was in those secret special moments that I thought, Nothing will ever be as brilliant as this, nobody in the world is as brilliant as her.

Cadbury was out the back and he said he was drawing up rotas but he definitely wasn't, he was snoozing away at his desk with slinky soul playing softly in the background so we couldn't hear his bear snores from outside the door. The two chefs were sitting outside on the damp step next to the bins smoking away and getting angry about nothing much at all, but they were just working themselves up ready for the dinner shift because the angrier you are the better chef you are or something, seemed like that's how it worked anyway. Jenny the little waitress was in the kitchen chopping up lots of leaves for the salad garnishes ready for service, and stopping every five seconds to count the number of blue plasters on her fingers, but you couldn't blame her really after that one time. So it was just me and the two early-peakers in the corner and I was feeling proper restless, and even trying to work out when the optimum point to drop Soulwax's Krack was and whether putting that and Green Velvet in one set was being too much of a crowd-pleaser couldn't keep me busy. Staring sadly out the window I watched the blokes spilling out of O'Phalley's next door for fags and phone calls and so it must've been half-time.

Fate Jones was on the telly again. Her parents kept doing these press conferences with the same two fat coppers either side of them, her mum and her dad and her boyfriend, who was all greasy and spotty and tattooed and not anybody you might think would have such a pretty and giggly girlfriend. All the papers reckoned it was him that had done it so when you watched them on telly you knew that everyone was just staring at him and looking for clues, like a drop of sweat on the forehead or a pulsing vein and if you saw one you knew it would be in all the papers the next day. Some of the news channels had started up twenty-four-hour coverage by then, so you could get interactive and press the button for round-the-clock coverage – you know, press red for news, green for sport, yellow for celebrity and blue for Fate Jones, that kind of thing. There wasn't all that much to report so it was just live round-the-clock coverage of her parents' front door, which wasn't much to look at unless the milkman was popping by or the postie but other than that it was a bit pointless. But you still found yourself watching for ages just in case anything happened. Like you wouldn't want to miss breaking news so you had to watch all the unbroken news just to be sure. The telly was annoying me that day, though, with just the red door staring out at me and not even a pint of milk on the step for a bit of variety, so I turned it off and looked away.

I had a text on my phone when I had a little sneaky check of it under the bar, and there was still nobody around so I looked at it. It was a picture message from my sister, Hannah. It was of her face cos they'd been having another go at it, I remembered then. It did look a bit better even though it was still all red and tight and scarred and her eye still drooped and gaped in a weird way and it still wouldn't move with the other, I knew that even though obviously I couldn't tell just from a photo but they'd told her all along that it would never work properly again and I think she'd just got used to that. Her face probably looked loads better but it was hard to judge when the photo had half the normal side of her face in it, half her nose and half her mouth and half her forehead, all normal pale smooth skin and then the jagged monstery part across her cheek and her eye. You couldn't see the arm in the picture, just a close-up of her face but that didn't really matter cos they'd done all they could do with the arm, they'd already told her that, and it didn't look all that bad when it was in her sleeve; it just wasn't much good for anything any more, that was all.

It was weird, thinking about how it wasn't all that long before that all the news had been about the bomb and now it was about Fate Jones. In a weird way I sort of knew how Fate Jones's family felt, but when it was Han's face on the screen it was with loads of other people's pictures too, flashing up as they listed the injuries and even worse the dead, and later as they filmed her and other people attending court to testify and to hear the verdict of the inquest and all the other stuff that dragged on and on long after it was over. Fate Jones was on the screen on her own and that must have been a lot worse. I looked up at her front door again and thought about the people behind it and whether their TV was on and showing the same picture and whether they ever pressed blue for Fate Jones.

Thinking about what it had been like back then and the horrible sadness and worry of it all, I felt terrible thinking Hannah's face still looked bad and that I hadn't seen her for a long old time, so I texted her back and said nice things about how good it looked and then I put two kisses instead of my usual one. The lunchers were finally staggering out and they'd have headaches by teatime, I reckoned, but I smiled and waved 'bye and then I went over and started clearing their table.

Well, I was right about being late, that was for sure. Must've been after three by the time I finally took the drawer out of the till and shut it in the storeroom and said night to Cadbury. By the time I got to the house I was knackered and I knew I needed to get in the mood quickly or I'd just end up curled in a corner of the sofa all night like a right miserable git. Al was sat on the front step and she looked dead pleased to see me but her whole body was bobbing to the beat and her eyes were like big black marbles and she looked pretty spangled all in all, so I just patted her on the head and carried on up to the front door, leaving her conducting the beat with one finger and smiling at the little moustachioed guy next to her. Inside it was all a bit much for my fragile tired mind. It was just one of those things. I knew if I'd been there from the start I'd have been having a whale of a time cos it was pretty impressive: the whole hall had giant sheets of paper taped up and all of it was covered in doodles and slogans and lyrics and love, and all these different-coloured lights were creeping out from under doors with snatches of bass line and people were milling about looking at each other and the walls happily. But because I was sober and shattered I couldn't be arsed with it all, really, even though I wanted to be. I felt a bit out of it so I sort of waded through the crowds into the lounge, grabbing a can bobbing in a wastepaper bin on my way past. I caught a glimpse of Delilah stomping about in the corner with a tall brown-haired girl so I headed over, stepping round another girl casually gagging into a plant pot on the way.

'All right, Lilah,' I said, tapping her on the shoulder for a bit until she finally turned round.

'Ooooh, Fitz,' she goes, all squealy. 'You're here! Isn't it great? Have you met Meg?'

'Yeah, it's awesome,' I said, half waving at Meg. 'Saf about?'

She looked at me all confused and gurning her chops off and said, 'Who? OhSafyeahsheiscoursesheissorryforgot! She'supstairs-intheotherlounge.'

A little tiny warning bell went off in my head in between the bass of the music. 'What?' I said. 'Are you serious?'

'Yeah,' she goes. 'It's nice up there, allpinkandplinkyplonk-music!'

The warning bell quadrupled in size and started ringing cheerily against the back of my head. 'No,' I said. 'The other lounge is a ket party – you've not left Saf with a ready supply of K, have you?'

She'd stopped listening ages before cos she just nodded and said, 'IdunnoFitzsorry!' and then she carried on grunting the beat with grinning Meg, sloshing their mugs of wine about and hugging each other and the people around them loads.

I gave up and wandered off up the stairs, stepping over people sprawling about, mumbling at each other and trying to focus on each other's faces. I made for the pink glow at the far end of the landing and pushed the door open, feeling weird and nervous and scared about what I was going to see without knowing why.

The room felt empty even though it was full. Nobody was DJing, someone had just stuck an iPod on shuffle, but some bald bloke off his head seemed to think he was, listening dead serious to one of the headphones round his thick neck and grinning round at the room really proud of himself. Everyone else was melting into sofas, giggling and stretching themselves out, a leg or a finger at a time, pawing at each other or the air. In the middle of the room were these two guys, one of them I thought I recognised and he might've worked with Al but it was hard to tell because they were lying down with happy looks on their faces – well, the one I thought I recognised was face down but the back of his head looked happy anyway. They obviously couldn't move and that's why I didn't do K – apart from this once in the summer holidays when I was a kid – I've got a fear of being still. Spike, Alice's rescued Staffy, was sniffing about them with a bow of tinsel round his neck and this toy in his mouth that Al had bought him a few weeks back. The dog had chewed one end and when it looked up at you with the toy in its mouth the bit sticking out had on it a big cartoon grin so it looked like the mutt was smiling at you. It would've been funny but Spike didn't like being laughed at so you wouldn't chance it, you just smiled along politely like he was telling you the joke not like he was the butt of it. There he was, trotting around the two blokes, grinning like the Joker and sniffing around, getting his nose right into some unfortunate places. He casually cocked a leg against one but that was okay, I reasoned, because it didn't look like the smell'd make much difference to him if I'm honest. But then he was looking round with mischief on his cartoon grinning face and he was sizing up their heads and while I was stood leaning against the door and he knew I was watching, and he was glad, he mounted the poor bloke's face and began humping it, I mean really going at it, and there were a few squeals from the rest of the room and a few people sat staring at the scene like it was one of those toga fellas being eaten by a lion and nobody was moving, even I couldn't for a minute, his stubby tail bobbing up and down in and out was hypnotising me and I'd only had half a beer. I stared at the tinsel rustling away on his neck and the bloke's floppy foot, which was rocking back and forth ever so slightly with the movement, and then at all the people around the room staring all transfixed and it all seemed unreal and slow, like things are in a dream. But when Spike leant onto one paw to get a better angle, the spell was broken and I steamed in and grabbed him by his tinsel collar and yanked him off. He dropped the grin and it rolled next to the skullfuckee's face like a crazy old lady's false teeth and he looked up at me sadly and then up at my finger pointing to the door and I said, 'OUT,' just to really get the point home, and he did slink out, looking longingly back over his shoulder at his new love.

The room around me went back to melting and pawing and stretching and I finally saw Saffy's black boots poking out from behind the sofa, so I marched over there and there she was, with her yellow hair sticking out around her face, and it was all short and wrong and I realised someone had cut it as a joke while she was in a state and didn't know any better and I felt like finding the scissors then and poking whoever it was right in the eyes but there was no time for that. Her fingers were flexing to a beat that wasn't there any more and her eyes were rolling back in her head. I knelt in front of her and I touched her face gently and said, 'Saf,' as quietly as I could, because I didn't want to scare her, 'Saf, you idiot, wake up, it's time to go home.'

And then her green eyes rolled back into view and she looked at me in confusion and wonder. 'Fitz?'

'Yeah, it's me,' I said, pushing hair out of her eyes, 'Thought you were hardcore, you numpty.'

She smiled but it was all weak and pretend and her face looked droopy and she was chewing at her lips, mashing them against her little white teeth. I picked her and her handbag up and she put her hands round my neck and nuzzled into me. By the time I got to the bottom of the stairs her eyes were gone again.

## SAFFY

Sometimes, if you stare at something for long enough, you can make it into whatever you like. You can do it with the clouds in the sky, you can do it with the Artex on a ceiling, you can do it with shadows on the ground. You can do it with swirls in the snow and ripples in wet sand.

I stared at myself for years and years and the things I saw never changed.

As morning came, I lay on the bed looking up at the ceiling. I was waiting patiently to see if pictures would form, willing the lines and swirls to show me a story. I hadn't been to sleep yet, even though Fitz was flat out in a contagious kind of floppy sleep, warmth and dreams wafting off him into the room. The room looked so glaringly dirty and dusty, mould spots speckling all the walls brown and green. I wondered why we never cleaned more. The skirting-boards were thick with scum and the light fixture had a rust-coloured tidemark around it, left over after a leak from the flat upstairs months before.

Everything seemed to be running away from me, the longer I looked, as though new layers of dirt and decay were forming right in front of me. I could see mould crawling over the walls, taking over everything. The TV would explode and my laptop would stop working. Quin's copy of *Brideshead* would become all

39

bloated and misshapen, pages soft and mildewed. All our clothes would get wet and putrid, even my favourite dress, which lay on a chair from Fitz undressing me the night before. I knew it was getting damp even then, all scrunched up and abandoned.

I looked away, back to the ceiling, but the dress kept flashing into my mind, brown spots over its lace. It was happening at that second, the fabric drawing moisture out of the air and soaking it up like a gorgeous frothy sponge, and I was going to end up like some poor man's Miss Havisham in my Miss Selfridge dress and my forgotten flat. I leapt up and grabbed the dress, clutching it to my chest. My head was spinning and the fabric felt far away between my fingers. I slipped it onto a hanger and tucked it carefully between two others in the wardrobe – not between jeans, in case they left a blue stain – and made sure it was hanging down straight so mould couldn't form in the creases. I squeezed some of the other dresses hanging there, the blue denim pinafore and the pale pink tea dress and the polka-dotted one with the sticky-out skirt, and they felt wet. Everything felt wet suddenly, even my hair and my scalp. And they felt cold, but maybe it was my hands that were cold. I wondered how you could ever tell. How could we ever know whether it was our hands that were cold, or wet, or hot, or dusty, or the thing they were touching? Do we make things happen or do they happen to us? I walked out into the living room, feeling the carpet soggy between my toes.

I liked silence in the house sometimes. On days like those, it was a soft silence that you could almost reach out and touch. It was peaceful; the house and I were at peace because he was there, sleeping. Everything was in its place.

Quin's duvet was turned back and his pillow still had the oily dip where his head had been. He spent a lot of time away from the flat, but it didn't matter: the room felt warm and safe even with just his things in it. Quin and I were like two leftover bits of the same puzzle. We fitted together even though we were misfits. I straightened out his sleeping bag and smoothed down the duvet, making his corner nice for him.

The rest of the room was tidy, everything put away. I stood in the middle and looked around. Though I tried to pull away, the corner kept calling me back.

The canvases were stacked neatly against the wall, backs to me. The papers and loose sketches were piled carefully underneath the desk. My sketchbooks sat on the desk, big, medium and small fitting one inside another. I sat down in the foldout chair and ran my finger along the edge of each one. I liked the way they lay together like this and looked like a shrinking version of one item, the stages laid out for you to see; the large original to the perfect miniature. I took the small one down and opened it, letting the fat cover flop over on its spirals. Here are the things that lived inside:

*Portrait of a Lady*. Picture of Fate Jones torn out of the free paper and taped in. Pencil question mark across left half of page.

*True Love Never Dies*. Still-life of a bed of roses with a junkie lying among the flowers – work in progress. Outline of arm, three unfinished flowers. Half-page torn out.

*Things I'll Never Say*. Crying child. Half a head of hair, one eye, unshaded lips, outline of nose. Jagged biro line through centre of page.

*Untitled # 1*. Blue dots of paint, flicked with the edge of a paintbrush. Work in no progress.

*Untitled # 2*. Circle drawn with black kohl. Artist's intention unknown.

*Stick Man Feels Sad*. As described.

*Self-portrait #1*. Blank page, faint traces of pink eraser over surface of page.

As I turned the pages, I felt my skin begin to creep and crawl with all of the feelings that couldn't get out and swirled half-formed and stormy. I grabbed hold of the pages, tore them out and slammed the notebook against the wall. It slid down all the way and when it reached the carpet it tipped over sheepishly. I grabbed a handful of my hair and pulled that instead. I felt the newly shorn shortness, the uneven patches and the way it brushed my shoulders where before it had trailed down my back, and I remembered it in a rush. How the day before had started and how the party had ended. I started at the start and I thought it all through carefully like I was remembering a dream.

The silence in the house had been too loud for words that morning. It always was just after he left, as the sound of him loping up the stairs and across the pavement above me faded away. Sometimes there'd be the tinkle and fumble of him dropping his keys or his apron and bending down to pick them up, a quick flash of his thin fingers in the tiny strip of window and then he'd be gone. I had dropped the towel and stepped one foot, two feet naked across the little hall. The carpet had felt thin and cold between my toes, and the hairs on my arms stood up in a thick fuzz. I rubbed them hard to get rid of it and stepped carefully into the bedroom. Everything felt slow and dizzy, as if all the sounds had gone out of the flat with Fitz and I was left trying to balance in an empty room off-kilter and unsteady.

I'd stood in front of the cracked half of mirror, which was propped against the wall. It had been full-length, once, if you balanced it at the right angle and stood far enough back, but one night when we were drunk and silly and happy and kissing the kind of kisses you can't stop, when you keep raining kisses like butterflies on each other until you can't breathe any more, we'd stumbled into it and smashed it right in half. I had been frightened at the time that it was bad luck, that maybe we'd be cursed, but Fitz had said that if you didn't look in the pieces you were all right. And so I'd sat on the end of the bed as he picked up each of the pieces, looking at the ceiling the whole time and humming, because he always did that when things were good or okay, and there was one piece left, almost a whole half, which wasn't cracked, so we kept that.

Looking at it then, alone and quiet, I'd wondered if we had been cursed all along. A draught blew in from the hall and I shivered, trying to shake the thought out. I turned away and went to the wardrobe. I ran the clothes hanging there between my fingers, denims and jumpers and soft dresses. When I looked down, my favourite lacy dress was in my hand. That happened sometimes; I'd told Fitz once that it must like going out, but secretly I wondered if sometimes I made it jump out of the wardrobe just by thinking it.

I'd pulled the lovely, frothy loveliness of it over my head and wiggled it down. Kneeling back in front of the mirror, I drew on fat lines of black liner without really looking at my face. I stuffed my hair up into a kind of knot and stuck some pins in to hold it up, and then I fluffed at my fringe a bit until it started going static in my fingers and I had to stop. I bounced on the bed a few times, but it wasn't fun with nobody there, and the creaking of the springs echoed around the room, so I flopped down and lay in a heap of duvet. My phone was hidden in a little coil of the smoky quilt and I picked it up and checked the time. Three thirty. Still two hours before I could go to Lilah's because she was at work, and nothing left to do.

I hadn't wanted to go to Alice's party all that much. I didn't even like her really. She was always shouting and burping and talking about sex or shitting. She made me feel or seem shy, which I wasn't. Always wearing leggings and tops that were too short, so that all you could look at was her crotch, which was perhaps the point. She wore her hair in a tight bun on the top of her head, held up with chopsticks, which made her face look huge. I could never say these things out loud because she was a good friend to Fitz and he loved her. She wanted to fill Hannah's spot, to support him and care for him when he had suddenly had to become so many things to so many people. And, really, *I* wanted to be everything to him. And she was in the way.

I'd sat up and fiddled around in the duvet some more until I found the packet of tobacco and papers. Then I sat on the edge of the mattress and rolled a cigarette in my lap. Alice threw parties all the time, like she was Father Christmas or Hugh Hefner, so this one wasn't exactly special. But with the quiet house and all the time to wait, I felt full of a weird curling anticipation and baby butterflies started circling in my belly.

I had sat out on the front step to smoke the cigarette. The concrete was cold on my feet, and rain was slowly colouring the steps dark. It was beautiful rain, the soft misty kind that hangs in the air and sits in your hair in tiny diamonds. I'd looked up at the pavement but there was nobody there, just the occasional swish-splash of a car driving past on the other side of the road. They only ever drove past on that side of the road, out of the city, and never on the other, never on the way in. Sometimes it seemed like the city must be getting empty, all the people leaving and nobody coming to take their place.

I wondered what Fitz was up to at work. He'd be making up set-lists, probably, bent over an order pad on the bar with a pencil in his hand and his hair falling in his eyes. Filling up the big glass jar of pistachios, green in their pink shells, or the olives, all glossy and black, chunks of garlic and chilli floating in the oil. Stacking the crisps on their shelf, checking there was enough of each bright colour, crackling the foil bags closer together to fit more of them in. Cleaning the pumps for the soft drinks, sticky with sugar and bubbly in the drip tray. Another car drove past up on the street out of sight, leaving a little trail of faint music as it went.

My cigarette had gone out in the damp fuzz of the rain, so I lit it and lay back, head inside on all the post, wiry doormat tickling my back and legs stretched out in the wet. Smoke drifted upwards and I looked up at the ceiling with a pizza flyer slippery under my head. That day there were no patterns or shapes to be made, just miles of meringue stretched from corner to corner.

The cigarette ran out again after a while, and I stood up and wandered into the lounge. I was shivering: it got cold in the flat when it rained, damp patches on the wall seeping through silently. I went over to Quin's rail and pulled out one of his millions of blazers, a sailor's one with white piping and braid and stripes on the shoulders. It was too big for me so I rolled up the sleeves and snuggled into it. My favourite blazer was missing; a red velvet one, which was soft like a hug when you put it on. Quin would have been wearing it; it was his favourite too. It was still cold, so I crouched on Quinnie's sleeping bag and pulled his duvet round me. It smelt like him, of posh cigarettes and hair oil and just a tiny bit sweaty. There was a DVD case on the arm of the sofa with a bit of a line left on it, so I dabbed some and waited and waited for a high.

Time crawled by, until at last I could escape the emptiness. I left early and walked slowly to cheat it. Delilah's flat was in a big old building with pretty windows and tall steps leading up to the front door. Every time I climbed them I felt pangs of jealousy. Lilah always told me that from the inside the windows were draughty and there were mice in the basement where the bins went, but as outsiders we can see things only as they seem. Envy was a feeling I collected as a diehard habit so truths like these often fell around me unheard. I pressed the buzzer and shifted the bag with the little bottle of vodka Fitz had bought me from one hand to the other. Molly, Delilah's flatmate, answered, a blue paisley apron tied around her waist and a pan in one hand, a spoon in the other.

'Hey, Saf! Come in, come in. You look gorgeous!'

I liked Molly. She was clever and pretty, with round pink cheeks, and she always had nice things to say to everybody. 'Lilah's in her room,' she said, stirring the pot. 'You want some bolognese?'

I shook my head, touched my stomach. 'No, thanks, I just ate. Smells amazing.'

She smiled and went back into the kitchen, trailing hot tomato-garlic-wine scent behind her. I walked down the hall, looking at the framed photos on the bright white walls as I went. Lilah's door was half open, music playing out, so I knocked and opened it at the same time. She was crouched in front of her mirror, straightening her hair and spraying each strand wildly as she went.

'Hey, gorge,' she said. 'How's it going?'

'Good,' I said, sitting down on the end of the bed and taking the bottle out of the bag. 'How you doing?' And before she could answer, I added, 'Glasses?'

We'd sat for a while like that, me with my back against the wall and my legs stretched out on the satin duvet, Lilah kneeling by the mirror, preening and powdering and straightening and shining. She had started seeing a man at work, a client, and she didn't want her boss to find out.

'He's so beautiful, Saf,' she gushed, her gold eyes widening, her own beauty reflected back in the mirror.

'I'm happy for you,' I said, and I was, the vodka warming my heart and making the room pink in the lamplight. I racked up two lines on the cover of a hardback book, but as she turned to look in her huge toolbox of make-up, I snorted one and quickly racked up another.

'Here,' I said, as she turned back round. 'Let's celebrate.'

I held out the book and the note and she grinned, 'Little fairy with your pixie dust.' She scooted forward and knelt at my knees to do the line. I watched the tiny particles zip up her nose as her hair swooshed across the cover. She handed back the note and squeezed my boot. 'Thanks, baby.' She went back to the mirror, turning up the music as she passed. She started to sing, humming the beat aloud in her beautiful sparkly voice.

The thing with Lilah was that she started off each night like this. Full of happy, fun and glossy pretty. I'd look at her and feel so ordinary sat on the sides. She was shiny and new and I was growing-out roots and scuffed boots. She looked like the kind of person anything could happen to, like in fairytales and rubbish films, like she might drop her purse in the street and a prince or a footballer would bend to pick it up and fall in love with her. But as the night went on she'd get bored. She'd look around the room and she wouldn't see anybody she liked or wanted to talk to and she wouldn't know the music and she'd feel out of place. And her glossy would look too much, too bright in the dark loveliness of the night. And she'd sulk and start to whine, and she'd take her shoes off because her feet hurt, and she'd pull her hair back because it was too hot, and it made me realise that even beautiful people are only beautiful in their own place. Fitz thought that Lilah was a bit up herself, but I knew that she cried herself to sleep sometimes. I knew that she hated her job and I knew that she could never tell her parents about the abortion she had had or the married men she slept with and so I found a bit of her to love.

We did the lines and then we stood up and straightened ourselves out and then we left. Molly was pouring bolognese onto two perfect nests of spaghetti as we passed. There was a man's shoe poking out from the kitchen table, but the door hid the leg and the body and the face. 'Who is it?' I asked Lilah, as we walked down the street, waiting to feel cold through the vodka but staying cosy in its warmth. She shrugged. 'James, I guess.

Someone boring like that.' To Lilah, anyone without beauty or wealth was boring. It made me cross with her but it also made me feel relieved, because I knew that she couldn't see the real wonder of Fitz and so he was safely mine.

The streetlights had been starting to come on as the sky turned darker grey, little globes of orange glowing along the long street. I took poppers from my pocket and offered them to Lilah. She shook her head. 'God, no. What are you – sixteen? You'll be sick …' I laughed and put them to my nose anyway. The rest of the road rushed by in a warm lurch, lights brighter and cheeks warm, Lilah chattering away about everything and nothing.

I could feel the bass throbbing through the pavement as we walked up the drive, beating up through my feet and into my heart, leaving me short of breath and anxiously happy. The door was open and we stepped through into the dark. All of the light bulbs had been swapped for the coloured ones you could get in the pound shop, red in the hall. The walls had been covered with giant sheets of plain white paper, which people were already scrawling messages across.

We headed naturally for the kitchen, the place where everybody begins and ends a party. It was bustling busy, people perching on worktops and crowded around talking and reaching for things and filling glasses. The light bulb in the kitchen was green, everything and everybody suddenly seeming as if they were under water. I was already high and happy and didn't want anything bringing me down, so I floated through without stopping, smiling at people and feeling the music rolling around my head. Alice was at the far end of the kitchen table, crotch glowing in the green light, and she jumped up excitedly and pulled me into her arms, showing me off to the rest of the table, like I was her pet, and then slipped a pill into my hand and danced off.

When we had gone into the lounge the light was dark blue, and people were dancing in a little clot in front of the decks. We danced in the blue dark for a while and I could feel my eyes starting to roll back behind my lids so I took Lilah's hand and we sat down on the sofa. She was drinking wine slowly from the bottle, watching nobody in particular, and she ran her long fingers through my hair sending shivers over my rushing skin, tight and tiny pearls. My face and my mouth were dry and hot. The beat was pounding in my ears and I couldn't breathe, like the darkest blue was shrinking in on me and the beat was growing and growing until it would crash down and cover me like a wave. Around me people were changing, shimmering gold glasses appearing over eyes and disappearing again, strange masks looming out of dark corners, faces melting into screams. I closed my eyes but the darkness sent me spinning. I stood, and the carpet lurched underneath me as I hurried out into the angry red of the hall and then into the toilet. I had to peel away a corner of white paper to get into it, and when I shut the door behind me, I could hear squeaky pens scribbling and scrawling messages on the inside of my skull.

The light was a normal greenish yellow in there, and I thought somewhere far inside my head that Alice must have run out of colours. I looked at my face in the mirror. My eyes were black and my skin was greenish yellow too, disappearing into the reflection of the walls and the door. My hair had come loose from its knot and was sticking to my scalp and cheeks like straw, falling limply down on my shoulders, and I pushed it and pulled it, disgusted. The bass pulsed through the door and in my veins, and as I pulled and tugged faster and faster at my hair and face my image blurred in the glass and the light seemed to shiver in its socket. I scraped my hair back and tied it with the band I kept round my wrist, but it was no good. I looked on the shelves and I found a tiny pair of nail scissors and I got hold of the ponytail between my fingers and hacked clean through it, the soft sound of the scissors snipping echoing around me in the pale light. Bleached clumps of fluffy hair fell into the sink like feathers. The sober me was stirring in the back of my head, panicking and fluttering anxiously, but I ignored her, shoved her back down. I left the hair feathers in the sink and pulled the band out so that my hair splayed around me, rough and uneven, and looked at my face for a long time until it stopped being my own and then I went back into the party. I went upstairs where the light was pink, and silvery strains of techno were spilling out and I did not look back.

I sat at my desk, still pulling at the new short chunks of my hair, the sketchbooks lying forgotten around me. I wondered, for the first time since I'd remembered cutting it, what it looked like but I didn't get up to check. I sat, and I waited for Fitz to wake up.

There are places and rooms where everything can be taken away from you; words and thoughts and strength, until you are a child again, small and adrift. You feel invisible and caught in the headlights all at once. The things you have tried to build up around yourself, the things people have said you can be, fade away in the shadows of others around you. At school you are instantly comparable, instantly assessable. There are suddenly other players in the game you play with yourself.

I looked around the room but there was nothing to see except the tops of bowed heads as people pored over their work, scribbling notes on sketches and leafing through pages torn from magazines, scraps of fabric and glossy photographs. I rolled a pencil slowly back and forth along the table enjoying the dull clatter it made each way. The tutor, John, sat in a chair by the window playing on his phone. He was young, with blondish curls and an earnest enthusiasm for most things. If he'd had a tail, it would always wag. On the board behind him, he'd cheerfully scrawled the number '14' in scarlet. This was the number of days we had left to work on our final pieces, weekends not included, and it glowed against the bright white of the board. The degree show hadn't meant anything to me when I'd first begun, not like the others, the serious ones like Millie, who'd tagged along to the show each year even though we didn't have to, making notes and talking to the students who were graduating.

But now, with the red numbers on the wall and the feverish energy around the silent room, I felt the pangs of real panic rise. I looked down at the blank page in front of me, and I wondered how I'd ever thought I could do this.

*I'm too old to be a student. I'm miles older than everyone else.*

*He bounces onto the sofa next to me. Don't be silly, he says, rubbing my back. Only a couple of years. Bet you nobody even knows if you haven't told them.*

*I know, though, don't I?*

*He ruffles my hair. You've come this far, babe. You're brilliant, Saf. You're gonna knock their socks off.*

*You think so?*

*I know so. Now give us a cuddle.*

With my eyes closed, I could see him so clearly and feel his arms around me. But I knew if I tried to open my eyes and draw, he'd disappear like steam, float away out of reach and be gone. With my eyes closed, everything was in its place in my head, the ground was still and the desk was in front of me. I knew if I opened them the buzzing in my head would get louder and everything would start to spin out of control and away from me.

John had got up and was pacing slowly around the room, offering his services, which seemed primarily to be the aforementioned enthusiasm. He stopped to talk to Grant, two seats away.

'So how will the videos work in the show? You don't have masses of space, you know.'

'I've got three little plasmas from Hardy's downtown, on loan. They've said they'll fit them as well. I want them in a diagonal, you know, left to right.'

'Great, yes.'

'And I'm adding in this footage, the CCTV, see?'

'Fate Jones? Great, great. Perfect.'

'Yeah.'

The sound of patting on the back, footsteps moving on. I didn't have any electronics in my work. I didn't know how to make films. I could take photographs. That was all. I had been out the weekend before and taken pictures of things and people who caught my eye without thinking too hard about them. When I looked back through the pictures at home there was shot after shot of people eating, food in their hands and hanging out of their mouths, empty wrappers on the street, pigeons picking at a takeaway, a baby with ice-cream smeared over its face. These things did not sound great or perfect.

I felt the first familiar prickles of anger. It wasn't fair to move the boundaries, to include videos and CCTV and free TVs. It was the same story but with different rules, different people pulling the strings – I was used to moving my own goalposts, but having someone else to edge them away made my skin begin to crawl and my chest feel tight. Everyone else was filling space so fast there wasn't time or place enough to fit everything they could do. My pages were blanker than ever.

John was talking to Millie now, little Millie who was a year younger than everyone else because she'd skipped a year of school, and two years younger than most because she hadn't had a gap year, and four years younger than me because I was backward, Millie with her study in still lives, objects taken from people she'd met in the street, in interesting places, and arranged together and painted to represent a cross-section of modern society in an old style, and John thought that sounded great, great, perfect too. I closed my eyes tighter.

*The flat is cold and lonely, so I turn on the radio and start to fill the sink so I can wash up the dirty plates before he gets home. This will make him happy, and as the sink begins to fill with bubbling water, I imagine his dimple and the hair falling in his eyes as he reaches down to cuddle me.*

*The radio plays old songs, it's Motown hour, they say, and I hum along as I put the plates on the draining-board. A song comes on that I know. My dad used to sing it to my mum when I was little and she'd get annoyed and flick at him with a tea-towel, even though she wanted to laugh really. It's 'Let's Get It On' by Marvin Gaye and I begin to sing along.*

*I hear his voice behind me. He puts his skinny arms round me and we sway along and sing even though we don't quite know the words, my hands in the soapy water and his cold against my skin.*

*He turns me round and suds run down the back of his neck as I hold him close and we dance, round and round, in circles. We dance for the whole of Motown hour, with Marvin Gaye, Stevie Wonder, the Four Tops and the Temptations spilling out of the little radio and him and me dancing round, spinning and clicking our fingers, wiggling and laughing and kissing. When Quin finally comes home he laughs and joins in and the three of us sing until Crazy Bob and Ket Kev next door start knocking on the wall.*

John moved past me, invisible me, and began leafing through Gennifer's sketches of her handmade dress, formed of photographs printed on fabric, painstakingly stitched together. I opened my eyes and looked down at the page in front of me. I knew that I had to be better.

The smallest things can be the biggest jobs, if you let them. Fitz liked to take his time choosing which song to put on, weighing one up against another and fretting about whether people would like it, watching their faces in fear as the first bars began to play. Quin could never choose an outfit to wear each day. He'd spend ages putting things on and then pulling them off, leaving them in tiny piles on the carpet like shed skins. Lilah spent an hour every day straightening her hair, over and over again, tiny strand by tiny strand. My mother found it difficult to tell someone awkward or unpleasant news. You could hear her on the phone, skipping and skirting round what she needed to say, tripping up on the words and jumping out of the way of questions. When my sister seduced her maths teacher in the store cupboard, my mother told everyone for months that he had assaulted her. All of them were just putting off the real thing they had to do; the going outside or the telling of the truth or the letting yourself be seen. They reminded me of my sister Lulu when she was tiny, when she knew that putting your toys away was the thing you did before you went to bed, so she'd put the things back in her toy-box, one by one, then take them out, one by one, and lay them on the floor in neat rows, then start all over again. If you watched her from the doorway, without her noticing, sometimes you'd catch her giggling to herself; maniacally happy that she'd beaten the sequence of things.

Sometimes I wonder what life would have been like if we'd all just done the things we were afraid of.

Fear was the feeling knotting my belly that evening, though I didn't realise it then; a weird creepy feeling all over my skin and crawling in my insides. I was standing by the counter with my hands just floating above the surface, frozen. The sound of Fitz singing in the shower and the water hitting the tiles were the only noises in the flat.

The things were lined up on the counter. They were staring at me.

This was not how it was supposed to be. These things were my routine, my security. I chopped and sliced and created and looked and saw and did not eat, and in this way the world stayed upright and Fitz was happy and I was strong. I looked at the globs of chicken in their purple polystyrene tray, the plastic peeled back. I looked at the knife in my hand. I reached out and took a pepper instead, holding it in my hand like a grenade. I tried to ignore the feeling of its skin against mine, ignore the smell of it, sharp and green. I sliced it, singing a song in my head, wishing the radio was on. When it was done, when I had won, I slid the strips onto a plate and looked again at the chicken. I reached out to pick up the first thin slab. I imagined the feel of it in my hand, the wet it would leave on my fingers, the thin white veins of fat stretched across its pale, flabby flesh. I put my hand down. I put the knife down.

The peppers and the purple tray of chicken went to bed in the bin.

By the time Fitz came out, I had put the telly on and turned off the main light and turned on the lamp. I held out ten pounds, crisp and dry in my hand, safe.

'I think you deserve a treat,' I said. 'Fish and chips? Kebab? Proper pie and mash …?'

His eyes lit up and he looked at it like it was a million pounds. 'Where'd you get that, lovely?'

'My mum sent it to me. Think she knows I'm working hard. Here, go on. You deserve it, for looking after me when I'm being such a pain.'

I loved the way his face creased up all the way to his ears when he grinned.

Later, as we sat in front of the soaps with our feet tucked up under each other and our fingers laced up together, I tried not to smell the scent of frying fat on his skin, or feel the grease on his fingers, seeping into the edges of mine. On TV they were showing a special programme, a live show about safety in the city, a woman's guide to avoiding crime. I leant my head against his shoulder and tried not to breathe.

When you take drugs, things that were once opposites become the same.

Too much = Never enough
Standing still = Spinning around
Feeling at ease with someone you know well = Falling head over heels in love all over again
Just one more = Please never stop
Night = Day (but day still equals day, and that's what sends the world sideways)

It's important not to get too hung up on drugs. They're just a tangent to anyone's story: at best, an accessory, just a minor character; at worst, a symptom of a deep dark that hides behind the high. To me they had become both, though I didn't know it, not really. They were a big fat block and an opening; they shut out hunger and emptiness, and gave me ideas, thoughts, feelings. These were things that filled white pages.

I climbed the steps to the pavement and I climbed the short steps to the flat next door. I knocked on the door because I knew the bell didn't work, and I waited.

When I first met Fitz, I realised instantly what a true high feels like. This kind of high didn't come from inside, wasn't affected by your mood or how much you wanted it. It just took you over, all over, in a warm, glowing fuzz, from head to toe. It could come from the smallest things, the way he pronounced a word or the way he danced around the bedroom when he was drying himself after a shower. Innocent and uninvited and always welcome. A real buzz, as he'd say. But it was a dependency all the same. A need. And life is nothing without needs.

There were footsteps in the hall, slow, confused, and the sound of a bolt unlatching, a chain undone. The door creaked open.

Rufus was tall and always walked like doors were too short for him and ceilings too low. He had curls of sandy hair that were never washed and he was always unshaven. He'd worn the same red hoody every time I'd seen him. He never remembered my name and I wasn't sure I hadn't made his up. He never looked surprised to see me.

'Hiya,' he said, and he left the door open and wandered back down the hall, leaving me to follow. It was a normal flat; bigger than ours, with new carpets and a framed poster in the hall. The kitchen always looked clean and there were blinds on the window instead of the nets everybody else had, or the bars that we did. I followed Rufus into the living room.

There were three of them. Rufus returned to his seat on the leather sofa, picking up his controller and carrying on playing whatever shooting game he was halfway through. Playing against him, in the other corner of the sofa, was Jackson, who was wearing a black leather jacket that matched the sofa and was stare-at-me beautiful, with smooth dark skin and hair shaved short. He gave me a dreamy smile, then looked back at the screen.

'What you after today, babe?'

I shrugged and leant against the door. 'What you got?'

'How much you got?'

I smiled at the side of his face. 'I get paid tomorrow. I'll settle up then. You know I'm good for it.'

He tsked. 'Give her some drone. No more of the good stuff.' He turned briefly to give me another grin, a no-offence-meant flash of perfect white teeth.

'Here you go.' I didn't know the third one's name. He was sitting on the floor, back against the wall, holding a wrap out to me.

There are certain people you pass on the street or on a plat-form or in a shop. A sudden inexplicable shot of fear hits you, though if you looked at them again it would be gone. Sometimes you see a person glance at you as they walk past and you think of the people who kill strangers and bury them under their houses and gardens, who chain girls up in their cellars or who remove their breasts or feet. There is an electricity in those almost encounters, as if you have accidentally and unnoticed skimmed the surface of a secret underworld of evil. He was one of those people. I stepped forward and took the wrap.

'You know,' he said, fixing eyes with pink rims on mine so that all the noise of the game faded away. 'There are other ways you could pay.'

He didn't look away and I felt my skin turn to ice all over. The spell was only broken by an explosion on the screen and Jackson's tsk.

'Kay, man, don't say things like that to the poor girl. Jeeeez.'

I laughed. 'In your dreams, mate.' I turned and left, but I felt Kay's eyes follow me even through the wall.

'Money tomorrow!' someone called after me.

Inhaling white dust fills the empty space hunger makes, but it doesn't replace the white noise inside your head. Hunger is a cavity, carefully hollowed out, but emptiness is a void, borderless and infinite. The pages remained blank.

I listened to my footsteps echo in the silent space. There were no windows, just the spotlights above, so that I was temporarily without time, though I knew that it was bright daylight outside. Time was never my friend: it stretched out away from me and then ran past too fast to keep up with. It was always waiting for me just ahead, sometimes hiding round a corner and sometimes just waving at me from far away, teasing me. Walking through the empty hall, it was both. I was alone and the clock was stopped, but once the spell was broken it would spiral wildly away again. I had nothing, blank pages still. I'd stared at the wall for hours and hours the day before and all the night, Fitz moving around me and the light changing, and there was nothing but the hole inside me and the roar of half-formed nothing thoughts buzzing and banging against my brain.

When I was small, pictures flew out of me with just a twitch of my little fingers; pictures and paintings and stories and games, all appearing out of nowhere into the air and onto paper. I didn't know when they had abandoned me. By then I was even struggling to watch the TV for more than ten minutes. There was no peace for me anywhere.

I looked at the names pinned neatly on each of the boards. My footsteps sounded suddenly like a clock ticking, and for once it was as if I was making my own time. If I could stop, find my place, all would be silent again. Somewhere in the distance an ambulance or a police car wailed past. I found my name and stopped. Two plywood boards, painted white with emulsion and fixed to make a corner, one where my work could be mounted and pinned, where people could stand around hushed and look, some of them to point at a thing that captured their eye or their heart and whisper to their friend before moving on. I reached out a hand and ran my fingers over the smooth surface.

Earlier that day, I'd stepped into the workshop and sat without taking any work from my bag. I'd wanted to capture the anger I'd felt before, to see what the others were doing and spur myself on, light a fire in my head that would burn away the blur. There were only a couple of them there, Gennifer hunched over her sewing machine, Millie studiously guillotining backing paper. I sat and watched her hand move back and forth along the board, sliding the blade along its runner. I fished for my camera in my pocket, captured by the thin strips of the paper being sliced away, the borders brought in nearer and nearer, the edges coming closer to the centre. She turned as I raised the lens and I looked down again, pretending to flick through pictures, hearing her neat step and hair swish behind me.

'Whoops!'

The sheets of thick paper fluttered to the floor in their perfect squares. She had caught her foot in the strap of my bag, spilling its guts onto the dirty grey tiles. I bent to pick up the things and felt my head spin.

'Sorry, Saffy, I didn't see you there,' she said, crouching down with a hair flick to gather her perfect paper. 'Gosh, what are all these for?'

There is a time and a place for stealing cutlery. It's mid-lunch-time on a weekday and it's in the branch of Scoff nearest the Tube station, where the cutlery station is near the door and not the counter, and where the sets come shrink-wrapped, folded in a napkin, bedded in with a pinch of salt and a twist of pepper in their paper packets, sealed. You can slip through the door with as many as you can fit in your hands and your bag and nobody will notice.

My fear of forks, and of knives and spoons too, though that doesn't sound half as lovely, had started in earnest a few weeks before. I'd watched Quin do the washing-up, with the cutlery left till last in the bottom of the bowl, mayonnaise and butter and sauce and potato and fat all greasy around the teeth and the handles. I'd watched him run the dirty sponge over them once, a fat fistful of them, then dump them on the smudged metal draining-board. And I'd known, right away, that I would never be able to put one in my mouth again.

I took the plastic packets from her and shoved them back into my bag.

'They're for a piece,' I said. 'About consumerism.'

'Wow,' she said, straightening up, hair falling back into place. 'Sounds amazing.'

I wondered if Millie had been to see her boards, if she'd stood there in the silence and stared at the space, like I was. The wall was flimsy to touch. I could push it over if I wanted to. Push it over and make it all go away, make everything stop whirling and stop the white panels staring at me. But I didn't. I stepped back and I stood there for a very long time, staring at my tiny printed name and the blank space beneath it.

*The music is loud and I don't know anybody here. I've taken all my coke and still haven't found anybody I want to talk nothings about nothing with. I keep drinking my drink for something to do, but the ice is cold and it hurts my teeth. I came with Abby but she's gone up to a bedroom with some guy who spilt a drink over her white dress and whom she kissed as a reward. I'm wearing a top I love, although I lose it somehow a week or so later. It's covered with heavy sequins; not sparkly but dull, used sequins, like armour. It makes me feel small and light, like the top is the only thing holding me on the ground. I could take it off any time I want.*

*I lean against the bookcase, watching people dance and drinking my horrible sweet drink. A couple in front of me are dancing slowly together. He is biting her ear, she's laughing. Her skirt has ridden up and his hand is sliding up the back of her thigh. He says something to her and she stops laughing and they leave. In the space where they were, I see him. He is sitting on the windowsill, scratching a CD case with a library card and looking around him for somebody. He sees me too, and we stare at each other as if the rest of the room has faded away into nothing. His eyes are dark and his hair curls around his ears and neck. He smiles and stands up. He has one dimple when he smiles. It makes his face look crooked in the loveliest way. He's tall; it only takes three of his long steps to get across the room. His fingers bending around the beer bottle are crooked as well. When he gets up close he smells of beer and cigarettes, cold houses and cosy beds. I think I would like to look up at him like that for ever.*

I stood and watched him at the sink, washing two mugs to make tea. His hair curled over the collar of his top by then and his elbows bent out at odd angles as he scrubbed, humming along cheerfully to a tune being played in his head. He often looked surprised or pleased at the track he found there, as if he'd just wandered into a bar and found they were playing his latest favourite album. I wanted desperately to reach out and touch him, to wrap my arms around him and bury my face in his back. I wanted, for the first time in a long time, to talk. To tell.

And then the hammering began. At first, in the strange second it takes for your brain to find the meaning of a sound, I thought it was coming from inside me. Fitz turned off the tap and turned to look at me.

'Who's that gonna be?' he asked, but I couldn't find any words. He hurried through to the hall, leaving me to trail behind him. I stopped in the doorway because suddenly I couldn't go any further. Fitz wiped the suds off his hands and opened the door.

It slammed inwards in a movement so violent that I felt the world shake, and before I could scream, Fitz was pinned to the woodchip wallpaper by his throat.

'Time to pay up!' Kay's knuckles were red against Fitz's white neck, and the veins in his arm stuck out blue against the greying evening. His face was sweaty and his eyes had turned from pink to red. With each word he banged Fitz's beautiful curls against the wall.

There was a terrible moment of complete still, when it seemed as if Kay's outstretched arm had us all pinned in time, his veins pulsing, Fitz's words gurgling and trapped at the back of his throat, my legs shaking me against the doorframe. And then Fitz managed to choke a sentence out.

'Pay up for what, mate?'

Kay dropped him and he sagged against the wall. 'Your tab,' he said, and then he turned and grinned at me. Two of his teeth were pointed. 'Pay it,' he said, and then he grabbed Fitz's face in his meaty fist and slammed his head back against the wall. 'Or things are going to get nasty.'

'We'll pay,' Fitz said, squeezing the words out through squashed cheeks. 'Tomorrow. We'll have the cash tomorrow.'

Kay let him go, his head rocking forward. Kay grunted, and left without another word, leaving the door wide open behind him. We stood there in the dying light without saying a word.

In chaos, there is often beauty. Exploding lives can be seen in a million tiny parts, each one beautiful as it passes before you, as it is violently snatched away. In the centre of a hurricane, things are still. I sat at my desk and let the music play out, and I saw my life whirling away from me and the page still blank, and everything seemed far away, like a dream.

Love:

> Will Tear Us Apart
> Is a Losing Game
> You Always Hurt The One You
> All You Need Is
> And Happiness
> I'd Do Anything For (But I Won't Do That)
> Is All Around
> Me for a Reason
> Can Build a Bridge
> Grows (Where My Rosemary Goes)
> Fight for This
> It Must Have Been

So many voices, spilling out of the speakers, telling me what love was and what love meant, how it could hurt you and how it could save you. None of them told me what to do when you were the one doing the hurting and you were beyond saving.

I sat at the wonky table and listened to the system pick songs at random for me, for hours and hours, hearing nothing, seeing nothing, lost in the lyrics. When I finally looked down at the page, there was just a fat black bleed from the paintbrush hovering in my hand. I was in the dark, in more ways than I had ever been.

I got up to turn the lights on. Fitz would be on his way home, and while I was waiting there was still the lovely possibility that things would be okay, that Cadbury would have agreed to give him another sub, that we could pay Kay and then we could find our way back.

The sound of the key in the door made all the love I'd listened to leap up into my heart. Things were possible once again.

When I saw his face, I knew I was wrong. In a fairytale or a crap film or a love song, there would be some tiny magic, some fortune, that would make things happen for us. But all our magic was gone. We were alone.

He shook his head. 'Sorry, lovely. No more subs.'

And then he held out an arm, making a space for me to fill in the way he always did. I felt as if it was impossible to get close enough to him, with my arms wrapped round his waist and his cheek resting on my head. 'Hey,' he said, 'don't worry, lollipop, it'll be okay. We'll just tell him we'll give it him next week. He probably won't even remember, you know – he was wrecked.' He kissed the top of my head. And just like that, the magic was back.

We sat on the sofa and twiddled our fingers together. As the evening wore on I let my head fall to Fitz's shoulder, tucking myself into him. In the sixty-second news round-up between programmes, *Top Idol* was being accused of rigging phone lines and Fate Jones was still gone. Life was carrying on, and so would we. Fitz sleepily reached up a hand and stroked my cheek. He was reading my mind without even trying, and he was next to me. Even as things changed around us, that was true.

And then the knock came.

I felt my body go weak, and I wanted to cry out and grab Fitz by the hands, keep him in his spot and bury ourselves in Quin's corner, but it was too late. He was standing up, straightening his jeans. He ruffled my hair. 'It'll be all right,' he said. 'Leave it to me.' And then he was gone, and the front door was opening, and I was clinging to his words even as they were fading.

I could only hear Fitz's side of the conversation; Kay's was muffled by the walls into a deep, growling hum.

'Hiya, mate.'

'Look, about that …'

'No, no, mate, nobody's fucking you about!'

'I swear, honest, I'll get it for you!'

'Come on, can't we just be mates about it? Let's have a beer, shake on it, yeah? I can get it to you next week.'

'Please …'

There was a dull thud as the door was shoved open, a faint wheeze as air left Fitz's lungs, and a sudden rush of chill as the cold outside found its way into the flat. Kay swaggered in. He gave me a little wave in a way that made me feel sick all over, then strode over to the telly, his dirty boots leaving marks that would stay there for days. He knelt in front of it, looked it over, his face right up close to Simon Cowell's hyperwhite smile as the rerun of *Top Idol* got into its stride. Fitz was standing in the doorway, bent almost double.

'You guys need a new telly,' Kay said conversationally. 'Need a microscope to see anything on this piece of shit.' He strolled around the edge of the room, looking at the furniture, weighing each thing up. As his eyes rolled round, I felt my heart sink.

'Ah,' he said. 'Here we are.'

Fitz's decks had their own table when they weren't being used. It was an old coffee-table, one he'd rescued when they'd been chucking it out of the bar. It was too low for him to play on, but it was big enough for them and the stereo to sit on, out of the way of the kitchen and greasy fingers. They gleamed in the low orange light from the tiny kitchen window, and for a second I could see every pound he had spent on them, every tiny bit he had saved up, all the songs he had played on them, all the songs he could have played on them.

'These will do nicely.' He stacked them together, scratching them, tugging them free of their home. He grinned at us cheerfully. 'Laters, guys. Cash. Next week. Don't fuck with me.'

And then he was gone. This time, he closed the door behind him.

Sometimes, when people say something to you, the reply whispers itself in your head before you can stop it.

'You look tired.'
*You mean I look rough.*

'You're looking very thin.'
*Jealous?*

'You're looking very thin.'
*Liar.*

'I went off him a bit.'
*He dumped you.*

'We want different things.'
*He dumped you.*

'We're just worried about you.'
*You're worried about what people think of you.*

'I love you.'
*No, you don't.*

'I love you.'
*How can you?*

After he'd gone, the flat was silent again. I tried to look at Fitz, but he was squinting up at the ceiling and he didn't look at me at all. When I tried to say something, he blinked once, hard, and then he squeezed my hand.

'It's okay,' he said. 'Don't worry.'

I wanted to disappear.

We sat on the sofa, and though he put his arm around me there was a mile between us. The news was on, and he didn't get up to turn it over. He wasn't really sitting in the room with me any more. We were both alone.

Police had released new CCTV footage of Fate Jones, and the news was playing it on a loop as they read the latest statement from her family and from the fat detective who was working on the case. It was grainy, black-and-white, and showed her leaving the doors of the pub at the top of the screen, and walking down to the Funky Chicken, the takeaway place at the end of the street whose cameras had caught her. She walked down our screen again and again while we sat there in silence, with the buildings looming black at the edge of the picture and her blonde hair turned white and her face grey in shadow.

In the fuzzy image, we looked almost alike.

# FITZ

I was looking down at my chips, and that didn't take long because there were only three left to look at, wondering if any of our cards had money on and if Saf had been paid yet. I had a couple of quid left in my pocket, which I thought I'd get changed up into silver and play on the fruities with. I've got a soft spot for the fruities. They may not be the most fancypants in the casino and maybe you don't ever win or if you do you don't ever win more than a fiver and that's the jackpot, the big guns, but they'll stay up with you all night long and flash nice lights at you to make you feel better and all they ask is 10p a go. They even have a little cup-holder, see, where you can stick your drink. Nice little stool to sit yourself down on if you're so inclined. Everything is easy when you're sitting at a fruitie; nothing is dark or sad. I put two of the chips in and looked down at my battered cards. It wasn't going well but I didn't mind that because in some little part of my little brain I still thought there was always a chance of things turning around.

And then I heard a crash and a bang and a tiny little, 'Whoops,' and my leg's all dripping wet and smells a bit like beer. I looked down at my wet leg and there was a plastic pint glass rolling around in a white frothy fluffy pool of lager on the grim carpet and a sticky tray with chewing gum on the bottom taking a little spin around the floor before falling down ring-a-ring-a-roses-a-pocket-full-of-posies. When I looked up again there was this girl stood there looking about as red as a bus and a phone-box and a postbox all rolled into one and she looked at me and said, 'Whoops,' again but this time even quieter. All her hair was falling out of her ponytail onto her face, and her white shirt, which all the waitresses had to wear, had these big wet patches under the arms.

'I'm so sorry,' she said, and she looked like she was about to cry.

'No worries,' I said. 'Bit of beer never did anyone any harm.'

And that made her smile a bit and she was probably just bus and phone-box red by then. And then there was a bang from over by the bar and a fat sweaty man who looked like he might be the manager started hotfooting it over, making all the floor wobble as his chins went from side to side.

The waitress went white as a sheet and the tears started popping back up. 'He's going to kill me,' she said. 'He's going to take it out of my wages.' Like they were one and the same thing, which I guess for a lot of people working shitty jobs in the city they are.

'Here y'are,' I went, taking out my last two pounds and holding them out so as he could see. 'My fault,' I said, nice and loud so he could hear me over the thundering of his chins. 'Sorry about that, miss.'

He stopped and looked at us for a minute, then he made a little huffy noise and turned around and wobbled all the way back. The waitress stood there with the two pound coins clutched in one hand and the tray still lying where it had fallen across one of her feet, and she was shaking like a little leaf all over and she was just staring at me.

'Why'd you do that?' she goes. 'You never had to do that.'

I shrugged. ''Sall right. I do things like that all the time, a right butterfingers.'

She looked down and saw her tray but she didn't pick it up. She looked back up with eyes like saucers. 'Thank you,' she goes, and her voice was all little again. 'Thank you.'

I shrugged again. It was only a couple of quid. I thought I should probably be getting back to Saffy anyway. I really was worried about her the more I thought about the party and the bloke from next door and this debt we were gonna have to pay and I didn't think all of it was going to go away this time. Every time I looked at her hair all hacked off I had a little shiver, even though it did suit her. The gap where the rest of it had been made me even sadder than the gap where my decks had been. The waitress was looking at her feet, well, the one without the tray napping on it – tracing the patterns on the minging carpet with her toe and going red again. 'I've finished my shift now,' she goes, looking really hard at a sicky yellow spiral. 'I get free chips if you want to share?' and she pointed at the little noodle-chip bit under the karaoke rooms but without looking up from the floor.

Well, I'm never one to turn down a chip and when I came to think of it I was pretty hungry, plus she seemed a bit on the lonely side and I really don't like seeing people on their tod and I thought, What's ten minutes of my time to keep her company for a bit, in the grand scheme of things? 'Why not?' I said, and I hopped off my stool.

We walked over to the food bit and I sat down at a table while she talked to the man behind the counter. There was a fly walking across the plastic table, all little dots of salt stuck to its feet. I blew at it and waved it away with my hand and it zoomed off up into the greasy air and into the bits of song that were floating out from under the karaoke-booth doors. She sat down opposite me with one of the squeaky white trays of chips. 'I didn't know what sauce you wanted …' she goes, and her voice trailed off. We both looked down at the plain yellow chips.

'Looks good,' I said. 'Maybe just some salt, eh? Can't go wrong with the classics.' And I shook the salt with a little flourish and dug straight in to make her feel better. She held one between two fingers like she was afraid of it. It's not as if I wasn't used to girls who didn't like to eat in front of people and so I said, 'Best hurry up if you want any, I'm starving.' And gave her a grin to show I was only messing. She smiled back and chomped down on her chip.

'What's your name?' I asked, to try and get her out of her shell and make her feel a bit more relaxed.

'Win,' she goes, looking at the floor. 'It's short for Winifred.'

'That's an ace name,' I said, and I did mean it. 'Fits right in here, with the gambling and that, you know.' She nodded like she wasn't all that sure and then she popped the rest of the chip into her mouth. 'I'm Fitz,' I said. And then there was that bit of weird silence you get when you meet somebody new and the introductions are over but the knowing each other hasn't arrived yet.

'You come here often?' she asked, and then she went a bit red again and laughed into her hand, like a weird chuckle. 'I didn't mean it like that. But do you?'

'Yeah,' I said, shaking more salt on the chips, cos we'd eaten the top ones and none of the salt had snuck through like it should do. 'A fair bit, yeah. I like it here. You been working here long?'

She shook her head and pushed some sticky bits of hair away. 'I used to work at their other place. You know Wheel of Fortune?' I nodded, cos I did, but I didn't like it much. A bit posh for me. I like a place where your feet stick to the carpet if you stand still too long; where nobody's pretending to be something they're not and everyone knows what they're there for and you know where you are. 'I used to work there. But I kept dropping things and getting into trouble, so they sent me here instead. Same owners innit.'

'Oh, right,' I went. 'You like it then, waitressing? I work behind a bar so quite similar really. I don't mind it. The free drinks are good. Get to chat to people. Not bad really.'

She poked at her fingers with the points on the little bendy plastic fork. 'I'm not very good at it.'

'You just need a bit of practice.' I folded the lid over on the empty tray and brushed the salt off the table top. 'Honest, it's like when I started at the bar, couldn't even pour a pint, you know, all fluffy and foamy like a cloud and people getting moustaches every time they even sniffed it. And now it's like people come from miles around just for a fine golden pint poured by my fair hand.' I gave her a little wiggle of the fingers so she could see. She was a bit of a starer, actually, like she'd forgotten she was meant to talk when you'd finished or she was just frozen into place waiting for the words to catch up.

After a minute, she shrugged and said, 'Maybe. Hopefully I'll get better.' And then she sat and waited for me to say something.

There was a little telly up over the counter, kind of pointed so as we could see it and most of the empty tables could see and the guy scraping the silver hot bits you keep the food on could see it too. The news was on, same as it was everywhere, but it wasn't the front door any more, they were playing this dodgy short clip of CCTV footage instead, to try and jog people's memories, which I never understood really, as if you'd look at it and suddenly think, Actually yes, I did see that girl whose face is on all the buses and billboards and fag packets in the whole city and I'm just now remembering looking at this blurry little clip. It was playing on a loop while the presenters were reading headlines we couldn't hear because the volume was turned all the way down. It was like we were being hypnotised with this black-and-white video of a blonde-haired girl walking out of the pub, down past Wok Around the Clock and the Funky Chicken and then disappearing behind the bottom of the screen. I watched her go down the screen ten or twelve times and the whole time I felt more and more that I really needed to cuddle Saffy, and to kiss her, and to make sure things went right again. It bubbled up inside me until I had to stand up and say as politely as I could, 'I'm really sorry, but I've got to go. Nice to meet you, yeah? I'll be back, ha ha. See you.' And then I turned and hurried back out through the casino, through the doors, down the street and all the way home.

I trotted up to the house just as the sun was going down. I had a proper fizz of excitement in me, like I was going to see Saffy for the first time in weeks and I wanted to make a big fuss of her and smother her with cuddles and watch something crappy on telly and laugh about silly things that had happened that day. The key was all hot in my pocket and I had a really funny feeling like I was about to sing or laugh or maybe just smile. I hopped down the stairs two at a time and put my key in the hole and turned it with one fat click and let the door swing open.

The house was dark inside. I wandered in and let the door shut behind me, wondering if it was a trick and if she was going to pop up out of the pile of shoes that had collected in the hall or from behind the sofa and planned my surprised face just in case that was what was going on. Everything was quiet and dark and cold, so I went through the kitchen to wait for her to come home. I sat there for a very long time, watching the shadows in the corners and waiting for the sound of her key in the lock or her steps on the stairs or her laugh on the air. After a long long while I gave up and I put my glass in the sink and I put my shoes in the pile and then I went into the bedroom and it was too cold and dark and sad to even take my clothes off so I got into bed all dressed and hugged the duvet.

She stood at the sink that morning with a pint glass, filling it up and necking it down and filling it up and necking it down, just staring up through the skinny window and carrying on, until I felt like I had watching Fate Jones on CCTV, all hypnotised and jittery and confused for no real reason at all. When we finally got out and walked to the Tube she had to keep dashing into caffs and pubs to have a piss and I thought to myself she ought to get it all out cos they wouldn't like her doing that at work, dashing off the shop floor every five seconds to wee, but I couldn't say it because she was in quite a good mood and for a minute it was almost like all the other stuff had just been a bad dream. She was skipping along next to me in her little ballerina shoes, babbling on about painting the flat, which she did a lot but never actually got around to doing, so I just nodded and squeezed her hand.

'It'll all be white,' she was saying, turning on her step on the escalator and looking up at me. 'Lovely and white and clean.'

She was fiddling with a button on my shirt and I put my hand over hers and it was cold, really cold. I said, 'It'll fall off, hun,' and she looked up at me in surprise as if she'd forgotten I was there and said, 'Yes, you're right it will. Fall off.' And then she hopped backwards off her step onto the ground, laughing, and grabbed my hand again as we walked with the flow to the platform. We could hear the doors beeping as we tripped down the stairs, and by the time we rounded the corner, the train was sliding off.

'Oh, well,' Saf said, swinging my hand like my little cousin did when she was tiny and me and Han used to take her to the swings. 'Next one's in four minutes anyway.'

She was never in a rush Saffy, like time would wait for her like everything else did. We walked to the end of the platform like we always did – and you do, don't you? After a while, you work out which door is going to be the one that pulls up next to the exit wherever you're going and that's where you insist on getting on even if it's packed, I mean really packed, like everyone in the other carriages has got their La-Z-Boys out and their picnics in the aisles, and you're all cramming into one section of one carriage because you want to be the first one loping up the stairs at your station two at a time and it saves you like what two seconds off your journey but that seems really important, well, that's what the Tube does for you, it makes you crazy. It wasn't exactly my favourite place to be after Hannah's accident, which is what we all called it for want of a better word even though that makes it sound like she just fell down the stairs or got her hand-bag trapped in the doors or something boring and everyday like that. After that all happened I did find myself looking about at people's backpacks and parcels and that's not a good way to be. I just counted myself lucky that I'd moved to Saffy's not long afterwards so at least I didn't have to use the station where it happened, the one by my old house, which I'd lived in with Eddie, where Hannah had been coming to visit me, because that would just have been really shit, day in, day out.

So there we were, stood right at the end of the platform look-ing up the big black hole with all the little white lights running up it, and the screen said three minutes and it was hot down there like it always is, even in winter when you have to wrap up like the Michelin man to make it down the road without freez-ing mid-step like that bloke out of *The Shining*, but then once you get down the escalator into the Tube it's hotter than hell and in summer it's even worse than that. I blew up at the sweat on my face and pushed some of the hair off my neck. There was still ages till I had to be at the bar so I thought I'd walk Saf to work as a treat and also because I was really pleased she was actually talking again because even if none of it made all that much sense, it was still a step back in the right direction.

Two minutes on the screen and I suddenly realised the girls behind us were talking about sex and so I leant back to listen because I'm only human really and caught the words 'cum' and 'tongue' but then they started whispering and the giant round woman behind me and Saf started talking to the skinny tall man next to her about the roadworks outside and how she was sure they weren't doing anything much except digging holes and filling them back in again and she wouldn't be surprised if it was all a scheme to get us to spend money on the Tube, which as a conspiracy had a lot of holes in it when you thought about it but he didn't say so. Maybe he was scared she'd sit on him or maybe he agreed. There was one minute on the screen by then, which was a relief because I could feel my hair starting to get sweaty at the edges and stick to my face and when that happens I look a right prat. The bloke with the speaker thing was telling everybody to use the whole length of the platform although obviously nobody was listening because they already knew exactly which carriage they were getting on whether they had to flatten themselves against the door to get in there or not.

Saffy had taken her hand out of mine and she was wiping sweat off her top lip and when I looked down at her she was a bit grey and pasty, so I said, 'You all right, Saf?'

She nodded and wiped a bit more sweat off and the bloke was announcing our westbound service and the first flicker of light was just showing on the furthest bit of black wall we could see and I could hear the rumble of the train, and then I suddenly thought, OH FUCK I haven't got my fob and I was really pissed off because that would mean going back because I couldn't go to work without it, you needed it to work the till and to put orders in to the kitchen and to get in the stockroom. So I knelt down on the platform and opened my backpack up and started fumbling around in it, and there it was at the bottom of my bag next to my gimpy little apron thing, and I breathed a sigh of relief and zipped my bag up quick because the train was blaring round the corner now, lights in my eyes and roaring up the tunnel, and then there was a little plop as Saf dropped her bag and I picked it up and held it up to her but her eyes were closed and she was rocking forward, toppling like a skittle when you go bowling. And the train was rushing up behind her and someone was screaming and I realised the someone was me, as the giant fat round woman was rushing up behind her and grabbing her by her little twig arms and pulling her back and she fell backwards onto the platform and lay there still. And then time pinged into place and the train was in front of me an inch from my face and Saffy was sprawled on the tiles with her short hair spread out around her head like an angel's halo. And people were gathering around and some were filing round us like ants to get on the train and I was still kneeling with her little yellow handbag held up in the air to no one. I crawled forward on my hands and knees and peered over the round woman's shoulder and wailed. The tall skinny bloke put a hand on my back and said, 'It's all right, mate, she's just fainted, it's hot down here, she'll be all right,' and I nodded up at him and clutched at her yellow bag but really I wanted to yell at him, Well, it's not all right, is it, mate? It's really not, because from where I was sitting she looked like she was dead.

When I woke up the next morning there was a Saffy shape next to me but the covers were pushed back and she was nowhere to be seen. I could hear her in the next room with Quin so I lay there and listened to see what they were chatting about, not in a nosy way or anything like that, just pleased to hear their voices.

'Whose house are you going to again?' Saffy was asking.

'Freddy and Milo's. They've got a new puppy, did I tell you?'

'No! Cute.'

'Very sweet apparently. Anyway, it's Hector's birthday so we're all going to stay for the weekend. Walks on the beach, debauchery, that type of thing.'

Saffy giggled. I liked hearing them together like that because it brought out a lovely side in both of them, like Quin became all fatherly and jolly and Saf turned back into a little girl. When he was excited like this his sentences became big and grand and funny like he was saying them on a stage, and being around him it was quite catching, it made everything seem dramatic and glamorous and fun. I could hear him clinging and clanging hangers on his little rail as he put stuff in his bag and the good mood was sort of glowing through the whole flat. He'd been out the day before so he didn't know anything about Saffy nearly dying in front of the Tube train, and seeing as me and her hadn't even talked about it since we'd got back home, I didn't reckon she was going to tell him and I didn't know if I was either. She seemed happy enough that morning, singing along to the radio and occasionally saying, 'Yes,' or 'Hmm,' as Quin held up clothes he was deciding whether or not to pack. I could picture her where she would be, sitting in the chair watching him with her legs crossed and her hands bunched up in the sleeves of her hoody.

'What are you guys going to get up to while I'm gone then?' he was saying.

'Oh, I don't know,' she said. 'I'd quite like to go to the park if it's sunny.'

'That's nice,' he goes. 'Listen, can I have back that cash you borrowed? I wouldn't normally ask but I need it this weekend. Extracurricular activities, if you know what I mean …' I think we all knew what he meant but I was wondering when and why Saf had borrowed money off him and why she hadn't said anything to me so I got up out of bed quietly and started looking about for some kecks or jeans or joggers.

'What money?' she goes, and I could hear her eyes getting narrow and cross all the way through the wall.

'The money,' he goes. 'Fifty quid. It was in my blazer pocket on Tuesday. Now it's gone.'

I heard her shrug through the wall too. 'Nothing to do with me,' she said. 'You must've spent it.'

'Don't start this again,' he says. 'The lying is when it starts getting really bad.' I had one leg in my pants and one out but I stopped.

'What do you mean, start this?' she said. 'Start what?'

'You're not well, darling,' he says. 'It's getting worse again, isn't it?'

'Oh, fuck off. You've spent too much money and suddenly I'm getting "ill" again. Bore off, Quin.'

I put my other leg in my pants and then I opened the door very very quietly, *sssh*. 'Come on, Saf,' Quin goes. 'You know we have to do something about this.'

'About what? Your finances? I totally agree,' she said, and she sat back down arms crossed and looked at him like he was stupid.

'About this!' he said, and he stormed across the room and opened up one of his *Brideshead* videos. 'About this,' he said more quietly, and he lifted out a plastic bag with all chewed-up bits of meat and mashy chips in it, and it looked a lot to me like a dinner we'd had ages ago, back when things were still going okay.

She stared at it and you couldn't tell what she was thinking but then she stood up really quickly and grabbed the copy of *Brideshead* resting on the arm of the sofa, the one he found a year before in a special shop and he cried when he got it he was that excited, and she goes, 'Me? There's nothing wrong with me. What about you, wanking over your weird cad porn? All the pages are sticky, look! Surely with all the wanking it should be you who lost SOME FUCKING WEIGHT.' And she held the book between her fingers by some of the pages and the rest all flopped towards the floor like a beautiful word-filled bird, and we all stared at it for a second and then there was a horrible rip sound and the book fell on the floor and the pages she was holding fluttered down after it.

'Saffy!' I said, and I hadn't meant to but it just slipped out and she looked up, surprised to see me, but she didn't seem guilty or sorry. Quinton was still staring at the book on the floor and then he turned away but not before I saw the tears in his eyes. He picked up his bag and he didn't say 'bye he just walked out, and I looked at Saf but she just kicked the book and sat back down and she wouldn't look at me. I walked very slowly back into the bedroom and I sat down on the end of the bed for a very long time.

There I was, stomping home, and there was a bit of a breeze about and a few leaves on the ground so it must've been getting to be autumn. I did up my jacket, smacking myself in the chest with the pint of milk swinging around in the orange placky bags that were digging into my hands. I was fucked off and upset and I couldn't take any more, sitting there looking at Saf looking at nothing, thinking all the time of the money she'd given to me to get a takeaway or the little baggies that kept turning up in the house like they were creeping in off the pavement. She just sat there looking at the telly while I sat in our room and tried not to think about the horrible strange not-Saffy way she'd talked to Quin or the way she'd lied because I knew she *had* lied and I knew she *had* taken money off him and that in turn made me start to wonder just how much money she'd spent and how long she'd been keeping all of this from me, and all these questions started popping up in my brain and after a while I realised she was standing in the doorway behind me and I wanted to turn around and ask what was happening to her but I didn't because I was scared and it felt like we were suddenly in a different place and I had no idea where, and if I said something we might be stuck there with no way back.

I'd thought if I carried on acting normal maybe this would all go away and things would go back to how they were before, so I'd made myself stand up and pretend like everything wasn't falling down around us, and just said, 'C'mon, *60 Minute Makeover*'s on, innit? I'm not in work till six so let's have a duvet day.'

And I'd put on a happy smiley face and hummed a little tune as I dragged the duvet off the bed and into the lounge, and she trailed along behind me not saying anything and she sat down very still, not even making a dent, and I kind of tucked the duvet round her and kind of folded myself around her too, which wasn't all that easy, it was a bit like hugging a stick, and then we both looked at the telly and pretended that we cared. And I tried, I really tried, but I couldn't do it, just sitting there still as statues watching people dashing about chucking paint at walls and throwing up wallpaper and pulling up carpets and hacking into big sheets of pretend wood, and the only movement on our side of the screen was Saffy's eyes flicking from thing to thing, from window to sink to door to floor to telly to bookshelf to window again, and I swear I could actually hear them as they went round and round without stopping, click-click-click.

So in the end I threw off the duvet and got up to do the washing-up and there was loads of it, all sticky cups and mayonnaisy spoons and even though I loved Quin I was still a bit pissed off about that – there's nothing I hate more than a mayonnaisy spoon in the sink going all claggy and minging. But I got stuck in and Saf sat there without moving still, and then after a long silence, not a sound except the splosh of paint and the blow of the whistle for teabreak and the super-enthused presenter bird yapping on, I heard a noise behind me and just for a second I didn't want to turn round, I felt like I was in a scary film and as soon as I slowly swivelled round she'd be there chewing off her own leg. But then I told myself not to be silly, this was Saffy we were talking about, my Saffy, the girl who could have an hour-long chat about building a house out of marshmallows and whether it would melt in the sun and drip on your head or whether that might actually cement them and be a good thing in the long run, so I turned around, and she was still sat there, still as a rock, but she was laughing to herself, giggling away, and even though she looked a bit creepy I thought, Well, at least she's doing something. I wandered over with a wet plate and the scrubber still in my hand dripping suds on my feet and looked at the telly but there was nothing funny that I could see, nothing at all, just the presenter woman and the bald designer bloke looking at some pebbles he'd lined up on the bathroom windowsill and last time I checked there was nothing much funny about pebbles. And then she stopped laughing and just sat in silence again. I stood looking at her for a second, thinking, She's cracked, she's actually cracked, or maybe she's on something weird and what should I do and how long should I keep looking at her before I do something and what am I going to do anyway, wheel her out onto the street and say, Oh, excuse me, my girlfriend's gone mental, which way to the nuthouse please?

She moved a bit then, tucking her legs up under her and pulling the duvet up a bit and, feeling a tiny bit relieved, I said, 'You cold, babe? Shall I put the heating on?'

And she looked up sweet as sugar and said, 'Oh, I'm fine, thanks, honey, this duvet'll do me.'

And so I stood there a bit longer but she was quiet again and anyway the makeover was up to forty-five minutes by then and that's the bit where it gets good, so I sat on the arm of the other chair and watched it, and then I sat in the chair properly and watched a bit more and then it was *Loose Women* and the gobby one with the big boobs was on and she was my favourite, proper naughty you could tell, so I put my legs up and watched that a bit longer but I couldn't really concentrate. So then it was my eyes that were flicking about and I kept looking at the stack of videos in the corner and wondering how many of them actually had videos in them and how many had chewed-up chips or scraps of meat stashed in there.

I got up and started fiddling with the book, because I was sure Quin'd be back in a day or so and I wanted it fixed by then, and I couldn't get his little face out of my head and his hand half raised in a goodbye and the pages were so flimsy and I didn't know if I was going to be able to fix it and I was just making the holes bigger the more I tried, so I put the tweezers down and just looked at my hands on the counter for a minute. I looked at Saffy and she was still sitting there not paying any attention but, just in case, I slid the book and the pages into the drawer under a tea-towel and then I picked up my jacket off the back of the chair and said, 'I'm off to the shop, hun, you fancy anything?'

And she looked up a bit miffed, like it was a real pain having to tear her eyes away from the mouldy old biscuit tin on the auction programme she was watching, which is dead boring at the best of times, and said, 'No, I'm fine, thanks, love,' and as a bit of an afterthought gave me a squarish grin.

I nodded and waved as I went out the door, but she was already looking back at the screen at a close-up of the biscuit tin and it was pretty rusty if you asked me, you wouldn't want to stick your custard creams in that. I pulled the door shut quietly on my way out so the draught from the hall didn't get in and make her cold.

Out on the street the sun was still shining and there was just a bit of a breeze starting up. A girl was walking past wearing these big round sunglasses that made her look like a fly, and she had freckles across her nose and cheeks, like this rag doll Hannah used to have when we were kids. Saffy sometimes got freckles when it was sunny, but usually just on her shoulders. She hated them but I thought they were dead lovely, like little sprinkles. I'd tried joining them up once, we were sat in the park, me with my back against a tree and her lying between my legs like I was an armchair, with her jeans rolled up and the straps of her top rolled down and her bare feet wiggling in the grass and these heart-shaped sunglasses on. I sneaked a pen out and started joining them up, and she didn't mind, she was easygoing like that, or she was back then anyway, and when I was done, there was this biro blue lace over each of her shoulders. She didn't try and wipe it off; she liked it, she said, trying to see it properly in the reflection in my Aviators and she wiggled her toes in the grass and settled back down, arms on each of my knees just like you would a chair. She got sunburnt feet that day and all night I could feel them glowing away at the end of the bed like a little heater.

When I got to Sainsbury's it was ram-packed and I had a little sigh to myself and pushed my sleeves up as I picked up a basket, cos I knew it was going to be a right chore. I didn't have a list, and my mum always used to say you shouldn't go shopping without a list and as always she was right. I floated hopelessly through the aisles picking things up and putting them down and wondering what Saf actually liked to eat and thinking how bloody weird it was that I didn't know, not normal at all, and looking at cauliflower and celery and thinking that was stupid cos they're nobody's favourite foods, but in the basket they went anyway. I felt lost, pottering about the shop with everybody else powering around, chatting to each other and looking at wine and salads and making plans, and I couldn't even think of something that Saf liked to eat, anything at all, and that just seemed so stupid when you thought of all the time we had spent together, all the hours in bed looking at every inch of her from the squishy little half-nails on her little toes that never grew properly because of the pointy high shoes she liked to wear to the blonde hairs round her knees that she always missed shaving and you could only see in the mornings when the sun was coming in through the curtains across the bed to her sharp hips which pointed sexily down to the main attraction her little slit of a bellybutton and her little 5p nipples which she got mad if you laughed at, to her pointy chin and her little elf ears, just all of it, and it just made my head spin that you can know somebody and not know them at all when you really looked at it.

My basket had somehow filled up without me noticing, and who knows what I thought I was going to cook with it all, with celery and cauliflower and cheese and pasta and a bag of salad and a bit of chicken and milk and chocolate and pink fairy cakes and my old pals, those fucking pink apples. I was feeling all worked up by then, thinking about it and thinking about Quin and the book and the train and the water and the shower and her hair and the ket party and Spike shagging that bloke's face and Lilah just leaving her and Saffy not being able to be left alone and the money and the staring and the coke and the quiet and it was all spinning round and round and making me sick.

I paid for the shopping quickly and then I went to the cigarette counter to buy a couple of scratchcards and took them outside and leant against the dirty brick wall with all the shopping bags round my feet rustling in the wind. The sun had gone behind a massive cloud that covered most of the sky, and the air smelt like it does right before it pisses down with rain. I closed my eyes, counted to three thinking of three pound signs lurking behind that silver flaky stuff, and fumbled around in my pocket for a penny. I scratched them both without looking, making my eyes go all blurry on purpose, and then held them both out in front of me and looked carefully very carefully over each of the symbols, once and then twice. Not a sodding thing. The last symbol was a smiley face, and wasn't that just a right joke. I scrunched them up, picked up all the orange plastic bags, and stomped home.

When I finally got in with hands all red from the wind and the handles digging in, she was still sat on the sofa but there was a Jamie Jones CD next to her which hadn't been there before with fresh crumbs on it, and I wasn't pleased to say the least because that was new and that wouldn't usually bother me but what with everything else I guess my patience wasn't at its best. So I walked into the kitchen without saying anything and started putting the shopping away, and I threw the bag of brown apples away and put the fresh ones in their place proudly on the counter in her eyeline, and then I put the fridge stuff in the fridge and bundled up the plastic bags into a little ball and put them in the plastic-bag drawer.

I looked at her but she still wasn't paying me any notice, and she was poking at the crumbs with a credit card, and I must've seen red just for a second because I marched over there and snatched *Don't You Remember The Future* out of her hand and stormed back and slammed it down on the counter, and I grabbed an apple out of the bag and I knelt in front of her, right in her face, and I held it up between us like a magic ball and said, 'This stops right now, Saf, I'm not having it,' and both of us felt shocked and surprised at the way it had come out, so I lowered my voice a bit but I was still being really firm and I was still holding up the apple and I said, 'Eat this, eat this for me, because you can't go on like this, please, you just can't,' and she looked at it like it was poison and there was a moment of really horrible heavy thick silence, which covered us up until it was like time had stopped.

And then she looked away and her eyes went all blank, like she wasn't behind them any more, like she'd gone back into her head and slammed the door on me and I felt like crying and screaming all at once and I just wanted her back, just wanted whoever this was to give me back my gorgeous, happy Saffy, and my hands started shaking and my face felt hot and then I just took the apple in my hand and I said, 'Come on, Saf, just eat it just eat it just eat it,' and I was pushing it in her mouth and she was trying to pull away and I was holding her head still with my hand all tangled in her hair and then suddenly I floated away in my head for a second and I saw what I was doing and I let out a sob and stopped. And she was staring at me, scared, spit and bits of apple running down her chin and tiny toothmarks in the pink skin. And I started to cry and hugged her so tight, still on my knees, saying, 'I'm sorry I'm sorry I'm so sorry, Saffy. Please forgive me I'm sorry,' and she just sat there and let me wipe my tears on her.

I sat back on my knees and let the tears stop and I said, 'Please, baby,' and I tried to make my voice stop shaking, 'we can make this go away. We can be okay again. This is nothing. If you just eat the apple, it will all go away, I promise you. Do it for me. For me and you, babe. Please.' And I held out the apple and my fingers were numb.

She looked at the apple like it was about to explode, but in the end after a few seconds she reached out and took it and held it carefully in her hand.

I let out a breath and said, 'Thank you, babe, thank you, things can be normal and okay again, I promise you, I promise you. It's all okay.' And after doing a bit more breathing I stood up and said, 'It is a bit nippy, isn't it?' because I knew she wouldn't want me to watch, that it would take time but we had time, and if she could do that for me I would give her all the space she needed, and I clicked on the heating and I went into the bedroom and got my hoody and some socks out of the drawer and put them on and straightened out my windy hair in the mirror, and started thinking to myself what I could cook for dinner and then I strolled back into the lounge but she was gone. The duvet was still all whirled up with a Saffy-shaped hole in the middle like a walnut whip without the walnut and the apple was sitting on its own in the middle of the counter.

I went back to Lucky Chips that night and shuffled around a bit, wandering between fruities and tables, waiting for one of them to call over to me with their slinky green felt or their flashy bells and whistles, but none of them did. I was dead set on not thinking about Saffy, not for one second because I was tired of it all. I'd left my phone at home and for a bit being in with all the lights and the cards and the money did make everything else disappear. I sat on one of the tall stools by a fruity and spun around a couple of times, watching all the colours spin by going *wheeeeeeeeeeeeee*. Colours and lights and pound signs going hello, hello, hello as they blurred past until someone actually did say, 'Hello.'

I put my feet down and the colours and the lights and the pound signs all lurched to a stop. I shook my head a couple of times to get rid of the spinning and Win was standing there.

'All right, Win,' I said, once my head had stopped swirling. 'How's it going?'

She had on the same sweat-patchy shirt and skirt, which was shiny with those bits where you've held the iron too long but she was holding a tray with a pint on it and it was upright and still had beer in it all the way to the top, and she had a kind of floppy flower thing in her ponytail so I guessed things were looking up for her, which was nice.

'Hello,' she said again, shuffling her shoe along another yellow squiggle. 'Good, yeah, thanks. How are you?'

She said the 'you' all small as if I was a tiny tiny person hiding in the carpet. She was all pink in the cheeks again, looking like she wanted to hide in the carpet too. I didn't think I'd ever scared anyone before in my whole life, and I didn't like it, so I gave her a big toothy grin and said, 'Yeah, I'm sound, just a bit bored, you know? Thought I'd wander over for a flutter. Busy night?'

I could see that it wasn't but I thought if I started out with easy questions she might relax and we could be mates. It was nice to have someone who actually wanted to talk to me and even though that sounds a bit desperate and sad I just wanted to make the most of having someone to chat to. She was looking about like she'd forgotten she was at work, and as she did the tray hand tipped just a little bit to one side and the whole thing started to slide off. My hand shot forward super-slow-motion-style and caught the plastic glass as the tray clattered to the floor, slopping a load of beer over my foot but saving most of it. Even though I had a soggy leg once again, I couldn't help feeling like I was a superhero as she stared at my hand in wonder and delight.

'Easy there,' I said, handing her the pint as she slowly picked the tray back up off the floor.

'Thank you,' she said, with a bit of a stammer. 'I'm so useless.' She looked down at her feet like she hoped they'd just walk her into a corner so she could hide there.

'Don't be daft,' I said. 'Trays are hard. I can't do them most times. My boss showed me this thing you have to do where you always make sure the weight's in the middle. So if you have one pint, it goes right bang in the centre. And if you have two, they have to balance out, like *this*.' I put an imaginary pint on the tray. 'And then one here for three, and one *here* for four. See?' She nodded, but I didn't think she did if I'm honest.

Just then a big old hairy man in the corner piped up, 'Is that my pint? I'm bloody parched over here!' which made Win jump about six feet in the air and sent a fresh tide of froth over the edge of the glass. 'I better go,' she said. 'I get a break in ten minutes. Do you want to …' She fidgeted with the tray and her shoe and the edge of the table and anything going, and then cleared her throat and tried again. 'Do you fancy a Coke or something with me? You don't have to or nothing?' and then she went to run away almost, like her feet had finally heard the plan to hide and started making a move.

'Yeah,' I said. 'Why not?'

She smiled so wide the top of her head almost folded over and fell off, even the flower in her hair looked like it was smiling. 'Cool,' she said. 'Cool. I'll meet you over there in fifteen minutes.' And she backed off, bumping into a stool and knocking more beer onto the tray, smiling at me again all pink and then hurrying off to the thirsty man with the hair sticking out his ears.

I swung round on my stool a few more times and then I stuck 50p in the slot and pressed the button and watched the wheels whizz around, feeling the same little lucky butterflies flapping up in my belly. I could feel the twinkly lights shining right through my eyes and flashing pink and yellow and blue all the way inside me. The wheels slowed down, chugging away, and I wiggled the stool while I waited, making my trainers squeak on the bar, until they settled into place clunk-clunk-clunk. Cherries seven watermelon. A cheeky little cherry peeking down at the top of the third wheel, so close but yet so far. And that cheeky little cherry was the one that got the next 50p out my pocket, same as the flat top of a seven poking up from the bottom of the second wheel got the fourth one out, same as the two melons all juicy got the seventh one out, and before I knew it I looked up at the clock and then at the bar and saw Win wandering over to the empty table in the takeaway place.

I pottered over and sat down opposite her. She had two cans in front of her, one pink and one yellow, and she kept turning them one by one to look at the labels like she'd forgotten what she ordered. 'You pick,' she said, looking a bit scared. I was going to say that she could pick but then I thought that would probably make her feel a bit in the spotlight so I took the yellow one because she struck me as a pink sort of a girl and she did look a tiny bit pleased that that was what she'd ended up with so that was a good start.

'Cheers,' I said, and I clinked the can against hers, which almost made her drop it. 'You got much left to work?'

She looked up at the tiny clock on the telly, which was back to showing Fate Jones's front door. 'Three hours,' she said, with a little sigh. 'Ages.'

It was ages a bit, but I didn't say, just said, 'Hopefully it'll get busy when the clubs kick out. Always goes faster when it's busy, doesn't it? That's what I think anyway.'

I was talking a bit too much, filling the gaps so she wouldn't feel weird about being silent. I know what it's like when you feel like being quiet and everybody expects you to laugh and joke and sing and dance for them all the time. So I just let her be quiet and drink her can. After a bit, she said, 'Do you want to be a barman, for like ever?' Which really is a bit of a full-on question for a plastic table in a burger stall in the middle of an all-night karaoke and casino place, but that was okay, it was a bit of a full-on week all round.

'Nah,' I said. 'I want to be a DJ. Or own a pub maybe. Either would suit me.'

She was plucking at the ring-pull on the can, making a little *pling* noise each time. 'I hate being a waitress,' she said. 'It's the worst ever.'

I felt pretty bad for her, she looked really down about it all. 'You could go somewhere else?' I said. 'Somewhere with a nicer boss?'

She took a sip of the pink can and smiled up at me from under a long piece of brown hair that had slipped out of the ponytail. 'I could,' she goes, 'but I need the money. I got a little boy at home.'

She looked a bit like she wished she hadn't said that, so I said, 'Ah, ace. What's his name?' Loads of my mates from home had nippers so I wanted to let her know it was okay.

'Max,' she said. 'He's five now.'

I smiled. 'Cool name.'

She smiled too and pushed the sticky bit of hair away from her face. 'Anyway,' she goes, 'if I stay here they might teach me to deal.' I looked at her for a minute and I didn't like to say but I didn't think getting involved with bag and pills and that was a good way to provide for a kiddywinkler so I just went, 'Bit dodgy that. I'd steer clear. Good money and all, but sticky business.'

She looked at me all confused and then she actually laughed. 'No no no,' she goes. 'I mean cards, not drugs! I want them to teach me to work the tables.'

I laughed too, once I cottoned on, but she was looking all dreamy-eyed at the floor with the five or six croupiers shuffling their floppy cards. I looked too, at the one woman and the blokes, in their shiny waistcoats with their fingers moving in blurs over the decks of cards. After a bit I said, 'That's great. You should do it. Better uniform and everything. And you get mad tips when people are winning and that.'

She smiled a sad little smile and looked back at her can. 'Yeah,' she said, all in a sigh. 'But I'm shit at counting. I try and watch but I can't keep up. I was rubbish at maths at school.'

I drank some of my yellow drink and thought about what to say.

'Sorry,' she goes, like she wanted to change the subject. 'Should've got you a pint. I forgot cos I'm not allowed to drink on shift, you know.'

'No, all good, mate,' I said, 'Quite nice, actually. Refreshing.

'Look,' I said, after another sip, 'if you really want to do it, just practise. I reckon you'll get it in no time if you really put your mind to it. It's just one of those things that looks hard but once you get the hang of it it'll be a breeze. Don't put yourself down – you seem pretty canny to me. Go for it.'

She looked at me all agog and she didn't say anything for ages, and just as she opened her mouth like she was about to, the fat wobbling boss-bloke came stomping around the corner. 'Break time over!' he said, flapping his sausage-roll arms about and stomping off again.

She smiled at me, a very little smile that was hidden behind her hair again now like the spell was back on her and she was invisible again. She picked up the cans and took them over to the swing-lid bin, which squeaked like nobody's business as it creaked back and forth in the empty space. Then she tucked her hair behind her ears and walked back over and stood looking at me. ''Bye,' she goes. 'It was nice to see you? Maybe see you soon?'

'Sure,' I said. 'I'll buy the cans next time, eh?'

She touched the back of the chair she'd been sitting in very lightly like her fingers might make holes in the plastic. 'You're lovely,' she said, and then she walked away. She tripped over one of the table legs on her way, but I didn't really notice. I was too busy thinking how long it had been since anybody had said that to me.

Saffy didn't come back for two days. I knew I should've texted Alice or Delilah and seen if she was with them but I didn't, I just sat and stewed and sulked and listened for the door opening, which never came, and after a day or so I'd calmed down and I tidied up the flat a bit and put the heating on and a bottle of St Petrolsburg voddy in the freezer, and just thought to myself, Right, we'll sort this out properly now, we'll sit down and have a drink and chat all night like we used to, because at the end of the day, no matter what was going on, we always had each other and that counted for everything, it had to. So then I sat down and waited for her and waited and then waited a bit longer. And it was round about then that I started to worry and started sitting there running set-lists through my head like prayers and wondering how long is long enough before you start calling up important people.

But then I heard her key in the lock and that was a relief, but not for long because after that I could hear her stumbling about trying to take her shoes off. She wandered through and didn't even see me sat there all disapproving like her dad, just floated around the kitchen, touching the drawer handles and the cupboard doors one after the other, and when she'd done a lap she finally turned round and saw me. She looked a right state, her pupils all big and black and the make-up smudged round them into big panda eyes and her face all grey and sweating in the dodgy flickering striplight.

'Fitz,' she sang out, shuffling across the carpet swaying, and she touched my face and I blurted out, 'Jesus, Saf, look at the state of you,' which I didn't mean to, I meant to just think it but I was so surprised it slipped out. She never noticed anyway, just kept staring at my face and swaying away to herself, and in the dead silence between us I realised she was mouthing something, as if someone had hit her mute button and when I looked closer I could've sworn she was singing the Marvin Gaye one about sexy time we'd danced to in the kitchen a million years and miles ago, but the whole thing was so creepy that I had to look away and clear my throat all scared and awkward.

'You want some of this babe?' I said, holding out my cup of tea even though it was old and cold. 'Sort you right out. A brew's always good after a bit of a bender.'

She just stared at it all frightened with her pupils going in and out of focus looking boss-eyed, and then she started shaking her head. 'No no no,' she goes singsong, and turned and skipped out of the room, and as she went I could've sworn she was humming.

I stood and looked at the door for a little while and I heard her in the bathroom bouncing about and opening the cabinet door over and over, open close open close. I started thinking maybe she was just stood there smashing her face into it again and again, but then I heard the shower click on. I sat down and picked up her handbag where she'd dropped it and I fished around in there and I got out her phone and found the number I wanted, and I'm not ashamed to say a tear did fall out my eye when I heard that first ring.

# SAFFY

In our world today, the apple is a sign of progress and of wealth. It glows on the back of screens and phones and it reminds us that there are always new things to discover, new clever ways to be close to other people.

A long time ago a different girl, so the story goes, took an apple and betrayed her lover because of a whisper in her ear she couldn't ignore.

It's a different story, but really there's only ever one story. We let each other down.

We stared at each other in surprise. It was as if there had been thick glass forming between us for weeks and weeks and he had just taken a hammer to it. Things had cracked, things were shaking around us. He lowered his voice and it began to shake too.

'Eat this,' he said, and his voice was turning into a whisper. 'Eat this for me. You can't go on like this, please, you just can't.'

The apple loomed between us and I knew that if I reached for it things could never be the same. The silence keeping us safe and together would be shattered; things would have to be addressed, things would have to be understood, and I would lose him. I looked at the pain and the panic in his face and knew it was no use. I reached out and took the pink apple in my hand.

As he went to fetch a jumper, I slid out of my duvet and walked out of the door without looking back.

It was cool on the street and everything began to drain of colour as I walked away from my flat of warm and love and pink apples. The world stood still and everything was broken. Anger and hurt and sadness swelled and filled my head and so I just walked.

When I was little, my favourite place in all the world was the library. There you could lose yourself in dusty shelves. There you could be anyone you wanted to be, even if just for a moment. You could hide yourself between tiny printed letters on a page, tuck yourself behind the straight of a *d* or the curve of an *s*, lie down in the tail of a *g* or the bottom of an *o* and let yourself be carried away. There was a small wooden train in the kids' section, with books in each of the carriages and two little seats in the engine, where I could sit and read as much as I could before we had to pick our five books to take away, while my middle sister Jelli pushed me and poked me, and my mother chatted to her friend who volunteered behind the counter. The train took me a million miles all over everywhere.

I wasn't much of a reader after that. The things we read in school left me cold, the letters too small to fit between, and after that the reading in Happy Blossoms was so heavily supervised by the nurses that it felt like homework too. I couldn't remember the last time I'd sat down to read. I had other ways to escape and other ways to hide by then. But somehow I found myself in the library that day.

We'd never used our local library, even though it was close to the Tube and had DVDs as well as books. It had a pretty brick entrance with two dead lamps hanging one on either side of the door. It looked like somewhere Jack the Ripper or Oliver Twist might go to check out the Recently Returned shelves. Inside, the air smelt like unopened pages and rusks. There was a little metal gate with an arrow pointing upwards to show 'in', and a swooping desk that filled up the rest of the space, save for the little gate for 'out'. I pushed the gate open with my legs and wandered in.

Books lined up neatly around the walls, looping in and out of the U-bend shelves, faded colours and plastic jackets all muddled up and short and tall. In the centre of the room there were computers and swirly chairs, two long desks and old saggy chairs with wooden frames dotted around them. The children's section was in the far corner. There was no train. I found a book about magic, and then I went to the table and sat in a chair, crossing my legs beneath me.

The words on the page didn't look like a place to hide that day. As I stared at the type, the letters knotted together, locking me out. Something had begun to happen weeks before but it was only then, sitting terrified in the library, that I realised I could no longer read. Could no longer watch television or look at a computer screen. After a couple of sentences, a scene or a paragraph of a webpage, my brain began to shut down, like a computer left idle. I had no concentration left, all of my energy tied into the empty cavern I was cradling at my centre. This realisation sent a bolt of cold fear through me. All my life was about looking for an escape but, in searching for one, I had unwittingly trapped myself in reality. I held the book to my face, breathing in the pages. One by one, I was saying goodbye to things I loved. But perhaps that's all life really is: a long and drawn-out farewell.

I left the book on the table and went back outside into the weak sunshine. I walked until I came to a shop and I went inside and as the old lady behind the counter turned to answer the phone I slipped a bottle of vodka into my jumper and walked out again. I crossed the road and let the long grass tickle my legs as I cut across to the playground. The bench was old and chipped and there was rubbish in a perfect ring around it. I stepped over it and sat down, crossing my legs under me so that the flaking paint dug into my skin. The vodka was hot on my throat and thin in my mouth.

Two kids were playing in the park, too old for it really, a boy and a girl looking awkward about the fact that their friends had obviously left them to kiss or have sex or something magical and mysterious in between. He had hair that was cut too short around the front, leaving his eyebrows exposed and him looking permanently surprised. His jacket was zipped up too high; the lace on one trainer was a different colour from the other. She had drawn on her eyebrows with thick brown pencil; they both looked a bit startled and amazed to be on a jungle gym in a square of grey in the stubby green patch of grass in the middle of the city. She was wearing a skirt too big for her, and as she shifted on the bar she was trying to pose on, she had to shift it down and around, then up and around the other way. She had braces, which she was trying really hard to hide, so that all her smiles were only half-smiles and every laugh had to be corrected halfway through. I watched them and I fiddled with the hard red cap in my hands, and I drank my vodka. The sun was setting behind them, catching her braces each time she forgot about them, so that they had all the light in the whole park.

After a while the sun set, and their fingers, which had crept closer and closer across the chipped red bars until they finally touched, slipped apart. They left the park, the gate swinging closed behind them with a clang. At the end of the path that led to the road, they went different ways, waving to each other awkwardly, both turning back to look over their shoulders as they made their way home. I was on my own, only an inch of vodka left in the bottle, feelings still whispering around me in the half-light.

I stared for a long time, letting my mind go blank. And then I started walking again. Cars whizzed past me, lights tiny points of orange joining with the streetlamps in the pink and grey world. Sirens sounded far away and close by, hurt people all around. At the bottom of the road, the vodka was gone. I threw the bottle at the wall and it cracked clear in two instead of shattering; just two broken halves lying on the pavement jagged and sad.

Left, right, left, right, left, right, left, right. I concentrated until the hard ground underneath my feet at each step was the only sound in my head, covering everything else that tried to bob up in my mind as I walked. Rows and rows of the same house followed me along, looming over me until I felt small and squashed. I could see people inside them, blobby shadows behind their dusty net curtains, little slices of life through the ribs of half-shut blinds, skeleton people and skin-deep lives. Eating dinner, watching *Top Idol*, dancing, shouting at each other, talking on the phone, kissing, washing up, pulling each other's hair, pulling their own hair out. Crying at soaps, laughing at kids, poking people on their laptops and ignoring people on the sofa. I hated them. All of them and their stupid little living rooms and their stupid little lives. The wind pulled at my hair; my bag thumped my hip with every step. The whole world was moving with my steps. Left, right, left, right, left, right, left, right. A Tube station loomed up ahead. The news cart in front of it was shut, the scribbled poster still stuck in the mesh on its side – 'New Fate Jones Evidence Found!' – and I carried on past and down the steps.

I moved fast even though I didn't know where I was going, because if I stopped everything I was running from would catch me. Down the stairs, round and round, pushing past people and slithering over the thin ends of the triangular steps as they spiralled on. I got to the bottom and carried on without looking, not caring which line I was headed for and not stopping until I reached the far end of the platform with the big black mouth waiting to swallow me. I leant against the tiles and looked into the darkness. My brain was going a million miles an hour but my heart had sunk down into silence and I was empty. The billboard opposite me was broken, not flipping between images of Fate Jones and mobile phones and a rubbish film nobody wanted to see like the others were doing, just a plain black screen. I could see my smudgy outline in it, just a shape in space, white for a face and a short, squat body that tailed off into nothing.

The platform was quiet, just two boys kicking a can around at the other end, and a tiny mouse running in circles behind me. They get brave, the mice, when nobody is around: up on the platform and running in wild zigzags and spirals and loop the loops, high on being up off the dusty track and free. I wanted to kick it. And then, just as suddenly, I wanted to pick it up, to kiss it and kiss it again, to put it in my handbag and keep it for ever. I didn't do either. I left it to be free.

The train was rumbling in the distance, and for a moment I looked at the rails in front of me. I put a toe to the edge of the platform and ran it along the chipped edge. Two white lights pierced the darkness, still far away, and as the rumbling grew closer I imagined the roar, the rush of air as I fell into the gap between us, the bang and burst and then the silence. I should do it, I thought, but even as I did, I was stepping back. This is the thing about life. The things you want most are the things you are never brave enough to grab when they're right in front of you. The train shuddered past me, brakes wailing. The carriage was empty; the doors creaked open and gaped at me. I stood and stared back for a second, and then, as the beeping began, I stepped in.

I sat in one of the dirty seats, sinking into the saggy cushion and letting up a puff of dust. Crumpled pages stirred in the breeze as the train began to move, empty lines of print and smudged pages, words that people didn't want to read just left behind. I looked up at the map, at the little flashing light that showed us moving along the line. It seemed impossible, the little flashing circle moving so easily and quickly across the city, while I felt heavy as a stone and sinking into the dark. I stared at my face in the black glass and I thought nothing. I sat and didn't move as people got on, sat down, got off. I was still as they moved, as the train moved, as the pictures in the paper fluttered in the wind. Fate Jones's face flittered on and off on papers across the carriage as the pages blew back and forth. Now you see her, now you don't. Now you see her. Now you don't.

The bar is dark. There are two empty glasses in front of me. There is one with a dark liquid in it in my hand. There is a man sitting next to me, and one sitting opposite me. We are all laughing. I don't know why. One is wearing a trilby hat and an open-necked shirt and denim jacket. The other has long straight hair down to his shoulders, and a dark green T-shirt on with a band I don't recognise on it.

'You want another, Molly?' the one with the hat says, and I realise he is talking to me. I nod, and drink the rest of the one I am holding. It tastes cold, and sweet and chemical, like medicine. I cough as it chokes me with cold heat. We all start laughing again.

'We're going to a party, you wanna come?'

The party is darker. There is concrete everywhere, uncovered walls and uncovered floors. I don't know if the plaster has worn away or if it hasn't ever been there; if it is a house or a flat or a warehouse. I sit on concrete stairs and smoke the cigarettes and the spliffs that are passed to me. The boy with the green T-shirt is sharing a bottle of red wine with me. I don't even wish it was vodka.

Brick wall rough on my hands. Dress wet on one leg. I'm being sick. It's red and it splashes my shoes.

The sun is coming up. We're dancing out on a flat roof. The boy with the hat is holding my hands up in the air and we're singing. A girl with blonde and brown hair is sitting on the edge of a chimney pot and staring at me. The boy with the green T-shirt asks if we want to do some lines. The boy with the hat says we should do a pill first.

Lying on the roof looking up at the clouds. Stretching our hands and legs out and curling our fingers. I can't stop yawning. It feels as if my head might split all the way open if I yawn any more, but I still can't stop. The boy with the hat says taking another pill will help. We touch each other's hair and skin. The boy with the green top asks if I'm cold. I say no and we all laugh.

Toilet dusty with cement and dirt. Everywhere silent. I retch so hard I hit my head on the cistern. I laugh.

Walking through the deserted party to the roof. Everyone has left, just empty bottles and cans sleeping sadly on the floor. I find half a bottle of vodka and I swing it in my hand as I walk towards the sun.

The boy with the green T-shirt is being sick behind the chimney stack. The boy with the hat has his eyes closed. I close mine and drink.

Leaves in my face. Mud on my legs. A pill in my bra. Alone again.

There are certain things nice girls don't do. Nice girls don't swear. Nice girls aren't sick in the street or on themselves. Nice girls don't sleep with men they just met. Nice girls don't tell lies. Nice girls don't wake up in hedges with the sun high up above and no idea how they got there. Nice girls don't deserve bad things to happen to them. Nice girls don't end up on the news or on the side of buses. Nice girls should live happily ever after.

Sunlight shouting between the leaves burnt lines of white light across my face. In the distance I could hear the main road, and above, a sweet little bird that didn't know there was nothing left to sing about. I reached into my bra before I opened my eyes and swallowed the pill whole.

Perhaps everybody in the world but me understood how a tiny sharp pain could cover a deep dark ache. Then, with twigs digging into my skin and the world swimming and my head screaming, I felt strangely light.

I clambered out of the hedge on my hands and knees, listening to the strains of song that were still circling in my brain. It was mid-morning, the sun almost high in the sky and people passing through in a slow, unemployed kind of way, all the school-runners and walk-to-workers long gone. I sat cross-legged in the grass and held my handbag in my lap. All the money was gone, but my phone remained: silent, quiet, blank.

It was, I thought, the best way to be. I watched a little dog running frantically across the grass, long hair blown back from its face in the wind, paws flying high in the air as it leapt over the longer tufts, and I clapped happily. The sun shone down on my face and the pill picked me up and took me away and I closed my eyes and felt life stand still beneath me.

After what seemed like a moment but might have been an hour, I opened my eyes and stood up on wobbly legs. The park loomed ahead, sparkling like an impossible jewel in what had only a few hours and a lifetime before seemed like the darkest place in all the world. I wandered through the creaking gate and sat on a swing, picturing the young lovers on the jungle gym and smiling happily. Holding the chains and leaning back, I let the phantom hair I could still feel weeks after I'd cut it hang down behind me. I lifted my toes and swung gently with my weight, watching the clouds sway softly back and forward.

When we were children, there were too many of us for the swings. Swings in parks come in twos – two alone or two big and two little. We were three, Bluebell just a pinhole in a condom in my mother's distant dreams. Just three, Ella, Anjelica and me. And somehow I was always the only one on the swings. Ella and Jelli liked to be moving, always, running up and down the climbing frame with the slide and the fireman's pole and down again and on the see-saw and across the monkey bars and back again. They'd swing but only for the shortest of times, jumping off at the highest point and running away again. I stayed there for hours and hours, or so it seemed, swinging back and forth. What they didn't realise was that you could get so much further in that one spot, further than your legs could ever take you, higher and higher until you were flying. I'd swing and swing until the rusty chains left orange crowns on the palms of my hands.

There aren't many places where you can really lose yourself, but the few there are will always be in a still space, a silent spot. In a chair with a book, on a swing, in bed next to the person you love more than anything in the world. You can be taken away further than you'd ever dreamt just by staying still.

There will always be something that brings you back to earth. Like a low wolf-whistle cutting through the warm air.

I turned my head, the ground lurching back and forth beneath me as the swing slowed. And then I saw him.

Kay was leaning against the railings.

The swing creaked to a stop and my eyes were trapped in his. Waves of the ecstasy were still rolling over me but the goose-bumps on my skin had turned to ones of chill. He lifted the cigarette he was smoking and took a long drag, blowing it out slowly. I stood up, leaving the chains shivering, and staggered a few limp steps towards the gate. He watched me go without moving, just kept smoking. I wondered if he was really there at all.

The gate loomed in front of me and I reached my hand for it two or three steps before I was close enough to touch it. I didn't look back, just opened it with stiff fingers and wobbled out into the park. As I went, I got faster, leaving him further and further behind, tripping on the uneven ground and letting the strap of my dress slip off my shoulder.

And then he was walking alongside me.

'All right,' he said, looking at the cigarette between his thumb and finger. 'That was a bit rude.'

I didn't say anything, just kept walking, trying to keep putting one foot in front of the other and feeling as though I wasn't moving at all.

'Not very friendly today, are you?'

We were nearing the main road, and suddenly I could hear the sounds of the rest of the world through the straggly trees. The thin dirt path that led through them seemed to glow in the grey shadows. Kay flicked the cigarette away from him. Things were going slowly now, my body heavy and dragging, and as I broke into a stumbling run, he grabbed me in a flash.

'Ah ah ah,' he said, his fingers tight around my arm. 'Stick around a bit. Let's be friendly, shall we? Neighbour.'

So much is hidden from people driving past a place. Trees and buildings hide the layers and layers of people and lives that are being and happening at any given moment. In one short stretch of road, you can be passing happiness, sadness, fear. Things forgotten, things lost. Lights on, fires burning, people left out in the cold. People at the end of the road.

He held me up against the trunk, one of his knees forcing mine apart. His breath was hot on my face.

'You stink,' he said. 'Dirty bitch.' He was fumbling with his jeans. 'Now, how much do you owe again? Let me think.'

*The day it happens is a Sunday. We're sitting in a caravan in a tiny terraced back garden with a plastic bottle of cider in the middle of the table and the Top Forty on the radio. Lick is holding my hand. I have never had my hand held before. I feel very special. He isn't the best-looking boy in year eleven but he is in year eleven and that's really quite old. Even Quin says so. I think Quin is going to be jealous squared when he finds out Lick has held my hand. I look at Abby, sitting on the other side of the table. She's a good friend. She found me Lick. Spoon isn't holding her hand but it's his caravan so he has to pour the drinks. Abby and me have been drunk before. At least, we think so. But this must be what being really drunk feels like, warm and cosy and lovely. I wonder when Lick will actually ask me to be his girlfriend properly. Having a year-eleven boyfriend – I don't think anybody else has done that yet. They will probably all want to be my friend. I know that Quin will still be my best friend, of course. Things like that never change.*

*Abby and Spoon are going to get cigarettes. I'm practising liking smoking. I hope it doesn't make the caravan spin like it did the time Abby and me tried it in her sister's wardrobe. Abby is laughing at something Spoon has said, and they're all looking at me and laughing. I smile back but I haven't heard what they said. My head feels floppy and my fingers are lovely and warm in Lick's hand. The door shuts and I can hear Abby giggling all the way down the garden path. Lick asks me if I'm okay and I say yes and he says good. Then he kisses me. He sticks his tongue in and pokes it about and pushes at my teeth. My face gets wet and his breath smells of cider. He moves his hand, which is still holding mine, down to his legs and he lays my hand on his zip. He puts both his hands round my head and squiggles at my hair with all his fingers at once. I don't know what I'm supposed to do with my hand so I give it a little pat and then I squiggle like he's doing, my face going all hot and pink. He makes a funny noise and then he pushes me hard onto the cushions and he starts squiggling his fingers under my skirt, which I only made yesterday from an old pair of jeans and it looks pretty cool, it really does, but the sewing isn't very good and I hope it won't rip. He starts poking at the crease between my leg and you-know-where with his finger and I don't think that's where he means to be poking but I don't want to say anything, in case he does and I just don't know anything at all. He's still making noises and getting my face wet and when he pulls down my knickers, which aren't even the nice pair I got for Christmas, and pulls down his jeans I say, 'no' but it's lost in all the wet and the teeth and the lips so I say it louder I say, 'NO' but his face is buried in my hair and he doesn't hear me and he pushes in anyway and so I look up at the dirty ceiling and I wonder if he's my boyfriend yet.*

I was frozen, only the rough bark at my back holding me up. In my head I had already drifted away. And then, somewhere, from deep in my heart, I thought of Fitz, and I thought that somewhere, in some tiny place, I mattered now. I had someone waiting for me. I brought my knee up hard into Kay's soft crotch, and as he doubled over, I brought it up again, harder, into his face. And then I ran.

I ran through the trees until everything was blurred, until I thought I was dead and everything was disappearing. I ran in the wrong direction, so that when I finally came through the trees, I was halfway down the road. And then everything really was disappearing. And then everything went black.

'You okay, love? That's it, open your eyes. Easy does it.'

The sun was on my face again, and there were stones digging at the back of my legs. Somebody with soft hands was pulling my dress down carefully.

'Get the water out of the car, Jo.'

I opened my eyes. I was lying on the pavement, cars driving past with their wheels turning softly on the sharp grey gravel, some slowing to catch a glimpse of the misfortune that had this time missed them. There was a red car parked beside me, hazard lights flashing, and a man kneeling beside me, rolling up a sweatshirt. He put it gently under my head.

'Keep still. You've fainted.'

The car door shut and a woman came back with a plastic bottle of water. She smiled at me kindly. 'Here we go. Such a hot day.'

I sat up and the world turned sideways and then changed its mind. The man unscrewed the cap and handed the bottle to me. I took a deep swig and sicked it straight back up on the woman's lovely shoes, clear and still tepid. I tried to say sorry, but she knelt down next to me. 'Here,' she said, taking the bottle. 'Small sips, that's it.' And she held it to my lips, once, twice, again, waiting while I swallowed. In the car a toddler pressed his face to the window. A fat baby sat strapped into a car seat next to him. The car's windows were rolled down, the radio playing faintly out into the warm air.

'Police have found the car they believe to have been used to abduct Fate Jones. Early forensic reports suggest that strands of hair found in the boot belong to the missing student. The investigation continues.

'Ex-England footballer Cayden Kingsley is today facing allegations that he cheated on his wife of fourteen years more than fifty times. An unnamed woman has claimed to a tabloid that he fathered three of her four children while captaining the squad – a team that prided itself on bringing family values back to the sport. A spokesman for Kingsley said there would be no official comment, but representatives from his various sponsorship deals, including childrenswear label Free Kicks, are expected to issue statements over the coming days.'

'Feeling better, sweetie?' the woman asked, screwing the top back on the bottle. I nodded. 'Come on, then,' she said. 'Let's get you up. We'll take you home.'

I let them lift me onto my feet. I looked at the two little babies in the back seat. 'It's okay,' I said. 'I'll walk.' And I walked away, leaving them standing on the pavement behind me.

*The day he moves in, I stand at the top of the steps and watch him unload his boxes from the back of Eddie's little car. I don't have any shoes or socks on but I'm so fizzy with excitement that I don't even notice how cold the November concrete is. We leave his boxes on the pavement and, as Eddie drives off, he picks me up and carries me down the steps and over the threshold.*

In the shower, warm water pouring down over me, soft like rain, beating out a relentless rhythm on my scalp and sending tingles down my spine. Turning the dial slowly, feeling the water turn from rainforest shower to cold drizzle and then clicking off. The drops of water on the glass catch the light as they run away. Picking two and watching them race, trying to guess which will reach the ground first. The drops on the tiles are different, tiny beads, still and silent. Smudging them into a long wet smear with my thumb. Furry black mould creeping round the edge of beige tile. Mould is all around, oozing out of every gap, sliding fingers around the edges of floor, crawling up old bottles and blunt razors. The air is thick. Stepping backwards out of the shower door quickly and shutting it tight behind me. The touch of the tiles on the soles of my feet, flat and solid and cold and smooth. Lying down on my front and feeling the flat solid cold smoothness of it all along my skin, from the tops of my feet to my cheek and ear.

*There is an evening once, just a normal evening, when we talk and talk. We sit together, then sit apart, stretching legs and arms over and around each other. We sit on the floor, we lie on the floor, all the time talking and talking as if we have never seen each other before. We move round and round, the streetlamp's light stretching through the tiny window and the sun slowly coming up over the grey of the pavement. As the orange of the lamp clicks off and grey dawn washes over us, we are lying with his face next to my hip and his breath hot through my thin dress. He kisses me gently through the fabric and I don't think he even means me to feel it. We stay there for hours, rolled onto our sides. We talk and we laugh until the sun starts to sink back down through the little window.*

Lying on the dusty floor, head spinning. That night seems to belong to a different lifetime, two different people speaking a different language. I'm an outsider, even from my own memories.

The last waves washing over me, stretching out the minutes and making every touch and every sound seem far away and strange. Walking naked to the bedroom, water cooling on my skin. Wrapping myself in an old jumper. My wet hair drying in curls around my neck.

Fitz on the sofa. Curling up next to him and pulling his arm around me and letting the music from the TV wash around us. The air is sparkling and the tips of my fingers are gold. I turn to look at Fitz and the tears on his cheeks are gold too.

Headlights from the road above shining on the wall, lighting up the flat and letting the outside in. Fitz lifting me, leading me to the bedroom. My legs feel weak and the world starts to swim. He lays me down carefully. Waiting to feel his weight on me, holding me down and keeping me safe. But he's gone.

Sounds in the hall, voices, footsteps. My mother and father. They loom in and out of view, the sounds of them muffled and far away. Clothes folded into a bag and clothes forced onto me as my eyes roll in and out of black.

Lifted, up and away. As the car door closes, my eyes do too. I don't even get a chance to look back.

I opened my eyes to flat white ceiling. No meringue, no possibility, no shape. For a moment I thought I was back at Happy Blossoms where everything was flat and white or flat and pink and everything and everyone was different degrees of dead. I lay there for a minute and imagined what it would be like never to get up, to lie there until I just stopped being. From outside the window I could hear Lulu in the front garden, riding her bike up and down the front path. I knew she'd have on a helmet, knee-pads, armpads, wrapped up in cotton wool just to ride back and forth along the twenty-three flagstones that led up to the house. They'd bought her these beads that slotted on to the spokes of her wheels, all beautiful blues and pinks and purples and one very bright green, and they clattered around as the wheels turned. Everyone was always fussing over how lovely they were, how unusual. Nobody remembered that I had asked for them for my first bike, or that my mother had said that the noise would bring on her migraines.

My window was open, the curtains lifting gently in the breeze. The windows in our house were always open; as if they were afraid that without an opening to the outside we would all suffocate. I could hear the sharp clip-clip of my mother's pruning scissors, and every so often Lulu would shout to her, 'Mummy, look at me!' They sounded close; as if I could sit up and peer through the window and see them right there in front of me, instead of a storey down and a world apart. The front door opened and Dad stepped out.

'Ginny on the phone for you, love,' he said, in a voice that was trying hard not to carry further than the privet hedges. The clip-clip stopped and I heard my mother sit back on her heels on the grass.

'Tell her I'll call her back, will you? She'll only want to go on about Georgie and the doctors. And it's so lovely out.'

'Right you are,' he said, and I heard rubber slipper-soles step carefully back onto parquet floor. 'Looking good, Lu,' he said, as the door began to creak shut, 'Maybe get those stabilisers off next week.'

They carried on for a while, the clip-clip of pruning and the clattering of plastic diamonds on shiny spokes and the singsong of birds in the trees all along the street. The ceiling stayed flat and white. No cars passed, the odd starling was the only traffic from house to house to the post office and back. I could hear the baby two doors down crying in his bedroom faintly. After a while, the squeak of a pushchair passed the window and stopped by the pruning scissors.

'Morning, Pippa. Hello, Bluebell!'

Lulu grunted in response and the diamond clatter barely slowed its cycle of sparkly sound, but the clip-clip stopped and I heard my mother stand up and brush her hands on the legs of her jeans. 'Hi, Una! How are you? Hello, little ones, hello.'

Una lived at the end of the street in a pretty white house in a leafy plot. She was beautiful in a pinned-back kind of a way, flicked hair and eyebrows and cheekbones all sprayed and pumped and pushed until they were fighting their way off the back of her head. Her husband Rupert worked in the City; when I'd first moved to London my parents had tried for ages to get me to meet him for dinner. They gave up soon after; or maybe they remembered it was better if I went unseen. The previous year Rupert and Una's third cycle of IVF had worked and she had become pregnant with twins. She'd waddled through the village in kaftans and leggings and flip-flops, skin stretched across her huge centre, ankles fatter and fatter and her face filling in until her neck was just the rest of her chin. You could hear the pavements creaking as she walked past and her muscles being slowly torn and pulled like Play-Doh over the things growing inside her and filling her up. The babies were born in the spring of that year, freakishly hot and feeling like summer in March. Two boys, fat and white and pink, paraded around the village along with the number of stitches and the hours in labour and the needles and the forceps and the stretchmarks.

'They're growing so fast,' my mother said, and I heard her hands fiddling with the stray stems of the privet, mentally marking them for head-chopping. 'Can I have a squeeze?' she asked, and before Una said yes I heard plastic buckles unbuckled. 'Ooh,' my mother said. 'Aren't you lovely? Yes you are, yes you are. Are we a bit windy? I think we are. There we go, there we go. All better. Isn't that better? Hello. Yes. Hello. Aren't you gorgeous? Yes you are. Ah yes you are. Gosh, so beautiful, Una. Just goes to show, doesn't it? Hello, baba. Hello. Who's that? Ah, who's that? Wave at him, Bluebell. Wave. He likes you, doesn't he? Do you like her? Ah yes you do, yes you do. Don't do that, darling. Don't teach him things like that. Lovely, aren't you? Aren't you lovely?'

Wheels squeaked over and over as Una rocked the buggy back and forth to comfort the abandoned and neglected twin. 'How's everything with you?'

My mother sshed and cooed in response.

'Terrible, isn't it,' Una said, over the squeak of wheels, 'about the car?'

'Gosh, yes.' My mother switched out of baby voice. 'Darling, go and see if Daddy's ready to go to the garden centre soon.' The bike and the diamonds clattered to the ground, the door creaked open and slammed shut. 'Awful news. You know, I really thought they'd find her one of these days. But this news about finding the car. Well, it doesn't look good, does it? Makes you grateful, doesn't it? To have your babies close.

'Ooh dear, you are a whiffy one, aren't you? Time for a change, I think, Una. I'd invite you in but we're just this second heading out.'

The sound of plastic buckles rebuckled. 'See you, Pippa.'

'Yes, see you, Una. Bye-bye, tiny ones. Bye-bye.'

The wheels squeaked their way back up the spotless pavement. I heard a few more privet twigs snap, my mother sigh. It was just us, this side of the house, her ten feet below me. She hummed two bars to herself and then stopped. Snap-snap. The sound of her wandering back towards the house, looking at the flowerbed as she went. I imagined her running one hand through her hair and then, carefully, one finger underneath her fringe. I knew she was standing just beneath my head, looking out at the Redleys' roof across the road, at the reclaimed pre-war tiles she had lusted after since they'd had them put on, and thinking about fat baby wrists and brand-new blonde roots. She was probably touching her own hairline, wondering if it was red or brown, or if grey was sneaking through. I heard her fresh white shoe turn in the grass and then one or two steps forward. She would be reaching up to fix her hanging baskets, one on either side of the door, one of them right beneath my window, where I would stub out stolen cigarettes when I was a teenager. She was reaching up to me, just inches from my face. I turned away and closed my eyes.

When I woke up an hour later, everything was quiet. My bedroom door was open, propped ajar with the tiny china house I used to play with for hours when I was a child. I always liked things that weren't really toys. Instead of my own presents I'd play with the boxes everyone else's came in.

There was a tray on the white desk in the corner, a straight silver rectangle with curly leaves on each corner.

The same things on it as ever:

- Jelly. Harmless, gentle jelly, shaped with a flower-shaped mould.
- One piece of bread and butter. Spread thinly with low-fat spread, cut into squares. Two crusts cut off, two left on: no discernible reason.
- Carrot sticks, five. Dry along the edges and most likely leftover from Lulu's lunchbox.
- One cup of peppermint tea, brewed so gently that the green was still just a swirl in the middle.

There would be soup on the hob downstairs, made from scratch. That was the next stage. I stepped past the tray and into the hall. The carpet creaked as I walked along, as if my feet were new and strange compared to my dad's hard skin and my mother's perfect pedicure and Lulu's dirty soft soles. I stopped at the stairs and looked at the pictures positioned every three and a half steps. Perfect portraits of each of us as tiny babies, the same painted blue sky behind us, the same pervy old photographer behind the lens. Here was Lu, on her front and gurgling cheerfully with a white china rattle clutched in one pudgy hand. Here was Jel, flat on her back on a white sheepskin rug, grinning at the camera with a wicked smile or a particularly violent bout of gas. Here was me, lying silently against a fluffy white bear. Here was Ella, the eldest, tiny white feathered wings strapped to her back, gazing at the camera with pink cheeks and an angelic smile. Down past the curve of the stairs to the seven straight steps that led down to the sitting room. Only two pictures hung here. In one, my parents were married in a cloud of batwings and puff-balls. In the other, the six of us stood in front of the house, the same photographer kneeling on the pavement with a black silk cloth over his head and just the camera eyeing us suspiciously.

*It's the middle of summer, the sun round and hot in the sky, all the windows open and the air inescapably thick, closing in. I have on a beautiful dress I bought from a market one day, on one of my wanders. Pale blue cotton, with a full, short skirt and a sailor collar, sleeveless with big white buttons down the front and white swallows printed over it. As I reach the door, feet bare, my mother springs.*

*'Put this on,' she says. She's holding out a white cardigan, thick knit with pearl buttons down the front.*

*I stare at her, the white jumper waiting between us. 'It's thirty degrees outside.'*

*'This is going to be on our wall for ever,' she says. 'You want to look nice, don't you?'*

Into the sitting room where the coffee-table sat at right angles to the sofa and two chairs, both facing straight ahead. I ran my fingers along the windowsills but there was no dust, nothing to leave a mark in.

Through the dining room and the kitchen, not stopping there.

*I sit at the table, arms crossed, trying not to shake. My dad stands opposite me, leaning on a chair, looking down at the table. He hasn't said anything in forever. There is just the plate between us. My mother stalks back and forth. 'We can wait here all day, Saffy. We've got nowhere to be. I'm not giving up today. Two spoons. Just two spoons, and then we can all get on. I'm sure you've got things you'd rather be doing. Something on telly? The others are watching telly. Wouldn't you like to? I know you can hear me, it's no use ignoring me.'*

*Maybe it's something I do. Maybe it's a slight curl of my lip or a flinch of my face. Maybe she just runs out of space to pace. But in that second, I hear her snap. I hear it, and I turn to look, and even as she's rushing towards me, even as she's picking up the spoon and jamming it in my face, even as the food is running down my chin and tears are falling down my face, I'm just staring. Even as my dad is pulling her away, even as the shouting fades deeper into the house, shut behind doors, even as I'm left alone with lumps dripping into my lap, I'm just staring. I can't feel anything any more.*

Into the garden. The sun was sinking slowly, the air dense and heavy. I looked at the wishing well in the corner of the lawn and wondered if I could fit inside, if I could pull the lid closed and sit there until I died. I thought probably not. Huck, my mother's basset hound, would smell me and give the game away. I went to the apple tree and walked the whole way around its trunk, tracing the ridges in the bark beneath my fingers. I climbed the six planks of wood, without needing to look where my feet should be put, grabbing at them and not caring if I missed.

The wooden porch of Lulu's tree house had once been big enough for two to sit and swing legs; now even she could barely fit. Green apples hung all around me and the sky was a clear, bright blue between the branches so everything around was bursting with quiet colour. When I was younger I would creep out there in the dark and listen to the rain falling softly around me. I hugged my knees and stared down at the grass, which grew long around the trees, short and uniform everywhere else in the garden. Up here things were wild and beautiful, a secret magic world away from everything else.

Beauty is a funny thing. In a tree it can be a colour or a bud or the way light dapples the leaves. In a view it can be the blue of the sky or the purple of sunset clouds or the curves of huge hills. But in a person beauty is not so simple. A single thing can't make someone beautiful. You can have nice hair or pretty eyes or a lovely dress and still be ugly. My mother told me once, when I was only small and I asked her to put make-up on me, that beauty was only skin deep. When Fitz would tell me I looked beautiful, that I was beautiful, I knew he was lying. Because beauty really is only skin deep but ugly goes all the way in. The more you peel away the more you find.

I wondered how long it would be before Lulu could no longer fit in the tree house and my mother got someone in to rip it out. I could picture her standing on the lawn, hands on hips as men with tools tore down the walls and took them away in pieces.

*We're walking down the high street. That's what I do at weekends, because I don't have any of my few friends left any more, apart from Quin, and he's being tutored at weekends and in the holidays by the university student who lives next door to them and who eventually introduces him to Brideshead. So I just wander around, sitting in cafés and bars, right at the back with a coffee or a water, and just watching people and seeing what they eat; looking at overcooked fried eggs split open to spill their still wet core over the browned and frilly whites, or burgers cooked too long, until the meat curls up at the edges, and the buns are shiny with fat and the lettuce translucent and dripping away onto white plates. Or I walk through bookshops and look at recipes and photographs, always flicking past the glossy author pictures or the scene-setting ones, the rivers or the rolling fields or the château, straight to the doughy pizzas and the fat fish and the carnival colours of peppers and red onions and fresh rocket. Rows and rows of symmetrical candy-coloured cupcakes with tiny sugar snowflakes and sharp crystals of sugar sinking into inches of icing. And I walk away feeling full.*

*That day, walking along with my mother, I'm wishing I could run into one of the shops, slide into the aisles and bury my face in one of the books heavy with food and stay there. It's a cool autumn day, the beginning of school, when people are growing up and moving on, and I am stuck. I just want her to be gone. Her voice is needling, poking at me.*

'I saw Kelly from next door earlier,' she's saying. I don't reply, pulling at a flap of skin over my hip through a hole in the pocket of my jumper until my eyes water. 'She graduates next year. Isn't that lovely? She's going to be a vet. She hopes she'll end up with her own practice. And a farmer husband! Isn't that charming? Now, will you look at that little dress? That would look so lovely on you. I've always said navy was your colour. Most things are, mind, you've got your nanna's colouring, though God willing not her temperament. Shall we try it on? That'd be fun, wouldn't it? You try on that and I'll give that green number a whirl, although I'll admit silk isn't always flattering on my thighs, but what is, eh? Saffy?'

I flick a hand instinctively, trying to swat the annoying noise away. 'No,' I say, with the greatest of efforts. 'I don't want to try it on. I hate it.'

She tuts. 'There's no need to be rude, Saffia. If you didn't want to come, you might have said. Bluebell needs new shoes, you know. I could've brought her.'

I stop watching my scuffed pump scratching the pavement and look at her. She's got older at some point when I wasn't looking – she looks pretty much the same, with the same round eyes as Ella and turned-under hair, which she sets with rollers every morning; but her eyes are creased deeper than before and lines run down the corners of her mouth. Her skin has a dry, velvety look to it when you're that close; powdery and crumbling. I feel a sudden hatred for her, for the too small handbag that hangs from the crook of her arm, for the lip-lined smile that never falters.

'You should have,' I say, pulling up my hood and stuffing my unbrushed hair over one shoulder, away from my face. 'I didn't even want to come.'

She rolls her eyes. 'For goodness' sake, Saffia. How long are you going to carry this on? The rest of us have lives too. You'll just have to snap out of it, soon enough.'

I look at her, at the tiny pearls in her ears, at the spirit-level straight of her fringe, at the pressed angora cardigan, and then I *look at the road behind her, at the cars and the buses heaving past, and I think about shoving her aside, about hurling myself under the wheels of the bus lumbering up the road, about the screech of brakes and the thud and the blood and the screams, and then the silence. The long-awaited silence. I picture her with a faint spatter of blood across her dusty cheek, as my skull smashes against the asphalt and my hand falls flat against the road, fingers closed as hers reach out for me too late. I almost smile.*

I don't think she would have reached for me, looking back. I overheard her, a day or so later, telling my dad that she couldn't take any more. Perhaps in that moment, hearing the bus shuddering up behind us, feeling me staring back at her, unfixable, she wanted to push me.

It wasn't long after that day that I was told I would become an in-patient at Happy Blossoms. It was a place I would come to dread and hate and dream about, but that first time, when I didn't know any better and was easily fooled, a tiny part of me was thankful for a way out, a new place to be. I'd left this house, and I'd hoped I'd never come back. And now there I was again, back up in the tree house hiding from a family who wanted me hidden. I felt like I'd slipped through a groove in time and ended up back in the past by mistake. I needed to get out, back to my life, back to my flat.

Leaning my head against the rough wood, I breathed in the green air. A bird fluttered through the leaves above my head, settling on the roof. I heard the squeak of pushchair wheels outside on the road and wondered if it was Una, walking back and forth along the road with nowhere else to go. A car pulled up outside the house. I opened my eyes. Heard the doors closing, one, two, three, and Lulu's voice wheedling something about a bunny. The sound of the boot opening. I slid back down the tree, over the doorstep, up the stairs and into bed just as the front door opened.

*The doctor looks at me wearily over fogged lenses, and then at his notes, and then at my mother. 'Your daughter, Mrs Truelove, is suffering from anorexia nervosa. An eating disorder.'*

*He lets the words sink in for a moment or two. I look down at the carpet and wait to leave. I seem to spend most of my life staring at ceilings or at floors, waiting for something or nothing to happen. 'There is a range of treatments available,' he says, as my mother's lips start slowly to form shapes, her eyes blinking slowly. 'It will depend on a number of factors,' he says, 'as to which treatment will emerge as the most suitable. Often, residential care is seen as most effective. But, certainly, we can offer the therapy you will both need to reach this decision.'*

*A funny thing happens then. My mother reaches over and takes my hand in hers, and squeezes my fingers between her cool ones. I feel a sudden surge of hope, though I don't know what I'm hoping for. And then she finds the voice to speak.*

*'She doesn't have an eating disorder. My daughter does not have an eating disorder.'*

*She drags me out of my chair and pushes me out of the door. 'Thank you for your time,' she says, pulling it to behind her.*

*'You do not have an eating disorder,' she says to me, marching out. As we pass the waiting room, she waves to a younger woman with two small children. 'Hello, Jane!' she calls out. 'Nothing too serious, I hope?' And then she pulls me out of the door.*

I could hear them piling in, carrying things bought from the supermarket or the garden centre, plastic bags piled at the foot of the stairs, the beep of the car as it was remotely locked. Lulu's cork sandals slapping on the tiles as she ran through the house as if she'd never seen each room, my mother calling after her to take her shoes off, to come and have something to eat. The TV switching on, the quiet sounds of the tennis, the squeaky springs in the worn-out spot on the sofa as Dad sank into his favourite hollow. I lay flat on my back and listened.

*The woman in the pink cardigan sits back in her chair and looks at me over her pearly glasses. The cardigan is the colour of the calamine lotion we've been blobbing on Lulu all week, little Lulu all scabby and sweet. I watch her playing on the carpet with an ugly doll's house, all bright colours and plastic edges, square furniture and block shapes.*

*'You can play if you want,' the woman says. I stare at her in silence. I'm fifteen.*

*'Tell me,' she says, turning to my parents, 'a bit about your day-to-day life. What kind of things do you do together, as a family?'*

*My father sits in silence, looking at his big hands clasped solemnly in his lap. He looks like she's a vicar or his headteacher. I hate her.*

*My mother clears her throat, a weird little noise in the silent room. 'Well, the girls all have their own interests, of course, but we like to go on visits at the weekend. Trips to see the family, that kind of thing. Sometimes we go out on a boat, sometimes to the library. You know, nice things.'*

*Jelli snorts. My mother looks at her sharply, and she goes back to fiddling with her lip ring. She's still grounded for that. She can't take it out yet, not until it's healed, but it will be whipped out not long after. A year later will follow the nose ring, then the tattoo. You can't whip off a tattoo, however hard you try.*

'And how about you, Ella?' The woman turns to her. 'What kinds of things do you like to do?'

Ella smiles at her sweetly, crossing her legs and folding her skirt around her, dainty and delicate. 'I read a lot,' she says. 'Sometimes Daddy and me – Daddy and I – read a book at the same time and talk about it over dinner. Or I'm busy studying. I'm going to Oxford in the autumn.'

The woman smiles politely at her, and looks back to my parents. 'I'd like to speak to you two alone now, if that's all right. Why don't you girls wait outside? There are mints on the desk at Reception if you'd like one.'

We wait. Jelli kicks me in the shin. 'We're missing Sweetheart High *because of you, twatface.*' I ignore her. Lulu knocks the bowl of mints onto the floor, sending them flying in all directions, like tiny blown-up bones.

After a minute or two, the door swings open and my mother comes storming out, two spots of red high on her cheeks. My dad hurries after her, carrying her coat and stooping under the door-frame. 'Pip,' he says, as she marches through the automatic doors. 'Come on.'

'No!' She shrugs him off. 'I'm not listening to any more. As if it's somehow our fault! As if we've done something wrong!'

We've reached the car, her in front, him clinging to her elbow, the four of us shuffling behind. He puts a hand on her arm as he unlocks the car. 'That's not what she was saying,' he says quietly. It's her turn to snort. I walk silently past them all and climb into my seat, buckle my seat belt, stare out of the window. Somehow, against all odds, they've managed to make it about somebody else again. It's never just about me.

Clinking ice cubes below. Iced tea and tennis were Dad's favourite things. There would be a piece of lemon in it, cut in a particular way, which made it into a spiral. 'A helix,' Ella used to say all smug. 'That's called a helix.' The rustle as the plastic bags were ferried into the kitchen to be unpacked. I heard feet on the stairs and turned to the wall in a hurry. The door creaked open.

'Saf-feee …'A pause. 'Is you sleeping?'

She was too old to say 'is you'. Nobody thought to correct her.

She was creeping up to the bed now, sticky fingers on my shoulder. 'Saf-feeee.'

I turned over. 'What?'

She hopped onto the edge of the bed, all gangly long limbs she didn't know what to do with. She still thought she was little, because that was how everybody treated her. 'Are you tired?'

I nodded. 'Yep.'

'Oh.' She swung her legs. She still had on the shoes. Cork soles with leather straps and plastic daisies glued on. She held out a packet of melting jelly babies. 'You want a sweet?'

*My grandparents always bring us jelly babies when we are little. I always wish they wouldn't. It means hours of sitting in my room, looking at them. I don't like the purple ones; the taste makes me feel sick. But if I leave them in the packet, I feel a horrible guilt right in my belly and I sit and apologise to their tiny sugary faces. It makes me cry to see them all alone in the yellow bag, unwanted. And so I eat them. I eat them and I say sorry.*

'No thanks,' I said, and I tried to smile at her. 'I'm just going to go back to sleep.'

'Okay,' she said, but she stayed where she was, swinging her daisies back and forth. 'Is you coming to live at home again now?'

I kept my eyes closed. 'No.'

'Mummy said you is. She said you was coming home.'

'Well, I'm not. I live with my boyfriend, remember?'

She was chewing a jelly baby, a soft mushing noise coming out of her mouth, like a cow eating grass. 'Mummy said you haven't got a boyfriend any more.'

I didn't remember throwing it, but the next thing there was water running down the wooden wardrobe doors, glass shards in my dad's spade hand as he picked them out of the carpet, my mother's hand on Lulu's head as she led her out. And then I was alone again.

*When you need the toilet, you have to wait until someone can take you. Someone with keys to unlock the two locks on the door. You can choose: you either let them in to watch, or you count very loudly as they wait outside the door, or you don't flush and let them do it for you. You can't say they don't give you choices.*

I locked the bathroom door and sat on the edge of the bath. Running the tap, I splashed water on my face and on my neck. I looked at the toilet and realised I didn't need to go. The house was quiet but I could hear the whispers in the kitchen without hearing them. I went back into the bedroom and lay down on the bed. I folded the duvet over myself, rolled up and closed in.

Soon afterwards I heard the footsteps on the stairs. I kept my eyes shut tight. They came in together, my mother sitting in a smudge of patchwork skirt and hairspray fringe on the edge of the bed, Dad leaning against the door and shuffling his feet. He had to stoop to fit through the doorway, and it made him look guilty and sorry. Her lipsticked lips were saying Happy Blossoms and Dr Anne and I wanted to scream at her, throw things, jump up and down – no, just no, just no nononono. But my legs and arms had turned to jelly flowers and it came out as a whimper and a whisper as my fingers gripped at the duvet. My mother stroked my fingers and laid a cool hand against my head.

'Yes, angel, that's right. You'll be just fine soon.'

And, for some reason, I found myself nodding. They turned off the light and shut the door and left me alone.

In the dark I waited and waited. When it was time, I stood up and walked out into the silence of the house, shivering and shaking. High up in the dark I could hear my dad snoring and the beach noises, waves crashing and gulls wheeling, from my mother's special sleep sounds machine. The tiles were cold under my feet but I knew I had to be quiet so I didn't hop. I kept going and I felt with my feet as I went along.

I'd stared at the walls and listened to them talk about me for too long and, no matter what else, I knew right then that I could never go back to that place, to Happy Blossoms. If I did I knew I'd never leave. I'd be force-fed, forced to talk, forced to listen, people shoving things at me from every direction, raped with forks and spoons and words and thoughts.

In the kitchen, shadows loomed and the green digits on the oven's display hovered in darkness. I could feel the things in the cupboards, alive, waiting. My hands felt blindly for the tin I was looking for, recoiling violently at the soft skins and hard flesh of the fruit basket, skirting cautiously over packets and boxes, dusty cardboard and crackling plastic. I found the small tin and removed the thin sheaf of paper inside, and then I closed the cupboard and stood in the dark. I listened to the floorboards creak and the people above me sleep, and I wondered when this had stopped being home. I wondered if it had ever even felt like home.

In the dark and the still I felt my way out to the door. Lulu's backpack was waiting there and I fiddled carefully with the key, twisting it in the special way so that the lock didn't make any noise as it slid back. I picked up the bag and walked out into the cool street as dawn was about to break.

'*Lost*'

# FITZ

I got bored of kicking my heels after about a day or so but I had no money cos it was Saf's half of the month to be keeper of the purse; she got paid in the middle and I got paid at the start and so we took it in turns to play Mum. So that left me a bit scuppered but I still had a tiny bit of cash lurking about, what with there not being any outgoings on food pretty much ever in our flat, and even though I knew I ought to be saving that for the next two weeks until payday started shining on the horizon like a beautiful beacon of hope, I thought what the hell? And I moseyed on down to Lucky Chips.

People walking past in the other direction had on their Find Fate badges and they all looked like they were part of a secret club. The badges got posted through your letterbox and everyone was meant to wear one but nobody had ever put one through ours so we weren't in the club. I waited at the crossing with a little old lady wheeling one of those little tartan trolleys, and when the green man started beeping to say off you go, I walked a bit slower than normal so she'd feel fast. It was kicking-out time for the schools and so there were sweatshirts and blazers all blobbing up and down the streets in this part of town, all queuing up to buy sweets and fags from the shops where they were only allowed to go in two at a time.

I nipped down one of the little alleys and wormed my way through the secret-maze route to Lucky Chips. There was the odd kid huffing deodorant here and there but mostly it was quiet, which was better. Even though I'd been lonely knocking about in the flat all on my tod, I didn't feel like squeezing past schoolkids all giggling and having fun and being young. So I just walked down the dark alleys and pretended in my head a little bit that I was a spy, having a peek around corners before turning them and occasionally swinging round to check I wasn't being followed, that kind of thing. And before long I was coming out of the alley next to the cash-and-carry and crossing the road to the big dirty yellow doors of Lucky Chips.

Inside it was pretty empty, which I guess is what you'd expect at just before four on a weekday. A bloke with a mullet was playing roulette and the clack-clack-clack of the wheel filled up the chip-fatty air. One of the karaoke booths up on the balcony had been stuck on 'Maggie May' since I'd been coming here, but in the evenings you couldn't hear it so much over the other ones and the fryers and the people talking and the fruities jingling. I could hear it pretty good then, but it didn't bother me too much as I was secretly quite partial to a bit of Rod. I fiddled with a pound coin and looked about at the tables.

All of the croupiers were sat round one of the tables right at the back, eating noodles and texting on their phones. Apart from the roulette there was just one table going, blackjack with Mao, my favourite dealer, who was short and a little bit fat and very very smiley, which is a quality I like a lot in people. There was one other person sitting there, a bloke in a suit with a sweaty head and dark eyebrows, which looked a bit like someone had drawn them across his face with a big fat marker pen, and a pint and a whisky next to his elbow both in steamed-up plastic cups. I went and sat at the spot two down from him and put in a couple of chips that had been floating in my pocket and a pound down to be turned into a couple more. Mao gave me a wink and a big smile. He never said much but he always let you know he was happy to be there. The guy in the suit smelt a whole lot like whisky and his briefcase had fallen on the floor and opened a bit so some papers were just slipping out onto the swirly-whirly carpet but he didn't seem too bothered.

I played a few hands and lost all of them, and the butterflies weren't even starting to stir or wave at me, like they were all asleep or gone down the pub. So I was quite glad when I felt a little tap on the shoulder, and when I turned round Win was standing there. ''Ello,' I said. 'You ever get a day off?'

She giggled and covered her mouth with her hand. She had a gap between her front teeth and I guessed she didn't like it. Hannah used to be like that when she was little and her front teeth were bigger than the rest but I s'pose those days she probably would've been glad if it was only her teeth she had to think about. 'I just finished,' she said, and she did have her bag over her arm when I looked down.

'Cool,' I said, 'I'll walk out with you.' It didn't seem like anywhere I was I'd feel happy so I figured maybe I'd be better off to keep walking.

'Okay,' she said, and she grinned and forgot about the gap between her teeth properly for a second. I gave Mao a wave and he gave me a smile full of dimples, and off we went.

Outside it was starting to cool down as the sun went to bed, and Win shivered. 'It's getting cold,' she said, and I nodded.

'You not got a coat?'

She shook her head. 'I need to get a new one really, before winter and that. I'm always spending my money on Max's clothes, see.'

I only had on a thin zip-up jacket thing but I whacked it off. 'Here y'are,' I said. 'Stick this on. I'll come round the casino some time and pick it up.'

She looked like she wanted to say no, but it was getting pretty nippy out so in the end she pulled it on and zipped it up and pulled the sleeves down over her hands.

'Max never see his dad?' I asked, cos it didn't seem right, her working all the time and still not having enough cash to even get herself a coat.

'Nah.' She bundled a bit deeper into the jacket. 'He's never met him.'

'Shame,' I said. 'He must be a bit of a knob jockey.'

She laughed into the neck of my jacket, which she'd pulled up over her chin. 'Yeah,' she said, a bit muffled. 'He is.'

We were walking down the main road by then, park on one side and houses on the other, cars driving past with their half-lights on because it was that weird dark but not dark time of the day. 'How's your week been?' she asked, and I had to lean in a bit to catch it, what with the zip and the jacket between her mouth and the outside.

'Pretty shit,' I said, and she looked at me all wide-eyed and I didn't know what to say, so I fumbled a bit and then I said, 'My girlfriend moved out.' Which was true and not even close to being true and made me feel a bit sick because I'd properly remembered again that she was gone.

'I'm sorry,' she said. 'Hope you're all right.'

I felt the backs of my eyes get a bit hot like I might cry so I just had a little cough to get my voice straight and I said, 'Yeah, I'm all right. It's for the best.' And then I said really quickly, 'I've, er, got to nip this way, actually, Win, gotta drop something off at a mate's. Catch you around, yeah?' and I jogged through the park and I kept jogging until my eyes felt back to normal and I could breathe again.

I'm not gonna lie, I was in a bad way the next day. I had the hangover sweats, the ones where you go hot and cold all of a sudden and your face turns all grey and your head goes light as a feather and aches like anything. After I'd got back from Lucky Chips I'd counted up all the change we had on the little change plate we kept next to the microwave, and in the end I'd had just enough to get a bottle of Mad Dog 20/20. I couldn't believe they still sold it when I got to the shop, like the taste of childhood, all magical. Except not magical at all because it tasted minging and it got me really miserable pissed. And I was there the next day with all the booze sweating itself out through my face and down my back and my legs felt all floppy and wobbly and I kept having a little groan and feeling sorry for myself and in the end I decided in my wise old head the best thing to do was apparently to tidy the house. Even while I was doing it I was thinking, This is a bloody stupid idea, where's my duvet and the remote? But still I kept on putting books back on the shelf and cups in the sink and still feeling sorry for myself. All I could think of was Saffy's confused little face looking up at me as I told her she had to go and that mixed with the 20/20 taste in my mouth, well, that was a sick-making combo let me tell you. And so I was doing what my mum did in these situations and sweeping away and rolling out the thoughts I didn't like, except we didn't have a broom and I couldn't make pastry so I had to settle for bleaching the bog and packing up Saf's things for her instead. I got all her bits out the wardrobe and put them in her big suitcase, which I'd nearly knocked my head off getting down off the top of the wardrobe, and then I got all her fluffy socks and little lacy pants out of the drawer and I didn't have to fold them so I bundled them up and put them in a corner of the case, and then I got all of her makeup bits and bracelets and earrings off the side and put them in a carrier bag and tucked that into a different corner and then I laid the bit of mirror that was propped up against the wall on top of it all and then I did up the suitcase.

Then I thought I might change the sheets on my bed so I stripped them off and yanked the pillowcases off and then stuck all that in the washing-machine but didn't turn it on because I wanted to watch the racing at four and the washing-machine sounded like it was gonna take off once it got going. I got the clean set out of the top of the wardrobe and stuck the sheet on first, that's the easy bit obviously, then stuck the pillows on because they're all right as well, long as you push them right in there otherwise you end up with that empty bit at the end and the case all twisted and that's a right bastard in the middle of the night when your head works its way off the plump bit. Then I decided to tackle the duvet. Saffy used to do this thing where she turned the cover inside out, picked up the corners of both and sort of flicked the cover over the duvet, but I couldn't get that to work so I sat on the floor and just tried pushing the corners right into the ends of the duvet, then tried to straighten it out inside without being able to see. Sat there shoulders deep in duvet, a load of stuff under the bed caught my eye. Once the duvet was buttoned up and not too twisted – although I had noticed a couple of tiny mouldy spots so I had to swivel it round a couple of times so they were at the bottom – I chucked it on the bed and started pulling the stuff out from under there.

Well, I must have sat there for an hour I reckon, going through it all with all this dust I'd set loose spinning around happily and a Bugged In Erol Alkan supervising. There was a load of crap under there but it was fun going through it, old magazines with the crosswords filled in all wrong on purpose, which she always kept if she'd managed to fill a whole one with different words or by putting the words back to front or by filling it in in froggy French *mais oui* or in the bit of Spanish she knew; I didn't know any. A daisy-chain that was all wilted and had hardly any petals left, just stalks and the little yellow bits, and it could have been from anything, she was always making them and wearing them round her head, but I knew she'd have known exactly when it was from because she remembered everything, Saffy, like that the cork on the dressing-table was from the night we drank red wine and I told her I loved her, or that the cinema ticket stub she found in her purse once was from the night we went to the cinema when we were worried she might be pregnant but it turned out she wasn't. And then I started thinking that maybe she'd have forgotten when this daisy chain was from or when all of it was from, which made me even sadder, as if she'd forgotten a bit of herself. A big photo of her and her sisters because she did love them even though they pissed her off, especially Anjelica, always going on about uni and how great it was, how she was going to be a doctor or prime minister or head of the world or whatever. None of them ever thought Saffy was going anywhere with art but I'd always known she would and even then, with her gone and it all disappearing, I couldn't bring myself to believe that she wouldn't.

One of the boxes had a big pile of old sketches and there was all of her sisters in there, Jelli again, a cool kind of anime Jelli, and a pretty little crayony type thing of Lulu and a pencilly sketch of Ella, who was really brilliant-looking, seriously fit, and then near the bottom a really bright painting of me and you could still see the pencil lines under the paint and she must have been going to frame it because the paint didn't go all the way to the edges, just faded out to white and she'd signed it in the

149

corner with a little Saffy squiggle and a little heart. Next to me, well, curled up on my shoulder to be accurate, was a brill bright green iguana. With the spikes all down its back and the googly swively eyes and the tail curled back up under my arm and a bright red forked tongue hanging out in a matey way. He had a collar on and that had more spikes on it, and on the yellow gold name bit it said in black letters, if you looked close enough, Lavelle, which was what I was gonna call him. I thought about all those times I'd made her go to the Lizard Lounge or Snake in the Glass – she never complained, just stood there merrily looking like an alien angel in the green light and nodded and laughed at their funny tails and the slow way they moved, and at this one shop there was a little chameleon and he was in love with Saf and if she stood in front of his tank and wiggled her fingers on the glass he'd stand on the edge of his branch and rub his little feet up against the glass trying to get to her, and from the outside it looked like he was raving, waving his weird forked hands around to the beat and when she took her fingers away he'd sink back down to his branch looking sad, so she'd put them there again and wiggle at him and back up he'd go again raving away, and even I was bobbing away to Erol thinking about it, and I'd always thought next time I had a bit of a win on the horses I'd buy her that raving chameleon. The thought of him all alone in his little cage waiting made me sit on the floor staring at the wall for a very long time.

I got in from work that evening with a crate of Stella under my arm and I'd even stayed late helping Jenny in the kitchen, I was that keen to steer clear of the flat, and then I'd walked home instead of getting the Tube and still there was forever for me to be sitting around thinking in the silence. But when I got my key in the door I saw Quin's shiny shoes, and I could hear 'And I Am Telling You' warbling out of the stereo and my heart went yaaay! and I strolled in with a spring in my step. I must have been grinning as I put the crate down on the kitchen table and turned round because as I was saying, ''Ello, mate,' he'd stood up and hugged me and I'm not usually into bloke hugs but I hugged him back and I was still hugging him when he let go.

I went and stuck my hoody on the back of the chair and got the last two cans out of the fridge and started sticking the ones out of the crate in there as I said, 'D'ya have a good time, mate?' and put one of the cold ones in his hand and opened mine. He was sat there in his silky dressing-gown thing and flannelly pyjamas and these slippers with curly toes, and he took a sip out of his beer with his pinkie stuck up in the air while I had a swig on mine and sat myself down.

'It was amazing, thanks,' he goes, and had another sip. 'And how are you?'

'I'm all right.' I had another swig and waited for him to ask about Saf, which obviously he did.

'I, er, noticed Saf's stuff's gone,' he said eventually, and I think we were both glad it was out in the open.

'Yeah,' I said, and the words felt all heavy in my throat. 'I called her mum, Quin. I didn't know what else to do. She was completely out of it.' My voice started to sort of wobble and crack and my eyes were getting hot at the backs again.

He nodded and looked all wise like an owl. 'I understand,' he said. 'I think you did the right thing.' Which didn't really make me feel better but I appreciated the gesture.

We sat in nice silence sipping and swigging for a while, and after a bit I said, 'So what'd you get up to in the country then? All clay pigeons and that, was it?'

'Oh, yeah,' he goes. 'All wellies and puppies and gin and tonics. I could've wept seeing the city looming up ahead when we were driving home.'

'I bet, mate,' I said, getting up. 'Another?'

'Yes, why not?' he said, so I grabbed two not-so-cold-yet beers out the fridge and handed him one in his other hand, cos he still had half the first one left, and flopped back in my chair.

'Here,' he goes, 'they still haven't found Fate Jones, have they?'

'Nah,' I said, pointing at the paper that was on the floor next to his chair. 'Boyfriend's still a suspect. Well dodgy background apparently.'

He tutted and had a drink of his beer. 'Terrible, isn't it? Poor girl. Her poor family.'

'Yeah,' I said, and had a swig myself.

'Do you remember that one a few years back – Polly, was it?'

'Molly,' I said, after I'd swallowed my beer.

'Oh, yes,' he goes. 'You're right. Awful that was. Just awful.'

'Yeah.'

The big-stack stereo started whirring as it went on to its next CD, which was Dusty Springfield as it goes. You could tell Quinton was back.

'Just awful,' he said again. 'They'll find this one any day now.'

152

'You reckon?' I was draining the last bit of my can by then.

'Oh, yeah,' he goes. 'They've got all those search parties out, haven't they?'

'Yeah, they've got all the contestants off *Top Idol* out there helping now. And the judges.'

'Well, that's jolly good of them,' he goes. 'God, imagine if one of them found her! Alive, I mean. Be a bit morbid if it was the other.'

I sort of went mmm and fiddled with the ring-pull on my can because I didn't really feel like thinking about bad news any more.

'So what happened on *Top Idol* this week anyway?' he said.

'Not much, same old. Actually, tell a lie,' I said. 'They lowered in that young one, what's her name, Lacey, isn't it? Yeah, they lowered her down on one of those swing things, you know like in the circus, only she fell off it.'

'Seriously?'

'Yeah yeah, but it was all right she had a safety thing on, she just hung there by her foot, only her hair caught fire a bit off the flame-thrower bloke they had on, but other than that she was fine, kept singing and that.'

'Oh, she's a proper little pop star that one,' he goes. 'What a little trouper.'

'Yeah,' I said, getting up to get two more beers. 'Yeah, she's all right. It was the older bloke that went this week.'

'The one with the peg leg?'

'Yeah, that's the fella.'

'Oh, that's a shame,' he said. 'I liked him.'

We thought about that for a bit and listened to Dusty and drank a bit more beer. And I remembered how much I'd been dreading being alone in the flat and now I wasn't and so I thought I'd better make the most of it and I scrolled through my brain for something good to say.

'And how's things with, erm, Igor?' I said eventually. That was the latest bloke Quin was loved up with, massive he was and always wearing big furry coats and big rings on his fingers like a Russian bear-hunter bloke.

He made this happy gushy face and said, 'Oh, he's so lovely, not much of a conversationalist but he does the sweetest things.' He didn't go into any details of what the sweet things actually were, and to be honest I couldn't imagine Igor doing anything nice except for maybe skinning you a rabbit, but then I'd only met him a couple of times so I didn't like to judge. He talked about him a bit more, and I started to sort of wish I hadn't asked cos I'm no good with giving advice or whatever, so I just listened and hoped he wouldn't ask me what I thought about any of it. I was starting to feel a bit pissed because I'd not had any dinner or any lunch apart from the odd handful of pistachios because everything was making me feel sick. Quinton had rosy cheeks and a bit of a slur too cos he was always a bit of a lightweight; it was one of his charms.

'Tell you what,' he said, 'do you fancy something a bit harder?'

'Yeah, all right,' I said, a bit wary I won't deny, and he went out to his bag and came back with this fancy black bottle of gin. He got out two glasses and we started doing inches of that each and it was all right actually, tasted like cucumber, and whether that's a good thing or a bad thing I couldn't say but it was interesting for sure. 'You Don't Have to Say You Love Me' had come on in the background and we sat there looking at each other misty-eyed.

'So,' he goes after a bit, leaning forward, 'is she coming back?'

Well, I knew who he was talking about obviously and it wasn't Fate Jones. 'I dunno, Quin,' I said, knocking back my gin and holding the glass out for more.

'Don't give up on her,' he said, looking me in the eyes as he poured a big measure for me. I opened my mouth to say something but he hushed me with his hand. 'She'll come back. And when she does, she'll need us.'

We sat there in silence after that, both with our glasses tipping to the side, feeling sleepy and full of thinking, and Dusty warbled on in the background, and when the song finished Quinton got up and turned the music off and squeezed my foot that was hanging over the arm of the chair. 'Night, hun,' he said, and wandered over to set his sleeping bag up.

'Night,' I said, and I got up and wandered in to sleep on my clean sheets.

The next night after work the flat was empty again. I sat on the chair and I put my feet up and then I put my feet down and then I hung them over the arm and then I stood up again. I straightened all the CDs on the shelf and took one down and looked at it and put it back and straightened them all again. I lined them up with their fronts at the edge of the shelf and then I lined them up with their backs all straight against the wall. I went to the fridge and took out the last sad little beer and opened it. It was cold and too fizzy and made my mouth taste all metally, like tears or like how your fingers do when you're a little kid and you've been holding pennies for ages and ages while you look at all the penny sweets. I went into the bedroom to tidy up but there was nothing left to tidy up and there were big gaps where all Saffy's things should've been, so I went back out and into the bathroom and looked but everything was tidy in there too, except for the four sucker holes where Phyllis the Fish used to live.

I went back to the lounge and drank some more of my beer and then I realised it was the quiet that was making everything so sad, squashing me down and making me feel all floating and lost at sea, so I put the radio on and that made me feel, well, not at all better but still at least I had something else to listen to other than the tumbleweed and memories in my head. I turned on the little lamp that Quinton had got from a car boot sale and which had weird fringy stuff all around its shade. It looked like if we were in a cartoon film it might start dancing around the drawers to cheer me up. But we weren't and so I just shuffled around a bit more, bopping my head a bit to the music and moving things around and putting them back and drinking my beer in tiny little penny sips.

And then there was a knock at the door which in my little world of my own confused me so much that I just stood still for a minute wondering what it was until it came again.

I went out into the hall, which was dark because it was nearly night outside, and I opened the door and Win was standing there looking a bit sheepish and also a bit red, even in the nearly nighttime.

'Hello, Fitz,' she said. 'You left your wallet in your jacket – you know, the other day – and I thought you might need it.'

I was a bit bewildered and my head was still all messed up and so I think I just looked at her a bit silly for a while before I remembered myself and said, 'Right, cheers, Win, yeah, thanks. Come in, come in.' I didn't even remember having a wallet and it had probably been in that pocket for months but it was just as well she had found it because I'd been looking for my driving licence for ages, and it was a new one anyway and I hadn't dared send off for another. So it was enough to put a very small smile on my face for the first time in what felt like ages. 'You want a beer?' I said, and then I remembered I didn't have any beers left. 'Or a vodka?'

She smiled like she wasn't sure. 'Okay, yeah, a vodka, thanks.'

I got the little bottle of voddy out of the freezer and got a glass down but when I looked in the cupboards I could see we didn't have any mixers. 'You all right with it neat, Win?' I asked. 'Or I could open a box of tomatoes if you like? Get some of the juice in for a Bloody Mary?'

She looked at the glass with the vodka in a bit nervous. 'Like that's fine,' she said. 'Yeah, that's how I like it. Neat.'

I handed her the glass and leant against the counter. 'So, yeah, thanks again for dropping that off, mate,' I said. 'I'd been shitting it about telling Saf I'd lost my licence already.'

She took a sip from her glass, a big one, and it made her eyes go all watery-runny and she pulled a face without meaning to. 'That's okay,' she said, when she'd got a nice face back on. 'I don't live far.'

That made me think for a sec and I said, all curious, 'How'd you know where I lived?'

This made her go quite a lot more red. 'Your address is on your driving licence.'

'Oh, yeah.' I had a little chuckle. 'That's clever of you, that.'

The radio was playing Motown now, which made me want to go and lie face down in a big pile of duvet and never come out again, but I didn't want to be mean so I said, 'How's Max?'

She got on this shiny happy soppy face and said, 'He's lush. Thanks for asking.'

I looked at my feet and tried not to listen to the song. 'I like kids,' I said, for something to say to cover up the music, which was making my heart feel all heavy in my chest and my eyes feel all fuzzy around the edges. 'Maybe I could babysit for you someday, you know, to say thanks for dropping this off.' I could feel my eyes starting to water so I watched my toes in their socks really really closely and scrunched them up and then let them go and then scrunched them up. 'I'm a good babysitter,' I said. 'The kids down our street were always asking for me when it was the Seventies disco for the parents and that. Or I could just take you for a drink maybe, just to say thanks, you know. There's a nice pub down that way …' and I pointed even though I was just pointing at the kitchen wall and my eyes were still all watery and my nose was tingling a bit and my voice felt a bit small. 'I'm not much company at the moment, but in a bit maybe—' And then I felt an arm sneaking round my waist and I thought, That's nice, I do need a cuddle, I really do need a cuddle, and I was about to say thanks when she leant up and kissed me.

Her lips felt soft and thin and for a second I almost kissed her back but then it was like my head had done an emergency stop on the brakes and everything went flying forward and I pulled away. 'What you doing?' I asked, stepping back across the kitchen.

Her eyes all filled up and she went pink in the cheeks in two blotches and she couldn't get any words out. 'I'm sorry,' she said, and she turned and ran out of the flat.

I felt terrible then, like everything was just a big whirl of sadness and the whole world was rubbish and I sat down on the kitchen floor and cried into my knees.

I felt squashed down with thoughts, like I was suffocating, on the train out of the city, but as I got closer to home I felt like I could breathe again and like maybe I might be okay someday. I thought, Yeah, that's better already, because even the air felt lighter and cleaner by the time I was walking off the main road on to our street. But that didn't last long because as soon as I opened the front door with the key that lived under the little stone beagle who sat on the step, and the yellow puff of fags and staleness and sweat and gravy hit me in the face, I suddenly felt myself sink again.

My mum came hurrying out, clutching her rolling pin, with flour dust following behind her. She looked tiny and even more like a mouse than the last time I'd seen her, bits of beigey brown hair falling out of the do she always had pinned up behind her head and flour dust and grey sprinkled in between. When she clocked it was me she grabbed at her heart and let the rolling pin down a bit. 'Oh, it's you,' she goes in relief. 'Hello, love.'

'Hi, Mum,' I said, bending down to kiss her floury cheek.

'I forgot you were coming,' she goes, looking confused. 'I must've forgotten to put it on the calendar.'

'No, Mum,' I said. 'Surprise visit today. That's all right, isn't it?' Which was a stupid question, I thought, as I took my shoes off and stuck them under the telephone table; it was pretty unlikely she had plans seeing as she hadn't left the house in over a year, in fact probably longer. Except the one time Dad had been off goose-stepping down the high street and the Jewish butcher had gotten a hold of his cleaver and started waving it about and the nice woman from the baker's with hair like a Chelsea bun had come and got Mum and she had gone out, but that was the only time.

Hannah was upstairs – you could hear the bed frame slapping the wall and the muffled moans even from down there. We'd all just learnt to ignore it and you did get used to it, after a while you wouldn't even notice it, which was just as well because it was a pretty regular occurrence. She didn't have a boyfriend but she seemed to have four or five or six special friends after the bomb, and whether we thought that was a good idea and whether we could see the link between surviving a terrorist attack and being struck with the urge for a good cocking didn't really matter. If it made her feel better then she could shag her way through the Black Country and I wouldn't mind. I just wanted her to be happy and if that was what she thought would do it then, yeah, it was all right with me, but I did hope that what would also make her happy was a new bed.

Anyway, not really wanting to hang around and listen to my sister's shagging noises any more than the next person, I hurried into the lounge where you couldn't hear it quite so much, probably cos the yellow fog blocked your ears a bit. My dad was sat at the computer but that was nothing new, he was a permanent fixture in that chair and if he ever got up to make a brew for himself, which was next to never, or go to the loo, within a few minutes the phone would start ringing off the hook. I wished he wouldn't give out the home number, it was bad enough with Mum's nerves, let alone having all these dodgy types ringing up for 'Griff'. Thing is, to me he was my dad, he was Griffin Fitzwilliam, postie and pub darts champion, but to the people on the other end of his chatrooms he was Griff and his opinion was really really important. He was sat there typing away, typing like dads do with one finger stamping out each letter like they were all very very important each and every one. The bald patch on the back of his head had got even bigger and he was peering over his glasses, hunched in his chair, so he looked a lot like one of the freaky horrible birds out of *The Jungle Book*, but I felt bad and guilty for thinking that because you're only supposed to think good things about your family and besides I was no oil painting myself. He didn't look up, just said, 'All right, son,' and I walked up behind him and put my hands on his bony little shoulders but I was careful not to look at the screen with its bright red and black letters because I'd learnt to pretend not to see that, not to see 'nigger' and 'paki' and 'allah' or any of the horrible words that popped up all over the place like nationalist Tourette's, which was what Saf called it, because even though they were sick and it made me feel sick, he was still my dad and it's hard to think bad things about your dad, not when there's a picture of you when you were five with a bowl cut and little flared jeans on, digging in the garden with him, up on the mantelpiece, so I'd just learnt to make my eyes go blurry and ignore it until I forgot it was there, just like I couldn't hear the thumping and groaning coming from upstairs any more.

'Journey okay?' he asked, because that was a dad thing to ask, especially my dad, who had millions of books of maps and would print directions off the computer for you if you were going somewhere, even though he knew shortcuts and better ways so he crossed off half the steps and filled them in himself in his spider's handwriting. He didn't get out that much now so all the maps were in the corner getting dusty, which made me sad right in the middle of my chest.

'Yeah,' I said. 'Train was a bit rammed at first but all right after Coventry.'

'Mmm.' He nodded, like to say he'd expected as much.

I stayed standing still looking at the pictures on the fireplace and the maps in the corner and the bald bit at the back of his head.

'Everything all right?' he said after a while and I said, 'Yep,' and took my hands off his shoulders cos that felt a bit weird and awkward and I couldn't think of anything else to say, but that was okay because one of his little conversation windows had popped up and somebody was asking him something and he was typing back looking serious so I just squeezed the back of his chair instead of his shoulder and went into the kitchen to see my mum. She was there, back rolling away in her little cloud of flour dust. There was always pastry in the oven, didn't matter when you popped your head in, an empty doughy bed would be in there baking away, probably another one sat on the window-sill cooling down. She looked up a bit surprised when I strolled in, probably'd forgotten I was there bless her.

'Cup of tea, love?' she said, clapping her hands to get the bits of pastry off them, and sending a big puff of white in front of her face.

'I'll get it, Mum,' I said, as she was blinking away the dust. I got her cup off the draining-board, remembered which one it was and everything. Han had bought it for her ages before, Best Mum Ever, it said with a big heart on it and stuff. They used to go shopping all the time, girly stuff and that, sit there in those mud things girls put on their faces and the big pink fork things in between their toes up on the coffee-table while we laughed at them. I got a mug out for myself and I didn't bother looking for mine just in case it wasn't there. I put tea in the teapot and that was nice, me and Saf didn't have a teapot, which was a shame actually cos Quin had a tea cosy, one of those ones that's a lady with a big woolly skirt to cover the teapot. While I waited for it to brew I leant back against the counter and watched her putting the pastry into its silver dish, prodding around the edges and slicing off the extra bits flopping over the side with a knife.

When she was done, she stacked up the knife and the rolling pin and the board next to the sink and starting wiping up the flour dust with a soggy J-cloth, putting it all into her little bird hand.

I poured the tea into the cups and got the milk jug out of the fridge and poured some in. I didn't sniff it cos it was best not to, Dad was quite bad at forgetting to pick up milk so it was sometimes, well, you know, a bit on the sour side, but Mum'd get upset then so it was best to just dump a bit of extra sugar in, give it a stir and hope for the best. She'd stuck all the extra flour neatly in the bin and was brushing her hands over the sink and looking a bit lost so I steered her over to the table and plonked the tea in front of her. We both sipped at it even though it was too hot, just sipping and smiling at each other while we tried to think of something to say. I was trying to think of things that wouldn't upset her, you had to be careful you really did because, even if you started off on something quite normal, before you knew it you'd somehow wandered on to bad topics and then it was too late. Don't get me wrong, she was definitely getting better, it was nothing like in the first few weeks after that day, when I'd come into the kitchen to make tea for the pair of them or to get ice for Han's face, because the burning carried on for weeks, her face was so hot it melted ice in minutes and so I was always running back and forth with peas and mugs and sympathy and brave faces, and I'd find her sobbing in a little heap of tea-towel on the table. Or when you tried to get her out down the shops or just a little spin around the block, just to get some fresh air, and even the sound of a car starting or a dog barking and she'd curl up on the pavement and you'd have to carry her home wobbling like jelly. She had nightmares about it for months, even though she hadn't been there; in the dreams it was her not Han and she was trapped. She'd wake up screaming and it would be me who went, because Dad was slowly rocking on the back step in the dark, smoking and thinking about murder and war and grinding his teeth, so it was me who went and cuddled her and told her it was okay, we were all okay, we were safe. No, she was much better by then but it was still definitely a case of being bright and breezy and watching very carefully to make sure her eyes didn't start blobbing up with tears.

'How's Saffy, love?' she said, and I looked at my tea.

'All right,' I said after a minute. 'She's been off visiting her parents as well.' Which wasn't a lie, was it?

'That's nice,' she goes, with a smile. 'Lovely girl she is.'

I nodded. 'What's new with Phil and Holly?' I asked eventually, and this is the thing, you see: when somebody doesn't leave the house the people in their life are the ones on the telly so I ended up asking after the bloody presenters on *This Morning* like they were real mates of ours, but I'd obviously hit on a winner because she squeezed my hand excitedly.

'Ooh,' she goes, 'ever so well this week. That Holly she's a lovely girl, she had on the loveliest dress the other day, beautiful curves, reminds me of when we were young. And that Philip, ooh, I've got a soft spot for him, William, I don't mind telling you.'

'Oh, yeah,' I said, winking at her and taking the cups to the sink. 'Well, I'm no Pip I'm afraid, Mum, but you need anything doing in the garden while I'm here?'

'Oh, you are a good boy,' she said, pinching my cheek. 'The beds do need doing – do you mind, pet?' and she started rolling out the pastry for the pie lid.

It was weird, grabbing my coat off the banister and shouting, 'BYE!' loud enough for Mum in the kitchen and Dad at the computer and Han and her guest up in her room to all shout, 'BYE!' back. It was just like I was a kid again, going out to play at the end of the cul-de-sac, back in time for my tea. Billy was waiting at the gate for me, just like when we were fourteen, and we did a sort of handshake-shoulder-pat sort of hug.

'Fitz, man, it's been ages,' he goes, he was always stoned, Billy.

'Yeah, Bill, good to see you,' I said, even though I was already getting to that heavy feeling you get on a night out sometimes, when you can't be bothered to talk to anyone and even smiling feels like a bit of a job and really you just want to sit in a corner and stare at your feet for a while, and I was starting to regret texting Bill to see if anything was going on that night so I could try and take my mind off Saffy. But when we got to the party I tried my best to smile and be happy and go, 'HIYA, MATE!' at everybody I hadn't seen for ages and try not to remember there was a reason for that. And everyone was ruffling my hair and patting me on the back and handing me beers and I kind of shiftied my way through without having to actually talk to anybody too much.

I got into the conservatory bit where everyone was smoking weed and I saw Petra sitting on the windowsill blowing bubbles.

She was the one person I didn't mind seeing, so I ambled over and sat down next to her. 'Hello, stranger,' I said.

'Fitz!' She threw her arms round me and gave me a massive hug and I thought to myself her hair smelt a bit like Saffy's, but then I put that thought away.

'How's it going?' I said, and as I did I thought she still looked nice, with nice curls in her hair and big curly eyelashes. She was my first girlfriend when we were like thirteen or something. We used to walk down by the river which isn't a river even though we all call it the river, it's just a dirty stream kind of thing with crisps packets and empty Coke bottles and sometimes nappies or johnnies floating in it, and hold hands and sometimes maybe a kiss on the cheek. After that she'd been a bit of a slag – at parties she was always taking boys off to the bottom of the garden for naughty fun with the Poddington Peas but I still always got on with her and it was always nice and never a chore chatting to her.

'All right,' she said, shrugging and drinking some of the blue bottle in her hand. 'Same old, you know how it is.' I did so I said yes.

'How's your family?' she asked, because she was nice even if she was a bit of a slag and I said, 'Yeah, they're okay, you know.' She did so she said yes. After the incident of Hannah and the fundamentalists I saw Petra in town once. It was on one of my last goes at getting Mum out of the house and I was walking her round to the baker's, the one with the nice Chelsea-bun-hair lady, holding on tight to her arm even though she was quivering away like a little jelly-person and trying to hide behind me or sit down I couldn't really tell which so I just dragged her along saying nice bright things like 'Ooh, I think I might have a cream slice, what about you, Mum? Nice éclair?' and tra-la-la-ing to myself because I was getting good at that. And then just as we were walking under the old church steeple, the clock went BONG BONG BONG for three o'clock and at the same time a dog that was tied up to a bench on the pavement jumped out from under it and started barking and my mum leapt behind me like she had little springs for legs and hid behind a parked car and cried. I tried for ages and ages to get her out but she wasn't budging and so I was just standing there like a lemon scratching my head, when Petra came along. 'C'mon, Mrs Fitzwilliam,' she'd said, in a lovely voice like angels have, 'let's get you home,' and she put pretty hands on my mum's arms and lifted her up and she'd walked us both all the way home.

I was thinking about that then and feeling a bit embarrassed about it but also I was remembering how nice she'd been and I felt a good warm feeling about her in my belly. I drank the rest of the beer in my hand and then I started on the one in my other hand.

'How's Hannah?' Petra asked, and she smiled at me and her lips looked like sweets or like red jelly.

'She's all right,' I said. 'She's had another operation on her face and that.'

'She still, you know …?' she said, and she didn't say the last bit, which was nice of her because what she meant was is she still going like the clappers. I nodded slowly and drank some of my beer so I didn't have to answer, because I didn't know what the right answer was without lying or without being horrible to Han.

'How's London?' she asked brightly, so I didn't have to answer the other question.

'It's okay,' I said. 'Yeah, it's pretty sound. What you up to these days?'

She was swinging her legs and rolling a cigarette. 'Working at the playgroup,' she said, licking the Rizla. 'Looking after the babies.'

'Oh, right,' I said, and I looked at her big eyes and her curls and her curly lashes and her jelly lips and the squidgy bit of boob showing at the side of her dress and then I leant forward and kissed her. And she kissed me back and it was all warm and jelly and squidgy, and then I got a sniff of Saffy hair smell and my stomach did a flip and a lurch like I was going to be sick. I pulled away from her and I ran out of the house and out of the garden and out of the street and all the way to my front door.

I got back and fumbled around for the key under the beagle, who was winking at me, which seemed a bit out of order after the night I'd had. I was trying to be quiet and I could hear my dad snoring upstairs, the weird squealy snore he made when he was lying flat on his back. I went to go to the kitchen to make myself a brew but the light was on, sneaking out under the door and into the dark living room. I felt creeped out so I creaked the door open all slow and peeped round it, but it was only Han, sitting at the table with a whisky. 'Hiya, hun,' she goes. 'Good night?'

'Yeah, all right,' I said, and sat down at the table too, but I never could lie to Han because she looked at me all sympathetic and got up and got me a glass and filled it with whisky from Dad's not-so-secret stash. 'Thanks, Han,' I said, drinking a bit and feeling it burn my throat. 'Just not in a party kind of mood,' I said, and gave her a little smile.

'What's up, love?' she asked, and her okay eye looked at me kindly.

There was no point pretending, Hannah'd always known what was what with me since I was mini. 'It's Saf,' I said, all in a big sigh. 'Her eating's bad again.'

'Oh, sweetie.' She held my hand across the table, with her good one I mean. 'What are you going to do?'

I wiggled in my seat cos I felt all weird suddenly. 'I called her mum,' I said. 'They took her away.'

Han swallowed her whisky slowly. 'Oh,' she goes. She didn't let go of my hand, but she stopped stroking it.

I drank the rest of mine. 'Was that wrong?' I said, super-quietly, and I thought she hadn't heard because she didn't say anything, just stared at the whisky in her glass.

'Gorge,' she goes eventually, 'don't you think maybe you're the best person to help her?'

I felt a bit hot. 'I don't know how, Han,' I said. 'I tried, I did.'

'I know,' she goes, taking her hand away to drink the rest of her whisky. 'But maybe you don't need to know how. Maybe she just needs you.'

We both thought about that and then she put her glass down and looked me right in the face. 'I'm gonna tell you something now, babe, that I've never told anyone before, okay?' I nodded. 'Okay.' She sighed. 'You remember right before the bomb?' I nodded even though I couldn't remember what it was like before the bomb, because not long before that was also before Saffy, and those two things had turned the world upside down in all kinds of ways. 'You know how I was in London a lot of weekends?' I nodded and I felt my heart start crying because I had never ever been able to say sorry for it, that she'd been there to see me and if it wasn't for me she'd never have been on the Tube at all, and it was all my fault and I couldn't make it better, just like I couldn't make anything better, only worse.

'I had another reason to be there all those times, sweetie. Apart from visiting you.'

I looked up from the hole on the table top. 'What?'

She smiled. 'I was seeing someone new. Someone I really liked.'

It felt like the light in the room changed, like it got lighter or darker just like that, except maybe I was just seeing things differently. 'Who?'

She took a sip and even though she looked calm her hand was wiggling a bit. 'A man I knew from work. Well, through work. James.'

'Why didn't you say?'

She put the glass back down. 'It was complicated. His situation … It was complicated.'

She didn't say any more and I didn't ask. Some things between brothers and sisters don't need to be said. Sometimes you need to protect the version of that other person who lives in your head. 'Well, what happened to him?' I said, and then I thought, Oh no, right in the middle of my belly, because what if he was one of the ones who died in the bomb and she'd been keeping that in her heart all this time and none of us had known?

She smiled but I could see that deep down behind her eyes she wanted to cry. 'I never heard from him,' she said. 'I tried calling after I woke up, you know. Texting. Nothing. He sent flowers to the hospital, but he never came.'

I remembered then all in a big flash a bunch of flowers in the bin outside the ward, all scrunched up and broken just like she'd been, and I wanted to run outside and run all the way back to the city and hunt him down and kick him in the shins and shout at him and make him cry. 'I'm sorry, Han,' I said, and I felt my voice start to wobble in my throat and then her eyes filled up and mine did too and the whole room was full of feelings just bursting to get out.

And then it was gone, and she cleared her throat and took a big swig of whisky and let out an embarrassed kind of laugh. 'Anyway,' she goes, 'what I wanted to say was that he didn't know how to help me. But I didn't need him to, not really. I just wanted him to be there for me, whatever happened.'

There was a long silence as I looked back over the last weeks and saw everything the way it should've been.

'Oh, I don't know,' she goes, breaking the silence and giving my finger a squeeze. 'You know what's best, hun. I'm sure she's getting the help she needs.'

I nodded slowly, even though I didn't feel yes. 'Your face looks good,' I said, and it did, in the low light from the lamp on the counter. The scars were going softer, the edges between them and the normal skin fading away.

She touched her cheek. 'You think so?'

'Yep,' I said. 'You can hardly tell in this light.' You could obviously. But that's what it's like to love someone, isn't it? You write your own truth to make them happy.

I got back to the city with what Han had said floating about in my brain, all words and bits of sentences repeating themselves over and over even when I was trying not to listen. I couldn't work out what to do with them, so I did what I could to make them go away and I stopped in on my mate Eddie after my train got in to buy some weed. With an eighth in my pocket and the sun back in the sky I started to be able to put the words away one by one, and as I got on Brixton High Street I found myself wondering if Quin was at home, and if he might fancy a few cans.

There were a load of schoolgirls milling around the high street at the end of Eddie's road, wearing short skirts and hoop earrings and shoes they couldn't walk in, and some Rasta guy with a ghetto-blaster on his shoulder, I didn't even know they still made ghetto-blasters, and an Iceland carrier bag full of beer in the other hand, and some horrible bloke with greasy grey hair and his pants way down and piss all over them and one shoe off, and his toes had all white bits over them and black nails and he was sweeping from each side of the pavement to the other as he went along, and a woman with a screaming kid, dragging the kid and his buggy along and knocking into shins all over the shop, even the pissed piss-guy's. It all felt a bit mental and I could feel myself getting all hot and annoyed, so I slipped into the bookie's just for a minute.

Everything was quiet and calm in there, blue carpet, blue stools, little blue biros, all very reassuring. Two blokes sat watching the screens, the footy scores were coming in now and one of them was bent over an accumulator while the other who must have lost already dipped into a packet of crisps, staring at the screen the whole time. Couple of younger lads playing the fruities in the corner. I looked at the scores rolling in on the vidiprinter at the bottom of the screen, and it was just the atmosphere of that place, it did something to me. Just knowing one day it would be you with the ticket clutched in your hand, jumping up and down like a prat, and even if it wasn't there's still the nice sadness of losing. I stood and looked at the odds on the horses instead of the footy because that was always more my thing, my favourite.

And there it was, the five-fifty at Kempton. Fifty-five to one. Saffire not Sapphire. Saffire. I'm not superstitious but that's a sign: when you get that itchy feeling about something in your belly, when you know if you try and walk away you'll have to go back, when your eyes keep going to that one line and you feel as though it's all meant to be, like it's a proper message from someone in the know, that's when you have to put that bet on. So I fumbled in my pockets and found a battered tenner and one dirty pound coin and filled out my ticket, got my ID out cos you get ID'ed till you're at least forty in the bookie's, you must do, and strolled up to the counter. The kid behind the desk, must have been only just eighteen himself, looked at it a bit funny but he printed off the slip and handed it over.

I wandered back over to the screens and found myself a stool a bit away from the two blokes who were quietly swearing and twisting at their accumulators. It was five forty so I played Tetris on my phone for a bit, and soon enough the horses were being trotted along the edge. Saffire had a green-and-yellow-checked jockey, which was bad right from the start, I prefer a one-colour jersey, blue or pink or red. More of a pressing concern, though, was the fact that she looked like a little donkey with legs like Twiglets. Eleven quid as well. I thought to myself I must be going nuts, but maybe without Saffy about someone had to. A few other people were milling around by then, probably just out of the pub because everything started to smell a bit like lager and chip fat, which is a nice smell, homely. And then they were off, pink number three haring off too fast, those too pissed to know better cheering and the others who'd betted on it and actually knew what they were on about sighing and muttering, red and gold slowly notching its way up the inside, blue number two was who you'd want to have your cash riding on, steady pace in the thick of it but no strain still plenty of go in the motor, and of course green and yellow donkey bringing up the rear with a weird bow-legged run, Tetris cubes raining down and I shifted a few, glancing up and down up and down, red and gold had fallen, dunno how it was a flat course beautiful weather, pink had slowed slowed slowed until overtaken by everyone pretty much, donkey aside, blue number two was still quietly storming away, some flash purple wanker was racing up the outside now pulling his weight but not enough to pass blue number two, I switched a red L-shape upside-down to slot between a T-shape and a block of little 'uns, blue number two was slowing, purple wanker showed no sign of a sudden burst but it must have been there, he had that wanky feel about him, a T-shape speeding its way down, no obvious gap for it, oh, here was the burst from purple wanker and still no gap for my T-shape so I flipped it and laid it on its back, now hang on what was this? The last straight. And my mangled little pony was making its way past pink past blue, and then suddenly, shit-the-bed unbelievably, it was neck and neck with purple wanker, Tetris blocks piling up I never even noticed, eyes on that stupid little horse, all the stringy muscles in its legs bursting out, spit foaming out its mouth, it was like it was talking to me going, Look at me, Fitz, look at me go, and purple wanker was even looking surprised if a horse can look surprised and it must have slowed down because suddenly Saffire the donkey was crossing the line and everyone was groaning, and I was sitting there sweating into my slip and then slowly going up to the counter and Johnny-Eighteen-Last-Week was looking at it and gasping and pretending not to and opening the till and handing me £616, and I was shoving it in my pocket and hoping no fucker saw me and walking out the door and thinking, Woah, what just happened?

I was laughing like a bloody loon in the middle of the high street and Pissed-Piss-Pants was still up in the distance and that made me laugh more, at the total weirdness of it, and a couple of dudes sitting in one of the bus stops were looking at me funny so it was just as well I managed to stop. And then I was walking towards the Tube with 616 hot ones burning a hole in my pocket. And right there, outside the station, was a man who was only dressed in a dodgy old parka and stained jeans, but who told me everything I needed to know, just by playing his battered old guitar. Maybe it was fate that made him think that day was a good day for a Marvin Gaye song, or maybe he just recognised it for the absolute tune that it was, but whatever it was it made me feel like the whole of Brixton High Street was staring at me and if there *was* anybody up in the sky looking out for us all then they were looking at me for sure. And the sun caught all the windows in the street and lit them up like the truth dawning and suddenly all of Hannah's words had set themselves free and they lined themselves up in my head for me to see and I knew then. I knew I had let Saffy down when I was supposed to be the one caring for her. I knew that this money was a chance to wipe the slate clean and to make everything better because if Quin was right and she was coming back then I would be ready and I would be waiting and I would have made everything safe and right for her again. I headed for the Tube and I knew exactly what to do.

It was strange standing knocking on the door and waiting for someone to answer and all the while looking down at my own front door tucked away below the pavement. The flats up there were bigger and some of the houses along the street were actually still houses instead of being split into flats. So I didn't really know what to expect on the other side of the door and now I was actually there I was starting to get pretty scared. I was about to scuttle off back down to the flat when I heard footsteps clumping towards the door. My heart started thumping in my chest but I took a deep breath and stood my ground and then a bolt was unlatching and the door was opening and Kay was standing there. He had pink eyes again and all the veins in his arms were sticking out blue. His nose was all swollen and out of place and his eyes were a bit black, someone had done a proper job on him. He peered out at me and gave this horrible little creepy grin with pointy teeth and beer breath.

'Howdy, neighbour,' he said. 'Won't you come on in?'

I followed him in and the door shut behind me with a quiet clunk and everything went dark after the bright sun outside. I blinked a couple of times until I could see properly instead of little coloured flashes appearing everywhere, and then I followed him into the living room. It was a right mess, empty cans everywhere and old takeaway boxes piled up in corners. On the table my decks were all laid out and they were turned on but without a record on them, just an empty can swirling slowly and sadly around to static.

Kay was slouching in a chair watching me. 'And what can I do for you?'

I swallowed and in my head gave my voice a little pep-talk about coming out strong and manly and not fucking it up for us. 'I've got your money.'

He raised his eyebrows and gave a gurning sort of smile, chewing the inside of his mouth. 'Super.'

'How much does she owe?'

'Three hundred.'

For a minute I couldn't say anything. It was so much money, and even though he could have been lying and probably just pulled a number out of the air right that second, a part of me knew he wasn't and things really had been that bad. 'Fine,' I said, and I got the wedge of notes out of my pocket and started counting them out, which in hindsight might not have been the smartest but I just wanted to get it done and get out of there quicksharp.

He stood up on shaky feet and went over to a little fridge in the corner and bent down to look in it. There was nothing in there so he picked up a half-empty bottle of whisky from the side and took a glug of that. 'You're lucky I ain't charging you for the rest,' he goes, and he was sort of slurring like one side of his mouth had given up the ghost and gone to sleep.

'Whatever she's had, we'll pay for,' I said, and I was feeling a bit braver but sadly that seemed to make my voice get a bit higher in a sort of Scrappy-Doo sort of way.

He laughed this weird single snigger. 'I'm not talking about gear,' he said, putting the bottle down on the table between us with a delicate little clink.

I looked at him blankly and he stabbed a shaky finger towards his face. 'Who'd you think did this?'

I was still looking at him blankly which really wasn't wise, sort of like how they tell you not to stare big dogs in the eye.

'Your lovely girlfriend,' he goes. 'Was just trying to get a bit friendly with her. *Neighbourly*.' He looked off into the distance like he was remembering. 'I was this close.' And he made a gesture with his fingers, which said that he was very very close, and then he licked his lips and smiled at me and I felt sick rising in my throat and blood rising in my face and a buzzing rising in my ears and I thought of him near Saffy, touching Saffy, hurting Saffy, and my fingers were closing around the bottle of whisky and the bottle was swinging through the air and the bottle was hitting him on the side of the head and the bottle was cracking and warm whisky was running down my arm and I was screaming words that were more like sounds and it was his turn to look at me blankly as he sat on the floor with blood and shock on his face and I threw the notes in my hand at him and they fluttered down like butterflies.

And then I was running.

I hammered on Eddie's door like a maniac until he answered it, looking all confused with his puffy sleepy eyes, letting a cloud of weed puff out behind him slowly.

'Fitz?' he goes, blinking slowly.

'How much for your car?' I said, not bothering with hi or anything.

'What?' he goes, and I wanted to poke him in the head but I just said again, 'How much for the car?' and then I said, 'I'll give you two hundred and fifty,' because I didn't have time for this.

'My car?' he goes, scratching his head. 'It's a heap of shit. Can you even drive? You all right, Fitz? You gonna whitey?' but he was so stoned it took him about five million years to get each question out.

'No, you idiot,' I said, shaking my head, and I probably did look a bit wired or mental or both in fairness to the boy. 'I need your car to go and get Saf.' I pressed a wad of cash in his hand and he was still stood staring at me like I was asking to ride him side-saddle all the way to Ipswich, but eventually his brain ticked round and he went and got the keys and handed them over.

'Be careful, Fitz, won't ya?' he said as an afterthought, and I already had one leg in the little banger so I just yelled, 'Yes, mate,' and slammed the door shut, started the engine with a splutter and reversed off the drive with a clunk, watching him disappear into a tiny white dot in the rear-view mirror.

As I drove out of the city, I could've sworn I saw Fate Jones wink at me from a billboard.

# SAFFY

There is a road that leads from the small market town and out into the open fields. As you walk along it, the big houses and their neat, manicured lawns turn into tiny cottages, round and crooked, and after that into empty spaces, a farmhouse, a greenhouse, allotments, spread out and lonely under the wide sky. After the fields of golden corn and the towering stacks of bales, the countryside is interrupted by a fat black line: the dual carriageway.

If you walk along the motorway at any other given hour of the day, at noon or dusk or deep dark midnight, you will be out of place, stared at, sworn at, horns beeped at. But if you walk along at dawn, you will be left alone, except for the odd cheerful trucker's friendly toot. You can watch the sun coming up over the tiny villages in the distance and the pretty fields and over the Quick Chef and the petrol station and you can walk, one foot after the other, away from everything.

When I reached the station, I sat down on the pavement to catch my breath. Sweat cooled on my face, and my hair was sticky against my neck. I put Lulu's backpack on the floor between my feet and watched cars pulling into the sloping car park, where the still-rising sun caught their colours against the grey asphalt.

People in suits and people in uniforms filed towards the doors like worker ants, stepping neatly through the ticket barriers and wandering onto the platform to find the little

183

huddle where their door would be when the first train to the city pulled in. I thought it must be nice to have such quiet order to your life: the same train every day, the same carriage, the same door. Maybe even the same seat. You could just stand calm and silent, cow-like, and wait for each part of the day to come to you. Same desk, same work, same train home.

I unzipped the bag and found the little roll of notes. Housekeeping money in our house was for the gardener who came once a fortnight, the cleaner once a week, the lady down the road who did the ironing. Before each of their visits, my mother would fly into a panic and ignore my dad's quiet muttering. On a Wednesday evening, in the dark, she would be out on her hands and knees, pulling out weeds. On a Tuesday morning, way before dawn, she would be dusting the skirting-boards, cleaning the hob. And on a Monday lunchtime, ironing clean clothes before putting them back into the bag that Lulu would trot down the road carrying in both hands. Housekeeping money for a house that was already kept but wasn't going to keep me.

The woman behind the counter was round in every way, all chins and folds with two round hands and sausage fingers sticking out like chubby stars. She had a thin fringe cut too short above her eyes and it was stuck into three or four sweaty strands, like claws reaching out of her head to eat her face.

'Sixty-nine pounds,' she said. 'Change at Peterborough, and then at Leicester for the replacement bus.'

I put four notes into the silver hole, careful not to touch the sides. The lid snapped shut. She held her hand above the ticket machine as it burped out the little orange card, and looked down at her magazine as she stuck the ticket and my change into the hole, sliding the trap open again without looking at me. I took them slowly, trying hard not to think about her sweaty sausage fingerprints on them, and then I walked through the gate and onto the platform.

The train pulled into Leicester and I stood up and stepped out onto the platform. My backpack felt heavy and I trailed along with the crowd, dragging its buckles along the tiled wall beside me. I didn't notice or care if I was bumping into anyone. I felt as though I had already run a million miles; my body was tired and my mind was empty. I climbed the stairs and when I got to the top I wondered if I should just sit down and wait to see if anyone would move me. Then I remembered why I was running. Then I remembered counting to twenty at the top of my voice with a nurse in blossom pink outside the toilet door; I remembered plastic tubing in nostril, down throat, later stitched into skin; I remembered long benches and long tables and girls screaming and girls crying and girls scratching at wood and arm and face so I pushed through the ticket barrier and into the forecourt.

The departure boards stared at me like square black spider eyes under the concrete legs of the roof. I found the board and bay number for the bus I needed and then I walked through the terminal, feeling smaller and smaller under the weight of Lulu's tiny pink rucksack.

I found the bus, idling next to the grey kerb, the air warm with diesel and late summer.

'Is this the bus for Liverpool?' I asked the driver, and he nodded and gave me a jittery wink. I showed him my little orange ticket and he nodded again without looking at it. He held out a hand for my backpack, one foot on the open luggage hold, a crooked rollie fizzling out between hairy fingers. I shook my head. 'I'll keep it with me. On my lap.'

He shrugged and slammed the hold shut, flicking the cigarette into the shallow gutter. 'All aboard,' he said, and I followed him through the folding door.

The bus smelt like old chewing gum and sweaty feet. I found an empty seat about halfway down the aisle and sat next to the window, hugging the shiny pink bag and smelling Lulu's little girl smell on it. The bus began to pull out of the station and I watched the grey floors and the grey people as they turned small in my window until I couldn't watch any more. I leant my head against the shaking window and closed my eyes.

I must've fallen asleep because when I opened them again we were stopping in another big bus station I had never seen before. The woman who had been sitting in front of me was standing and leaning over the seats to get her bag from the shelf above. Her top was too short and stretched up with her; in the dim light I could see dark scars stretching across her white belly. I looked away. She took her bag down and left. A mother and two children got on and rustled down the aisle all bustling plastic bag and shiny anoraks. 'Sit there and be quiet,' she said to them, and they hopped into the seats behind me as she sat across the aisle and started unpacking juices and comics and crayons. As the doors shuttered closed again, and I closed my eyes to match, four tiny trainered feet started kicking the back of my chair. Feet thudding at my back as the glass of the window thudded at my face and London disappeared unseen into the distance. I pulled my knees up under my chin and hugged myself into the pink backpack and sadness.

After a while the kids fell asleep and the bus pulled into another station. More passengers lumbered on, the wheels creaking and rain starting to patter on the windows. A fat man who smelt like sweating onions sat next to me and I shuffled closer to the wet glass. His legs swelled over the seat and closer and closer to me. There was a greasy stain on the front of his T-shirt and the fat around his neck was shiny in the last reflected sunlight. As the bus began to move again, I swallowed hard and looked out of the window, breathing in Lulu's smell from the pink straps and watching the buildings turn to darkness as we drove onto the motorway.

The radio was playing from the front, quiet news creeping through the quiet bus. The tinny woman's voice was slow and mesmeric, drawing words out and clipping others. I pressed my forehead against the cool glass again.

'... cloudy in the Midlands with a chance of thunderstorms later tonight. There's some patchy rain making its way across the south-east this evening, but this will clear up by the morning, with things looking sunny across England tomorrow. That's it for this evening – you can find updated reports for the next seven days on our website, or by texting FORECAST to 68887.

'And here's the headlines for this evening once more. The Home Office have once again raised the UK terror threat level to 'severe'. The Home Secretary has said that the move is intended to make people more aware and to encourage vigilance, not to scare the public.

'Footballer Caiden Kingsley has lost the last of his sponsorship deals following revelations about his infidelity. Sports drink manufacturer Thirst have released a statement thanking Kingsley for several successful campaigns before stating the company's recent decision to pursue a different direction with their new range.

'Police investigating the Fate Jones case have discovered a scarf, thought to be the one she was wearing on the night of her disappearance, in woodland on the outskirts of the city. Elsewhere, the Mayor of London has made a plea for the public to help put a stop to the recent trend of Fate Jones happy-slapping. There have been several reports throughout the city of teenagers filming each other jumping from walls or car roofs in order to damage the new electronic billboards that were introduced to London last year and have all been used to display the missing girl's face since the first week of her disappearance. Police say that they are seriously investigating claims of criminal damage, and that, worryingly, the trend is growing rapidly.

'Finally, the parents at Willowfields Junior School, the school that the younger sister of Fate Jones attends, have formed a security network against the paparazzi who flood the school gates each day. They are working on a rota to block the gates with their cars to prevent any photographs being taken of the children. Judy Jackson, whose two children attend the school, said that parents had become alarmed when photographers began passing sweets through the fence.'

I put my hands over my ears and buried my face in my knees. It was perverted. Why were we so interested? People were dragging Fate Jones into their lives – sticking her face over their windows and pulling her name around themselves. Everybody suddenly had a connection to her, it was all 'my-sister-went-to-school-with-her' or 'my-father-does-business-with-her-father' or 'I once walked down her street – imagine that! I could have been passing her on the pavement and I wouldn't have even known. Fancy that!'

It was horrifying, people pulling tiny scraps from her spectral image to keep for their own. One person had disappeared, and suddenly everyone was unstable, unanchored and vulnerable. Things that were previously safe and permanent – pub quizzes, fried chicken, plain-faced good girls – were suddenly snatched away, and the city had taken on a ghostly feel; as if you could reach out and touch the person next to you on the bus and feel your fingers pass straight through them. People were pulling Fate Jones to them, but not for her sake, for their own; as if by keeping her name on the air and her face on their lapels, they were securing themselves a space and permanence. By saying, 'Fate Jones is missing', they were all secretly shouting, 'I'm still here!'

It made me sick. I closed my eyes, and even though I couldn't sleep again I kept them closed the whole way.

# FITZ

Well, it took for ever to trundle my way out of London no exaggeration, with the window down to try and avoid dying of the fumes coming through the vents and slowing down instead of stopping wherever possible because it was pretty tricky moving off without stalling about five times. The radio worked which was a nice Brucie bonus, but saying that the channels danced off every once in a while and you had to twiddle the knob like a knobhead and chase them through the static. By the time I made it out onto the motorway finally it was actually still pretty hot and the sun was shining in through the passenger window, which wouldn't open, I'd only found that out when I'd tried opening it halfway through Croydon and it had wobbled outwards and I'd had to leap across and grab it, which nearly sent me into a postbox and a little dog piddling up it. It felt pretty good being out in the air driving, even though the car whined in fifth and made a weird screeching noise when you were in between gears. Having the wind on my elbow I felt like I was finally getting somewhere after so many stale days. I stopped at a service station and bought a bottle of Coke and some cigs and then I got back out there and felt pleased with myself, driving along smoking and swigging sweet Coke and listening to the fuzzy music.

I got to Saffy's parents' house around eightish after getting lost a couple of times. I'd only been there twice, most notably for a birthday party her parents threw her where she got drunk, did poppers in the loo and chucked up in the bushes in the garden, so I thought it was pretty impressive I got there at all. I parked the car carefully, not too close to her mum's little red number. You had to yank the handbrake up with both hands and even when you shut the door really gently the car wobbled so much it was touch and go if it was all going to collapse and just leave four wheels standing there. I straightened my T-shirt and combed my hair down with my fingers in the wing mirror and walked up to the front door, which had one of those big poncy knockers on it and no bell so I rapped on it a couple of times wondering how loud was too loud and waited, but nobody came and I felt a bit weird shuffling from one foot to the other and wondering if I smelt of cigarettes. I waited a bit longer and then I knocked again harder and more times cos I was beginning to think nobody was in, and then I heard quick footsteps and the door opened and Saf's mum was stood there with a wine glass in hand and very pink cheeks.

'Oh!' she goes. 'William.'

'Pippa,' I said back. She looked about her trying to decide what to do because she wanted to shoo me away but her manners were getting in the way. Her mouth was twitching a bit.

'Sorry,' she said in the end. 'We were in the garden. Have you, er, been here long?'

'No,' I said, 'not too long. I've come to see Saf. She about?'

Her eyes went all narrow and she said, 'I don't think that's a good idea now, do you?' and I felt like saying, Well, yes I do actually, PIPPA, otherwise I wouldn't have driven all the way here in the death trap now WOULD I? but I didn't, I just said, 'Is she okay?' in a weird small voice.

'She's fine, William,' she said, shaping each word out with her brick-coloured lips, 'But I have to say I'm surprised you care. Now,' she said, closing the door just ever so slightly, 'I know you've had a trip out here but I'm afraid you're going to have to go right on back there. Saffy's getting the help she needs from the people who love her.' And she shut the door but not before her English middle-classness had got the better of her and she said, 'Drive safely,' into the tiny crack before the door closed.

I stood there a bit longer like a lemon and tried to unglue my tongue off the top of my mouth. Well, what was I meant to do? This wasn't part of the plan, was it? I wasn't ever really one for fairytales but I never heard of a knight in shining armour who gets stopped at the door by the princess's mum. Then again I s'pose Pippa was a bit of a dragon. I looked in the window after a bit but it was dark in there so they were all still in the garden. I got a couple of pebbles out one of the barrels of flowers Pippa had sitting next to the door and chucked 'em up at the window I thought was Saffy's. But nothing. I thought I saw someone moving up there but then there was nothing again and so I kicked at the path and then I walked away. I got halfway up the road to the car, and I could hear them behind the fence in their massive garden barbecuing unicorn and sipping champagne and diamonds or whatever rich people do.

*Pssst.*

I looked about but there was nobody around.

*Pssst*, it goes again and then, 'PSSSST, Willybum!'

And I look about again and then up at the tree that's hanging over the fence and there's Lulu sat there merry as you like, with her head poking out the little window at the back of her famous tree house.

'All right, Lu,' I said, a bit taken aback.

She nodded. 'Saffy's not here.'

'Eh?' I go. 'What d'ya mean she's not here, Luie, she gone out?'

'No,' she goes, shaking her head so the whole tree house shook and all the leaves around it. She really was too big for it, I reckoned her arms must have been stuck out the windows at the side and her legs hanging out the door and standing on one of the branches. 'No,' she goes. 'She left.'

My head started to feel a bit fuzzy confused again. 'Left?' I said in a whisper so as not to be heard by the Lord and Lady of the Manor. 'Where's she gone?'

'She ran away,' she said, and just those three little words were enough to make me feel like someone had dropped an ice cube down my pants.

'What?' I hissed. 'What'd do you mean, Lu?' but before she could answer, Pippa's voice was right next to me.

'Bluebell! Dinner. Down you come, darling.'

And by the time I'd realised she was on the other side of the fence and not right behind me like in a horror film, Lulu was waving 'bye and shrugging her way out of the tree house.

I sat in my car and stared at the empty tree house and listened to Saffy's number ring and ring, and when it cut out I just pressed the green phone again and then on the twenty-fourth or maybe forty-third time of ringing it just cut out and after that it went straight to her answerphone and it wasn't even her little voice recorded at the other end but some horrible woman telling me the person I was calling was not available. I felt like there were millions of mental ants running through my head and carrying all my thoughts out my ears with them before I had time to put them together and think them through. Where had she gone? Why weren't they looking for her? Why were they having a flipping tosspot barbecue instead of getting the police and the army and MI5 to look for her? I banged my hands on the steering wheel and tried to get myself together and stop my legs shaking and my ears sweating so that I could go back up there and bang the door down and get some answers.

And then all of a sudden the front door opened, and like a dream a figure with blonde hair and a baggy jumper on came struggling out with two big suitcases, and my heart stood still and all the air started singing and I couldn't even move for a second and then I was opening the door and running out and running across the road to her, just as she got to the end of the path dragging the giant bags with her. 'Babe,' I said, and all my body was wobbling like mad. And then she looked up, and her hair was falling in her face but she didn't blow it up like she usually did, she pushed it off her face with her hand, and the face she pushed it off wasn't hers.

'Oh.' All the air sank out of me. 'All right, Anjelica.'

Jelli looked up in surprise, and one of her suitcases tipped over. 'Fucking hell, Fitz, what are you doing here?' she said, bending down to pick it up.

'I came for Saf,' I said. 'What's going on?'

She looked back at the house. 'Jesus,' she said. 'Right, come on. Give me a hand with these.' And she shoved both the suitcases at me and skipped over to a little silver car parked opposite the house. She clicked her keys at the boot and the door jumped up like it was well trained. 'Stick 'em in there,' she said. 'That your car?' She was pointing down the road at it.

'Yep,' I said. 'Don't mess about, Jel. I'm fucking shitting myself here.'

She waved me away. 'Follow me. If my mother sees you out here she'll probably call the police.' And she shut the boot with a sharp slam and tottered off to the driver's door. And maybe it was because there was nothing else to do or because Jelli was hard to say no to or because I was afraid to go and shout at Pippa, which was the only other option, but I did what she said and I jogged back to my car and started the engine, and I tried to make the fear nibbling at my stomach go away.

As I followed Jelli's zippy little car, I watched all the roads Saffy had grown up on flash past, all pretty houses and big houses and neat gardens and sprinklers raining down on silent grass and nobody around apart from mums with buggies and dads getting out of their flash motors in their suits and walking through their white front doors. Jelli's silver bonnet whipped in and out round parked cars and round bends in the perfect streets and then we were onto a main road and the neat and perfect people were fading away behind us.

The road turned dark, trees on either side and no cars coming in the other direction, just the warming-up streetlights to light the way. As we drove on with nothing in sight and all of Saffy's stories about how mental Jelli was starting to dance about between my ears, I turned the radio on so my fingers at least had a reason to be drumdrumdrumming on the steering wheel.

'Police investigating the spot of woodland where an item of clothing belonging to Fate Jones was found two days ago have begun moving in machinery to excavate the location. Officials say a significant area has been cordoned off, and the surrounding parkland is currently closed to the public. Digging is expected to begin today. A police source said

```
that parts of the ground showed signs of recent
disturbance.'
```

I felt my belly turn over so I switched the radio off. It's funny, isn't it? Your mum and dad spend all those years looking after you and keeping you safe from accidents and illnesses and paedophiles and sadness and all the other scary things in the world. All the time you looked around and all the mums walking along with their buggies and babies and their stroppy teenagers and crying toddlers and naughty kids had a little shiver every time they went past Fate Jones's face on tellies, posters, papers, billboards. Everybody was sad for her and glad for them because their kids were still safe from the bogeyman. But for some people, for Saffy, the monsters under the bed lived in a place nobody else could get to them: in her head. None of us could protect her and that made me feel like just about the shittest person in the whole frigging world. And now, thinking about what had happened to Fate Jones, it was hard not to wonder if something the same had happened to Saffy; if she hadn't run away after all or if someone like Kay but worse had found her, and the thought made my eyes well up and my stomach turn over, so I tried to just look straight ahead at the road and stop thinking of anything at all.

The trees along the roads were starting to disappear and then all of a sudden we were turning a corner and the sea was right there in the window, just a green slope and the beach between us. The sun was almost set behind it so it looked like the water was on fire and I had to remind myself to look at the road and not just drive *wheeeee* down the hill to stare at it. Then we came to some houses and the sea disappeared behind them, and we were back nipping in and out of parked cars until Jelli suddenly slammed on her brakes and pulled in to park next to a little bungalow. I drove on a bit and found a space and indicated and tried to parallel park, which has never been my strong point so in the end I just left it kind of pointing towards the pavement and got out and jogged back to the car where Jelli was sitting on the edge of the open boot waiting for me.

'Bloody hell, Jel,' I said. 'What was that all about? You could've said where we were going.'

She rolled her eyes and stood up. 'Get the cases,' she said. 'This way.' And she skipped off towards the bungalow, leaving me to swear but not so she could hear and lug the two cases after her. She unlocked the door and stepped in, waiting for me with the door open as she kicked off her shoes. 'Hurry up!' she goes. 'Stick 'em there.' And then she opened another door and stuck her head in. 'I'm back,' she said, and suddenly I felt my ears go hot and my heart start beating fast because I was suddenly starting to wonder what if.

'What?' Jel was saying. 'Oh, no, it's …' She opened the door properly and looked back at me and waved me forward with her hand. 'It's Fitz,' she said as I stepped towards the little square of light on the carpet. 'You remember Fitz, Nanna?'

So I had to follow Jel in and take off my shoes and leave them at the door and all the time she was shooting these little pointy looks at me but she couldn't say anything. It was nice and cosy in there and the chef my mum likes was swearing and chopping things on the telly. I didn't know much about Saffy's nan really except that Saffy liked her a whole lot better than most of the other members of her family. She looked more like Jelli and Bluebell, same fair hair and cat eyes. Ella and Saf were more like Pippa, big round eyes and darkish reddish hair 'cept Saffy made hers blonde obviously. I knew that her husband, Saffy's grandpa, had only died a few years before which was why she'd got this little pad and it was nice actually, lots of shells and pebbles about and big comfy-looking chairs.

'Hello,' I said, once I got in the room.

'Nice to see you again, dear,' she said. 'Is Saffia with you?'

Before I got a chance to get half a word out Jelli goes, 'No, Nanna, he's come to see me,' and then she thought for a second and said, 'We're planning a surprise for Saffy.'

Her nan raised an eyebrow but the chef bloke was letting rip at some shaking little waiter so she just said, 'That's nice, dear. Do you need to chat in here?' and Jelli said, 'No, that's okay, Nanna, we'll go for a walk on the front.'

'Come on, Fitz,' she said in a voice like sugar on sunshine, and I followed her out and wasn't that just the way with all Truelove women, I never got a word in edgeways. When we got out and away from the house and were walking down the green hill that went to the beach she gave me a shove. 'What the fuck is going on?'

'What?' I said, holding up my hands and standing back, cos there was no stopping Jelli if she got wind of a bit of drama she could milk.

'Where's Saf?' she goes.

'I hate to point it out to you, Jel,' I said, 'but if I knew that, why would I be asking you?'

She sulked on this as we hopped over the railing and onto the stone walk bit that ran along the pebbles. 'She did a runner,' she said, once we'd hopped down again and were walking on the pebbles.

'I got that much,' I said. 'When? How?'

'Night before last,' she said. 'Just walked out of the house in the night.'

'Well, where has she gone?' I asked, and she looked at me like I was the stupidest person in the whole world, which was probably true.

'How am I supposed to know?'

'Why aren't they looking for her?' I said, and I felt myself getting hot and shaky. 'Why haven't they called the police?'

She rolled her eyes. 'No idea. They seem ridiculously calm about the whole thing. And you know my mum, Fitz, she's never calm about anything.

'But that's not fucking right!' I said, and my voice got a little bit squeaky so I coughed it manly again. 'They should be looking for her, they should've called the police! What are they playing at?'

She shrugged, all cross. 'I don't know, Fitz! I'm not a bloody psychic! They're probably sick of her! We've got problems of our own, all of us.'

I got all hot in the face then, which was a bit because I don't like being shouted at or arguing but also a bit because I felt cross – because I was hard pushed to see what problems Jelli or Pippa had. But I supposed she had a point in her own Jelli way. Not everybody's world revolved around Saffy, and it wasn't their fault I'd only just realised way too late that my world really really did. I trudged over and sat next to her. There was a stone in my shoe so I took it off and shook it out while I tried to get everything straight in my head.

'Well,' she said, 'there's nothing much we can do. She'll turn up.'

'What are you on about, Jel?' I said, because I suddenly had this horrible sinking big cold feeling that Saffy was gone for good.

'This is what she *does*, Fitz,' she said, leaning back against the steps, bored. 'She runs. She hides. Sooner or later, and emphasis on the sooner, she'll be back and sorry and maybe they'll send her back to the cuckoo's nest for a few weeks and she'll eat up all her peas like a good girl and then they'll pack her off home to you and she'll be your problem again.'

'But I don't want her to hide,' I said, feeling a bit whiny and sad. 'I don't want her to be scared.'

'Well,' she said, 'not much you can do about that. Enjoy the peace and quiet while you've got it I say.'

'C'mon, Jel, you can't mean that. We should be out looking for her. Help me out here – where would she go? We could go look together, take my car, or yours, whatever.'

She turned to look at me with one pointy eyebrow raised. 'Do you actually not know my sister at all?' Which was starting to seem like a good question but I didn't need to answer because she just carried right on. 'Saffy does things her way or no way. If you go after her, she'll just keep on running. She's not coming back until *she*'s decided that coming back is a good idea.'

We both sat and chewed on that for a while and watched the sea licking at the stones. I wanted to tell her that she was wrong, but I wasn't sure I could. Jelli had known Saffy ever since she'd been alive; I'd only known her for a tiny time compared to that. Maybe waiting for her to come back was the best thing. Maybe she was already on her way home and when I got back she'd be waiting for me. I looked at my phone but there was nothing, just a plain black screen next to the plain black sea. I still felt all nervous and confused in my stomach so I tried to make conversation to see if it would go away.

'So what're you doing here anyway?' I said.

'Didn't you hear?' she goes, laughing. 'I'm in exile.'

'You what?' I said, cos I had a vague idea what that meant but I've been wrong about those things quite a few times and Jelli wasn't the kind of person you wanted to get your words mixed up around.

'Mum sent me away.' She was leaning back on her elbows and looking up at the stars. She was pretty, Jel, in a dirty sort of way, not good dirty more like a bit in need of a wash, with dirty blonde hair in waves and a T-shirt with the sleeves cut off and a greenish cardigan wrapped round her and bracelets jangling halfway up both arms. 'I'm hanging out here till the WI find something better to talk about.'

'Why?' I asked, and it was bound to be good, Jelli was always getting into trouble from what I'd heard off Saf: chucked out of school once for cutting off a girl's hair who was sat in front of her and then making her eat it, but she got back in because Pippa was on the board, whatever that means.

'Oh, just a bit of fun,' she said, but then she looked at me with a little cat wink. 'Mr Grubbins,' she goes.

'Grubbins! The old perv next door?' I was shocked I can't deny.

'Oi,' she said, giving me a little push but she was only messing.

'Jeez,' I said, getting my face together. 'He must be sixty, easy.'

'Don't be ageist,' she said. 'He's still got the moves.' But you could tell she wasn't all that bothered.

I laughed but maybe that was more out of surprise than anything else. 'Bugger me, Jel,' I said. 'Talk about pushing the boat out. You trying to get your mum in an early grave? She doesn't even drink tap water.' And then we both laughed.

'What's it like living with your nanna?' I said. 'Rock and roll, eh.'

She laughed again and dug her feet into the stones right up to the ankles. 'Nanna's pretty cool,' she said.

'Yeah?'

'Yeah,' she goes. 'She was a WAAF, you know.'

'A WAAF?' I said. 'Is that like a WAG?'

'Ha,' she goes. 'No. Women's Auxiliary Air Force. In the war.'

'Oh,' I went. 'Didn't even know that was allowed.'

'Oh, yeah,' she goes. 'Went off when she was nineteen, no intention of settling down and getting married like her parents wanted her to. She's always been like that.' Then she said, with a rare little real smile on her face, 'We've got a lot in common.'

'That's nice,' I said, with my own little smile because it was nice.

'Hey,' she said, sitting up to squeeze my arm. 'Why don't you stay here tonight? Go back to the flat tomorrow and wait a few days and she'll be back. You look knackered.'

'Oh, ta very much!' I said, but I nodded and suddenly I did feel really tired and being around Jelli was making it seem like maybe she was right and maybe everything would be okay and right about then I felt like clinging to that as tight as I could. 'Yeah, that'd be good. Thanks, Jel.'

By the time we got back over the railings and up the hill I really was knackered and the nanna had gone to bed so Jel grabbed a nannish flowery quilt out of the airing cupboard and I bedded down on the sofa. After she'd gone I lay there for a bit, and I thought it was nice for Jelli, having somewhere else to go, and I wondered where Saf was and if she was okay. And I thought about my nan a bit, which I never really did because I don't remember her, apart from this time when I was five and we got taken in to see her and I hid behind my dad's legs but Hannah was braver and she went up and gave her a kiss on her yellow wrinkly cheek but she cried the whole way home after. No one had really mentioned Granny Brown for years, not till Han and the terrorists, and then for weeks Granny Brown was all Mum would talk about, Granny Brown and the curse. Well, that sounds exciting, doesn't it, like I'm a council-estate Harry Potter? Well, 'fraid not, nothing exciting like that, no, 'Ooh, you're a wizard, William', although it would've been good come to think of it if a nice friendly giant had delivered the news that my family were batshit crazy, rather than my mum from behind a snotty tower of J-cloths. There's no point beating about the bush, is there? My mum's nan – well, you'd have heard of her. I hadn't but then I never did pay much attention to the news or history or anything. Charlotte Brown (Charlie to her mates) kiddie-killer and great-nan. Out on the moors and all over the papers and that. Anyway, for years and years people used to scratch things on the house or on her grave after she'd died, you know just 'murderer' and 'devil worshipper' that kind of thing. Well, it was a bit much for my nan to put up with, as it would be for most people, I guess. She started hitting the sherry and Mum'd always be coming home in her school uniform and finding her mam drunk and lying on the linoleum and that. One of the times, Mum told me once when she'd had a sherry herself, she went to go and move the glass out of her mam's hand when she'd fallen asleep with her head on the table, and just as she leant down her mum suddenly jerked up and her eyes were open and she goes, 'The devil's in you, Anna my girl, it's in us all,' and then she vommed brown sherry sick all on the plastic tablecloth. And that's gotta freak anyone out. In fact it was freaking me out then, lying in the dark with the flowery quilt up to my ears and the smell of sea-salty Grandma in the air, so I closed my eyes tight and went to sleep.

In the end I slept like a log on Mrs-Truelove-call-me-May's sofa. The next morning I found myself sat at the little table in the kitchen drinking milky milky tea while Anjelica was in the shower and her nanna was pottering about brewing yet more tea, which she put on the table and sat down across from me. I smiled at her and tried to think of something to say, maybe about Philip and Holly off *This Morning*, when she piped up, leaning forward over her cup of tea, 'So what's going on, then? Have you and Saffia split up?'

'No,' I said, a bit taken aback. 'Well, sort of, I s'pose.'

'She been having it away?' she said, looking wise.

'No!'

'Have you?' she goes, in a cross voice.

'No!' I said. 'Nobody's been having it away. It's just – well, she was getting ill again. And we thought she oughta go home for a bit.' I felt all sheepy and confused again but without knowing why.

'Oh dear. Have they sent her back to that dreadful place?' she said, taking a gulp of tea, 'Honestly, whatever is Philippa thinking? I'll never know.'

'Oh, no, Mrs Truelove,' I said.

'May,' she said, interrupting.

'Sorry, May I mean, no, she's not back in hospital … she's, erm, well, she's gone away for a bit.' I didn't know what to say and the tea was too sweet to think properly and I really wished Jelli would hurry up and get out of the shower so she could do the talking.

'Oh, right, done a runner, has she?' she said, patting my hand. 'Well, in that case, I wouldn't worry, dear. She'll soon be on the phone pining for you. She thinks she's full of fire, Saffia, like this one,' she pointed to where the shower sounds were coming from, 'but all she needs is love and care. She'll just want to come home. I'd bet you have a phone call in a day or so, if I were a gambling woman. Which I'm not,' she said, with a wink. 'Well, apart from the odd flutter on the geegees but we're all human, aren't we, dear?'

Couldn't argue with that so I just nodded.

'Well,' she said, standing up, 'you get her home, darling, and look after her, won't you? I've got my hands full taking care of the scandal *du jour*.' She looked over at the shower noises again. 'Always keeping me busy, my granddaughters. If only they all had a nice fellow like you to look out for them,' she goes, pinching my cheek. 'Just like my Archie you are.' And then she wandered out into the garden with her tea.

I sat and watched her out the window for a bit, looking at each of her flowers and picking off dead petals and stopping to smell one of them every now and again, sipping her tea and strolling around like it was a day in the park. I could just see her doing that with a little Saf toddling about behind her, maybe feeding the ducks, probably Jelli in the background somewhere killing birds or something and Ella off playing the harp or whatever. Nice to think of an old lady who did nice things with kids that didn't end up as reruns on the True Crime channel. Jelli came in then in cut-off-jeans and a strappy top with her hair dripping water all over and she had freckles on her shoulders as well, which gave me a horrible ache in my chest and for a minute I couldn't breathe.

'Morning,' she said, looking in the cup of tea May had left on the table and making a yuk face and putting it back. 'Sleep well?'

she asked, clicking the kettle on and looking in the cupboard and getting coffee out from right at the back.

'Yeah, good, ta,' I said. 'I'll be getting off in a min.'

'Back to London?' She got another cup down.

I didn't say anything then because either the ache in my chest or something else was stopping me and I couldn't actually make my mouth say yes, and neither did she for a minute, putting a spoon of coffee in the cup and putting the lid back on the jar and the jar in the cupboard and looking at the kettle while it bubbled away. It worked itself up and then clicked off and she poured it in and stirred her coffee and I watched May stroking a fluffy white flower.

'Give it up,' Jelli said eventually, leaning back against the counter and blowing at her coffee. 'Seriously, Fitz, don't waste your time. You're a nice kid,' she said, taking a sip and sticking her tongue out because it was still too hot, and I was older than her but I didn't bother saying. 'Don't get hung up on Saf. She lives on her own planet most of the time, her and Bluebell actually, but that's the bloody tree house I reckon. Find yourself someone new, hun, without any issues. Saf's sweet but she'll always put herself first, it's just the way she's wired.' She took another drink of coffee and crossed one ankle over the other. In the silence after that the ache in my chest grew bigger and bigger and my hands and feet felt itchy and I realised all of a sudden that the Saffy her family knew wasn't her – maybe it was the old her, maybe it was a her they'd just made up to explain it all away but whatever it was, it wasn't her. *My* Saffy was the real Saffy, and I knew her better than any of them ever would and there was no way in hell I was letting her just leave or be alone or be afraid and it was time that someone, for once in her life, didn't let her go or didn't just say she'd be back or that was just her, but went after her and didn't let her run and told her they loved her over and over until she believed it. My cheeks got all hot and I couldn't believe I'd wasted a whole night letting my whole life get away from me. 'Nice day, isn't it?' Jelli said, staring out of the window.

'Yeah,' I said, draining my tea and getting up. 'Well, I'll get off then. Thanks for letting me stay and stuff, Jelli.'

I stuck my head out the backdoor and shouted, 'Thanks for having me, Mrs – May, I mean!'

''Bye, love,' she said, looking up and waving with a rose in her hand. 'Pop round again soon.'

'Thanks again, Jel,' I said, pulling my shoes on. 'Hope you get things sorted with your mum and that.'

'Thanks, hun,' she said. 'Think about what I said, yeah?'

I didn't answer, just waved as I went out the door. The car started first time and I drove off down the road until I could see the green hill and the sea and then I parked and got my phone out.

Quin picked up on the fifth ring, and by then I was pretty much poking a hole in my cheek with one finger. 'Morning, William,' he said all chirpy. 'What's the story, doll?'

'It's Saffy,' I said. 'You gotta help me, Quin. She's done a runner and I have to find her. Fuck, I have to find her. Today.'

'Okay,' he said. 'Calm down. You've no idea where she'd go?'

I looked out at the sea through the dodgy window. 'I don't know,' I said. 'Is she there? Have you heard from her?'

Quin was silent on the other end of the phone. 'No,' he said, after a long minute, and for such a small word it made a big thud in my chest. 'Her phone's turned off whenever I try it.' There was a pause and then he said, in quiet words that made huge thuds in my heart, 'I don't think she's coming back, William.'

As I waited for Quin to call me back with a list of places or an idea of people or an answer to it all I laid my head on the steering wheel and tried and tried to stop myself punching the seat with both of my fists. All my head was buzzing and I knew if I sat there any longer I'd probably start throwing Eddie's collection of jungle tapes through the windscreen so I started the engine and drove back down the road I'd come along, feeling my lungs let in their first bit of air in ages as I kept going, following the road along the curve until I saw a turning for the town centre and I took it and parked in the first empty space along the neat little row of shops.

I got out with my phone clutched tight as anything in my hand, and wandered down the row looking for somewhere to buy more cigs and something with enough caffeine in it to keep me awake all day and all night for as long as it took to find Saffy. I told myself over and over that I would find her, I would, I had to, I wouldn't go back without her. But deep down inside my head there was a little voice who wouldn't shut up no matter how hard I twisted his arm or poked him in the eye or pulled his hair and he was saying that Saffy might have hurt herself or worse. He didn't say what worse was because he knew I knew. I told him he was a twat and I looked into the shop windows and watched the people going about their business to distract myself.

All the buildings around were little and old with dusty bricks and white walls and black wood but the row of shops were modern mostly, some of them with stripy bits outside to make them look a bit cuter. I walked past a little cheese shop and a baker's and a butcher's and a bike shop and a bank, and up ahead I could see a little swinging sign with a headline stuffed in, waiting for me on the pavement to show me where I could get a bit of nicotine to keep me going somewhere wherever that somewhere was. I hurried along, still holding my phone so tight it was making my palm sweat like a pervert. But then a flash from a window caught my eye and I stopped to look. It was an electronics shop, all big hi-fis and little gadgets and right in the window was a bank of TVs – two little flat screens, one wide-screen, one portable kind of one like posh people have in their cars, one weird old-fashioned one that could've been new and was meant to look old or could have been just old. All of them had Fate Jones's face on, with the word 'Found' underneath in a big red banner, and I felt my heart shrivel up. I stood and pressed my face to the glass even though I knew that the picture was bound to change any second to show the diggers and the police and the little white tent like they have on TV programmes. The sound was off so I couldn't even hear what the newsreader was saying, could just see the picture of her face and the word 'Found', which had never looked like 'Dead' to me before but now always always would.

And then the picture changed. It wasn't diggers or mud or yellow jackets or a white tent. It was a picture of a beach, with hundreds of people lying on sunbeds with colourful umbrellas dotted everywhere and a big belt of blue sea along the top. And I watched with my breath fogging up the glass and my fingers leaving sweaty prints as the little red line spelt out, 'Missing girl Fate Jones found alive and well on Ibiza beach'.

I don't know how long I stood there, staring through the glass, but I wasn't looking at the screens any more. I thought of Saffy's gorgeous little face and I thought, Seeing that again will be the best thing I ever see with my eyes ever ever ever. And then the phone started buzzing in my hand again with a text from Quin and I thought, Thank you, God, or anybody who's listening, thank you, and please let this be the answer, tell me where to go and find her and bring her home and cuddle her for ever. But before I could open the message, the phone started buzzing with a call so I picked it up without looking and said, ''Ello-'ello. Where is it? You reckon she's there?' But it wasn't Quinton on the other end of the phone. It was Jelli.

'Fitz?' she said, and for some reason my heart sank right into the bottom of my shoes.

'Jel?' I said. 'What's up?' I could hear the telly in the background and Jelli walking out of a room and closing a door and all the time my heart was sinking right down through my trainers and into the road.

'I just spoke to my mum,' she said, and she was being all careful with her words. 'After talking to you, I thought I might as well apologise, seeing as the rest of my clothes are there and it's not that long till my birthday.'

'Okay,' I said, and I didn't see what in the name of arse any of this had to do with me because I was happy for her obviously but I had to get going and I needed to pick my heart up out of the tarmac before I could do that because it was still sinking slowly down.

'Look,' she was saying, 'I'm not sure if I should be telling you this – I don't even know why I am telling you this – but … they're putting Saffy back into Happy Blossoms.' And my heart fell all the way through the road and through the super-hot core of the earth and all the way through the other side to Australia. 'She doesn't know,' she said. 'She's staying with our cousin in Liverpool, and she thinks they don't know where she is. They're going to collect her tonight and take her straight there. They thought it would upset her less if it was quick like that.' I could hear all this rushing in my ears and through that I could hear May coming into the room and saying something to her in the background and Jelli said, 'Look, I've got to go, Fitz. I'm sorry. I don't know why I'm telling you. I just thought – well, I guess I thought maybe it would be good if you were there with them. It's up to you. I'll text you the address.' And then she hung up.

I bent over and put my hands on my knees because all of a sudden I thought I might be sick and I let some of the wind blow in my face and let the rushing in my ears stop a bit. And then I held my phone even tighter and waited for the text to come through and while I did that I made a decision in my head. Jelli wanted me to be there to help Saffy know that it was okay for her to go back to hospital. But I was going to be there and I was going to run away with her and I was never going to let anyone take her away from me again ever and they could try all they wanted but I would put her in the front seat of that shitty little car and I would never let anyone in apart from us two and I would keep her safe even if it meant driving around the world three times over and never stopping.

And so I started running, running so my feet hit the ground hard and all the shops turned into a blur and all the time I was clutching my phone and waiting for Jelli to type out those few little letters that made up the rest of my life. And when I got to the car I closed my eyes and let myself imagine what it would be like to get to her first, to hug her tight and put her in the car and not let anyone take her away, because they didn't understand her but I did, and I would never let anyone take her somewhere she didn't want to be again. I could even smell her hair as I thought about it, and feel her little arms round my neck, and I banged my head against the steering wheel a couple of times until my phone vibrated in my hand and I sat straight up in my seat, reading the text and I was already flicking through the massive road guide Eddie kept under the seat with the other hand. And then I was off, and I was praying to myself over and over again that things could only get better from here.

Well, let me tell you, things got worse. The car was feeling as knackered and fed up as me, and after about half an hour she started chugging and whining and smoking as soon as I got my foot down, so I ended up having to take the back roads so that I could drive along at slow miles per hour. Being slow made me feel even more worried and even more fidgety, and with just winding road and bushes to look at my head, which is normally quite good at playing itself tunes and asking itself important questions like what is the difference between a raisin and a sultana, and more importantly, what is the difference between a raisin and a currant, kept slipping back to my mum and to Han and Dad and his computer and Charlie Brown and Saf and what I was actually going to do when, if, I ever found her. And so to try and get rid of all that, I spent some time thinking about the best sets I'd ever seen and then after that I thought about the best wins I'd had on the horses and on the fruities, where I was and when it was and how much it was, and then I started to feel a bit calmer.

After a bit of this, I realised I'd driven through the same village three times and I was probably definitely lost and this made me feel very pissed off, so much so that I thought I might just scream out of the window again and again so I pulled into a random car park and smoked my last cig to calm down a bit, which worked, or just enough that I wasn't seeing little dots

216

everywhere any more and just felt shit-the-bed panicked rather than throw-yourself-off-a-cliff scared. When that was done I thought, Oh, fuck it, and I got on the motorway just so I could get somewhere I could actually see on the map. It was going pretty well; seemed like the cig had perked up the banger too, and she was quite happy trundling along at sixty, which after the last couple of hours felt a lot like whizzing along in a rocket, so I got my sunglasses out my pocket, found a radio station and sang along to Britney, which might seem a bit girly but it made me feel more cheery, as cheery as could be expected anyway. Well, as we've seen, luck was not on my side and just when I was starting to feel a bit better, the car started whining again and the pointy thing that tells you the speed was shaking like it'd had too much Red Bull, so I thought, Best slow down but when I pushed the brake nothing happened. Nothing at all. The road kept rushing past and the speed dial kept going up, and I was chugging along with no way of stopping.

It wasn't a good situation by any standards. I had no feet on pedals but the speed was going slowly up anyway, so I shoved both my feet on the brake and that held the speed at sixty-five but still no sign of slowing down and by then I was beginning to sweat. By the magic of storytelling, let's have a quick little lookie at the scene. Here's me with both feet on the brake and a car that's steaming along the motorway. Luckily there's no car in front of me and I'm in the inside lane and there's a sign up ahead that says it's one mile to the next service station. I'm thinking to myself, What would my dad do? which is what I do when I need to make a sensible decision, and I thought that probably he would try and get to the service station instead of being stuck on the side of the road and by that time I was zooming past the sign with the two lines on it which, it just then struck me, looked like lines of chang, and by the time I'd had a crazy little giggle at that, one of them had gone up Saffy's nose because I was passing the sign with just one line on it and *whoosh* that was up her nozzer as well, and in my head my dad looked up from his computer peering over his specs and his beaky nose and said, 'Take the car out of gear and turn the engine off,' so I didn't ask questions I just did it and I steered the car into the lorry bit of the car park just as it rolled to a stop.

I sat in the car in the middle of the car park with a couple of lorries dotted about and had a little sigh and a shake and then I got out. I was trying to be like I was all hard and cool, like John McClane or someone else Bruce Willis has played, except for the bloke from *The Sixth Sense*, but really I felt like my legs had turned to jelly and I still might cry. The stink of burning tyres was awful and there was these little things inside the wheels that were glowing bright orange and I knew they must be the brake thingies so I sat down on the gravel and had another little sigh and a shake.

After a bit I heard someone coming up behind me so I stood up and rubbed the gravel off my hands and arse and turned round. It was a cheery chap who looked like he should be on a fishing-boat somewhere in his big jumper and his fuzzy grey-brown beard puffing out round his face.

'All right there, mate?' he said, and he had twinkly eyes and a flaky red nose when he got up close.

'I think so,' I said. 'Car's fucked, though,' and then I went oops inside at swearing but he didn't seem to notice. 'The accelerator's stuck or something,' I said, and he sniffed the burning-rubber smell and glanced at the glowy brakes.

'Let's take a look, shall we?' he goes, and he flipped up the bonnet and disappeared inside. 'Right you are. The coil's stuck. Hang on there,' he said, popping his head back up, 'Let me just grab something.' And he jogged off to his lorry, pulling up his baggy-arsed jeans, and came back waving some little spring thing. 'This oughta hold it, pal, just for fifty miles or so, though. And you can't drive for a few hours, not till your brake pads have cooled down. They'll need changing as well when you get chance. In a hurry, are ya?'

'Yeah,' I said. 'Sort of.' Which was the biggest understatement anyone had ever made in the history of the world and my toes were already tapping in my trainers and I was fidgeting inside my clothes.

'Well,' he goes, 'cool your jets, sunshine. But that oughta get you there.'

'Thanks,' I said, and I got a note out of my pocket, but he waved it away and goes, 'Oh no, mate, no worries,' and then we shook hands.

'Take care of yerself,' he goes, and walked away whistling and I don't know why but I watched him leave and wished he'd stayed.

I went into the service station and got a burger, which cost six quid and was horrible. I actually tapped one of the bun bits on the table and it made a noise, and then I wandered round the arcade probably a bit too long, like till people might've thought I was a kiddie-fiddler. Two little kids who were maybe brother and sister were sat in the race-car game just about reaching the steering wheels and having a whale of time, even though they'd not put any money in and the screen was doing the demo thing over and over, and I thought about me and Han playing on the Megadrive for hours and hours and I was Sonic and she was Tails and Mum used to bring us lemonade and sometimes those biscuits with the cows on them. A couple of spotty kids were having a snog up against the Slushy machine and their mates were all peeping out from behind the machine that gives you change and chuckling, and I thought, Well, I don't miss being young and awkward like that but at the same time wasn't it nice when all that was on your mind was touching a boob and your transfers on Champ Man?

I sat on the edge of the air-hockey table with nobody playing on it, and looked out at people walking past. There was a little old couple sat on the two metal seats outside the arcade eating a sandwich and drinking a flask of tea and gazing out cheerfully like it was a nice picnic spot they were looking at and not the bogs and the 50p massage chairs. I thought about how Saffy once told me that when she was little she used to play at being invisible and do naughty little pixie things like moving cups or books about and her mum and dad would play along and be like 'Ooh, I'm sure my cup wasn't there before! However did it get there?' and she would giggle away but then after a while she worked out they weren't playing along any more they'd just forgotten about her.

After a bit I realised that I couldn't keep staring at the two little old people while they were munching on their lunch, and the two kids who'd been snogging before wanted to use the air-hockey table so I hopped off and wandered out into the car park because there was nowhere else to go. I went over to the car with a little bit of hope in my heart, but you could still smell the burning rubber smell and the brake pads still looked scorchio. I felt really panicky again as I thought about Saf just chilling out, thinking nothing of anything and having no idea that her mum and dad were probably on their way right now to cart her off to the place she'd rather be dead than go back to, and what if she did decide to be dead instead? And that thought made me feel like I was going to be sick and scream all at once and I thought, I've gotta sort myself out, I can't be like this. Because I knew I was no good to Saffy in this state whether I was there or in the stupid services' car park, no use at all. So I unlocked the car and leant in and got my tin with the weed and all its accessories out from under the seat and then I went over to the grassy hill that went round the edge of the services and I sat down and felt the grass all wet through my jeans. I thought I'd only smoke a little bit of it, just enough to calm myself down so I could think straight and make sense in my own head even if I didn't make sense in anyone else's. As I rolled a spliff I tried to imagine how long it would take Saffy's parents to get to her and how they wouldn't have set out yet, and to tell myself that it was all okay. I got the lighter out of my pocket and lit the joint and I had a couple of long slow pulls on it and then I lay back with all the wet grass mixed in with my hair and let the spliff burn out with a quiet little sizzle. I took nice deep breaths and my head did start to clear but the panicky upset was still there at the back of everything. It was horrible not being able to set off, just being stuck, and I just wanted to jump in the car and drive as fast as I could even if I had to run the last bit or crawl it on my hands and knees but I knew really deep down in the sensible part of me where my dad gave me advice from like a control centre in the back of my brain, I knew that I really wasn't any use to Saffy at all if I was squashed in a crashed car on the M6. And I looked at the time on my phone and it was still early and Jelli had said her parents were coming *tonight* and it wasn't tonight yet. I still had time. *I still had time.* I looked up at the clouds and kept telling myself that over and over. Plenty of time. It's all right. Plenty of time. It's all right.

'All right?'

I jumped half out of my skin and looked to the left where the voice had come from and there was a bloke standing there looking at me smiling. 'Sorry,' he said, 'didn't mean to scare you. Just checking you weren't dead. Hard to tell from the car park.'

'Oh,' I said. 'Yeah, I'm alive, ta. Just killing some time.'

He plonked himself down next to me. 'Same here, mate. Jack,' he said, sticking his hand out.

'Fitz.' I shook it. He had curly ginger hair and loads of ginger stubble and he was pretty tanned. He had a big backpack, which he was fishing around in now for a bottle of Coke which he had a swig of and then offered to me. I said I was all right but then I changed my mind and had a bit and it tasted brilliant after the spliff, all cold and sweet.

'So what you hanging about for?' he asked.

221

'My car,' I said. 'Fucked the brakes and I've gotta wait for them to cool down or something.'

He nodded. 'Ah.'

'What about you?' I said, because even though my head was still whirling with thoughts and fears a bit too much to think about making sentences, I figured that making small talk with a stranger might help the time go a tiny bit faster.

'Just waiting for a lift,' he goes. 'I've got a mate who's a lorry driver who dropped me this far, now waiting for my sister to pick me up.'

'Where you been?' I said, because he'd obviously been on hols with a bag that big.

'Where haven't I been, mate? Been away for two years. India, Nepal, Malaysia, Vietnam, Laos, Cambodia. Stopped off in Bangkok for a bit and then did a bit of Oz.'

'Wow,' I said, and it was one of those wows you don't mean to do it just comes out because the thing you're saying wow about really is wow. I'd not even heard of three of the places he'd said.

'Yep,' he goes. 'It was top.'

We sat in silence for a bit and he swigged some more of his Coke. It was like we were just waiting at a bus stop except one that was made of grass and mud instead of metal and glass. 'So,' he said. 'You heading home or away?'

Good question, I thought. 'Neither,' I said after a minute. 'I'm going to pick up my girlfriend.'

He nodded. 'Very good of you. Brownie points in the bank for you then.' I smiled but it was very small smile that made my cheeks hurt.

'That a joint you got there?'

I'd forgotten the spliff still between my fingers. 'Yeah,' I said, handing it to him with the lighter. 'Help yourself.'

He lit it and took a deep toke. 'Not bad,' he said, and he offered it back to me.

I took it and pulled on it. All the feelings of darkness and despair were piling back in so I blew the smoke out extra hard and hoped they'd all go with it. Jack was fidgeting with his shoe so I said, 'What was the best place you went? Out of all of them?' and he thought about it for a while with his head on one side and I passed him back the spliff and he took a drag and thought some more and then he said, 'India, I think. Pretty amazing. And it was the first place I went so it was a bit special. Wouldn't mind living there one day you know.'

I nodded but seeing as I'd never been there I didn't have much to offer back in the way of a conversation so it just stayed put at the full stop. He had a newspaper rolled up and sticking out of his bag and all I could see was the word 'FOUND' in big black letters. 'Pretty mental, isn't it?' I said, pointing at the paper.

'You got that right,' he said. 'But you gotta admire her. If she's gotta point to make I mean,' he said, lying back in the grass. 'If she was just fobbing her dad off for cash that's a bit dickish.'

I nodded and then I lay back too. 'So you off again anytime soon?'

'Soon as I can,' he said. 'I've got the bug bad. Just need to earn some cash first. You ought to go you know. Take your lady.'

I pictured me and Saf in a lovely Beatles all-you-need-is-love flash on beaches and boats and snowy mountains and getting married in Vegas with one of those lacy things round her leg in her dirty jeans and flip-flops and I could practically feel the sun on my face. Jack was still telling me about the best places he'd been and I didn't bother remembering that I hadn't got Saffy yet or what'd happen when I did, and we just filled in a little imaginary travel plan instead and that was nice, it was like a make-your-own dream.

It was all lovely, building dreams, but then I remembered where I really was and all my dreams started wobbling and falling down one by one. 'The thing is,' I said, and it was easier to talk because I wasn't looking at him, just at the clouds and passing the spliff back and forth every now and again. 'Thing is, Saffy's not well. I don't think we'll be able to get away for a bit. Maybe ever.' And there was a little choke in my voice at the end of the sentence.

'Sorry, mate,' he said. 'I hope she's okay.'

'Me too,' I said. 'I just need to get to her and bring her home.'

He didn't ask any questions and I was glad. It was really nice to be able to say things out loud and have somebody else's ear for all of the words to go into instead of them bumping about inside your own head.

'What's going on here then, lads?'

The voice came from our feet and we both sat up and looked, me still holding out the spliff to Jack. Two policemen were standing by our toes.

It was pretty hot in the back seat of the police car and I was starting to sweat and stress and I thought I might cry any minute. The two coppers were having a fag outside. 'Where will they take us?' I said to Jack. 'What's all the fuss? It was only a spliff.' I fidgeted around in my seat and looked across the car park to where my car was sitting all on her own, like a dream, and then I remembered the eighth stashed in my pocket and I thought the police were looking at it too, like they could see it glowing away like a big beacon in the back seat.

'They probably think we're bums,' Jack said. 'I'll sort it, mate. Promise. We'll have you back on the road to romance in no time.' And he tapped on the window at the coppers and, when they turned round, smiled nicely and made an open-the-door face. The taller copper opened the passenger side front door and leant in.

'What's up?'

'Look, mate,' Jack said. 'Is there really any need to take us in? We've got a car. We'll be on our way. It was only a bit of draw.'

If I'd have said it I would've sounded really cocky and a twat but Jack made it sound pretty reasonable and friendly, like you'd do pretty much whatever he asked you. The copper looked at him like he kind of wanted to be nice but also like he kind of wanted not to be.

'Problem is, there's been a couple of reports of a nice big drug ring operating out of these very services. So you can see the dilemma for us when "a bit of draw" wanders right under our noses. Sorry. It won't take long, process you down the station. You'll be back on your way soon enough if there's nothing to keep you in for.'

I looked up at the grey roof of the car and drummed my toes inside my shoes and wiggled my knees back and forth. Jack looked at me and then back at the copper.

'Thing is,' he goes, 'Fitz here has got to get to the love of his life. Poor girl's really poorly. Isn't there anything you can do? I'm sure you don't want to stand in the way of true love.'

The copper raised an eyebrow. 'What's it they say about the path?' he said to the other one.

'Don't run smooth, think it is,' the fat one said, and they both chuckled and fiddled with their hats. But then they looked at me and I was trying a bit not to cry and they looked at each other again and then at Jack. 'You could say it was yours,' the front one said. 'Then we'd just have to take you in. Romeo here could be on his way.'

I opened my mouth to say no but before anything came out Jack said, 'Yep. All mine. Absolutely.'

'Sure about that?' the copper said, and before I could say anything, Jack said, 'Yep, course. Fitz here just stopped cos I asked him for a lighter.'

And the copper nodded and got out and walked around to my side of the car and opened my door. 'Off you go, then,' he said, holding the door open and waving his arm sarcastically. 'Your lucky day, Cupid.'

I turned to Jack. 'You don't have to do that,' I said, but he waved my words away as well.

'No worries, mate,' he said. 'Might even get a free meal if they drag it out down the yard long enough. Give my sister something else to moan about too, she loves that. Hey, listen, good luck. Hope she gets better soon.'

And I felt the tears wobbling up again. I hugged him tight round the neck, which was really wet but I just didn't care.

'Thank you thank you thank you,' I said, and then I got out of the car and I ran all the way over to my rustbucket and opened the door and jumped in.

I drove the car round in a couple of little circles testing the brakes and they seemed all right so I puttered out onto the slip road and back onto the motorway, which was empty and lonely but I whacked my hazards on just in case and stayed at forty, which felt a bit risky anyway. The sky was grey and I could see blue the way I was headed but the sign up ahead said there was still sixty miles to go.

# SAFFY

When you get off the coach the cold chills you right through to your bones. You pull your clothes round you tight and start to walk up the hill. Past the clinic where in the day there are always teenage girls smoking outside and inside is full of paper sheets and plastic gloves and swabs and advice. Past pigeons flapping around a burger and chips and a man in ripped jeans and a huge T-shirt who limps from person to person saying, 'Spare change, luv,' like it's not a question, just a motto, a thought. Past the windows of big suitcases, shoes, bedspreads. Up past the hospital, where people are standing outside in their pale blue gowns with their pale blue feet and their IV trolleys next to them, puffing on cigarettes and chatting just like they're at the bus stop, and a man is rolling out of a cab with a bloody tea-towel pressed to his head and his girlfriend hurrying after him screeching. Past a church and patches of yellow grass and kids hurrying up alongside anyone walking, saying in their little voices, 'Gizza pound for sweets, mate,' and past an offy with its shopkeeper in her red cage and a woman pressed up against the bars trying to check the prices on the different cans of lager and her boyfriend outside smoking a fag and telling her to hurry up and his fat dog tugging at the rope round its neck and some teenager pissing in a doorway and two girls giggling into their chips and cuddling plastic bags of wine and crisps and chocolate and hurrying back home in their joggers.

Past all this, to the postbox, which is how you remember where to turn, and down the long cobbled street, across the tiny T-junctions and crossroads, and past the group of boys with hoods and dogs and bottles and tiny orange fairy-flickers of cigarette burning in the dimness. To the gate, which squeaks as you open it, and to the door with the crack in one panel and the doorbell that doesn't work and the knocker you have to knock instead.

'Hello, stranger!' she says as she opens the door, and she pulls you in for a hug. 'What the hell are you doing here?'

She smells like flowers as darkness closes in around you.

My cousin Stevie was always the smart one. She wasn't book smart like Ella, or too-smart-for-her-own-good smart like Jel, but she was street smart, my granny used to say, sharp. She'd be the one who'd solve Granddad's riddles or find the Easter eggs first or work out how to build a den under the kitchen table that didn't fall down when you tried to get in. When I came round on her hall carpet I thought for a second we were back in one of those dens, hiding under miles and miles of flowery sheet in a happy nest of giggling and dirty knees. She was fanning me with an old copy of the *Echo*, and even there Fate Jones smiled awkwardly down at me.

'All right, babe?' she said, when she saw I'd woken up. 'Long journey, was it?' I smiled and sat up all wobbly lamb-like.

'Sight of you more like,' I said, even though my voice was shaking. 'What have you done to your hair?'

She punched me on the arm and then pulled me into another hug. 'You twat. Good to see you.'

We hugged for a minute, which seemed to stretch on for ever, and then she said, 'You need a drink. Come on.'

We stood up and she led me through into the little lounge. 'Sit,' she said, pointing at a sofa piled high with fluffy mismatched cushions. I sank into it and felt some of the heavy sad I'd been carrying with me float away. The room was stuffed full of things – stacks of DVDs in one corner, piles of folded washing on the tiny table and each of its two tiny chairs. Photos hung on each of the walls and a big clock with sparkly hands ticked loudly above the small table. Stevie came skipping back from the kitchen with a shot of vodka in each hand, and she handed me one as she dropped into the fluffy nest next to me. "Smeant to be brandy, I think, for shock. But we've not got any. Down in one!'

The vodka was hot and sharp at the back of my mouth but it slid down warm and filled me up and floated me away.

'Place is looking good,' I said, fiddling with a twirl of fluffy fabric. I'd only visited once, a year or more before, when I was still living at home and the idea of Stevie having a place of her own was too exciting to understand. She'd had a place of her own long before that, of course, but I'd been too out of it to notice. Too out of it to notice that everybody had grown up and moved on while I'd been trapped in a blossom-pink bed.

'Thanks, babe,' she said, and she put her arm around me and squeezed me tight. 'So good to see you.' She'd said that already so it must have been true. 'What's with the surprise visit?'

I thought of my homes. Broken glass on the carpet, whispered conversations. Fitz crying. Fitz sending me away.

'I needed to get away,' I said. 'Can I stay here?'

Stevie's mother, my auntie Peggy, was my mother's sister. They didn't get on. Peggy was divorced and living with a nice boyfriend who was only a bit older than Stevie or me. She always wore brightly coloured bra straps showing, and had the front of her hair bleached. She wasn't the kind of person my mother thought we should be mixing with. The only communication or connection they ever had was laced and looped up into six or seven words in a card at Christmas or on a birthday. I would have thought it was sad if I didn't know I would someday end up like that with my sisters too.

232

'So, you had a row with your mum and dad, then?'

I nodded, taking a sip of my drink and rolling my eyes to fill the space. 'Of course.'

She tutted. 'Not being funny, Saf, but your mum's a right nightmare. What was it this time, she not like your fella?'

I shook my head. 'No.'

'Surprise surprise. And I bet she's been on your case about what you're going to do next?'

'Yep.'

'Don't blame you for wanting to get away. You can keep me company for a bit – Jenny's away for a week anyway. Like old times, yeah?'

And that was it. I had given her the beginnings of a story and she had finished it all by herself. Sometimes it's easier not to tell lies, just to give people the pieces to make their own.

That night in bed, I thought how much Stevie had changed, though she was still herself. Life was always moving, the backdrop and the motives shifting. Every time you looked away, things grew, things changed. People moved into the gaps and feelings faded. In the paper on the table downstairs police were still searching for Fate Jones, still dusting the car in which they'd found a lock of her hair, still watching the same old CCTV footage of her over and over. Soon, though, there would be a new case, and the car would be forgotten and the CCTV would be forgotten and someone else would move into our minds and, slowly, Fate Jones would be washed over by the tide of day-to-day life, like footprints on wet sand.

I hated her.

I was jealous of her. Everywhere I looked, she was lost, she was gone. But I knew the truth, and it made a hole in my heart so big I'd fallen through it. You are never lost just by being gone; you are only lost when there is nobody who thinks to look for you. True loss is not the absence of a person or a thing, but the absence of a space where they fit. A place where they belong.

Fate Jones wasn't lost. They were still looking for her.

The simplest of tasks seem so easy when they're asked. They only start to unravel when you're left alone with them.

'Can you pick up some bits for dinner for me, babe? I'm in hospital all day.'

'Of course. Where do I go?'

Small streets in big cities have their own order of things. The cobbles the terraces stood on had their own world, a million miles away from the shopping and the clubbing and the rest of the world. The two ginger twins who lived two doors down were skateboarding in the road, the wheels back and forth on the stones sounding like waves on the beach. Across the road, the old man who lived in the house opposite stood at his gate, resting on his elbows, watching the street go by as if he were at the front of a ship. The telephone wires that criss-crossed the sky were heavy with pairs of trainers, laces looped together and flung over the thin black lines to signify some code I didn't understand. At the end of the street, the gang watched over it all, one creature with many heads, dogs in its folds, sitting on the dirty pavement panting as its many limbs smoked cigarettes and the heads spat into the gutter. And watched.

The road outside the terraces seemed colder. Maybe it was just the open space for the wind to cut across, but it seemed somehow like it was friendlier in the safety of the houses. Out here, with cars speeding past and people walking fast against the wind, I was alone. When I reached the automatic doors of the supermarket, I stood in front of the sensor long enough for them to open and shut twice. When they opened for a third time I stepped in, fingering the list in my pocket. I looked around me, at people dashing back and forth, pushing trolleys in zigzag lines and stacking things in their baskets without stopping. It was as if everything had been put on fast-forward and left me behind, trapped, an island in the middle of a million streams. I took the list out and held it carefully in both hands.

Don't be silly. How hard can it be?

The first things were vegetables. I felt relieved about this. Vegetables were good, simple, safe. The vegetables and fruit and salad things were at the front of the shop, which seemed stupid to me – as then these things, which were softest, would be at the bottom of the busy baskets and would get squashed or bruised by everything else, all the jars and the tins and the bottles. The thought made me feel sick. I stood in front of the rows of green and looked again at the list. Lettuce. I stared at the boxes stacked up on the slanty shelves, full of curly heads of pale green and yellow. The edges of the leaves were turning brown, the plastic sleeves spotted with condensation. I felt impatient with myself.

Just take one.

Lettuce is on the list.

I reached out a hand, put it down again.

That one. That one looks fine.

The hand reached out again.

There's dirt on that one. It's dirty.

The hand went down again.

You can wash it, you idiot. It's only dirt. Lettuces grow in dirt.

Dirt, dirt, dirt.

They grow in dirt.

They soak up dirt. They're dirty inside. You can't wash them inside.

I turned away. Two children were playing next to the shelves, their parents chatting over crooked trolleys in the middle of the aisle. The toddlers were lining up the brightly coloured peppers, stacking them on the dirty lino like toy blocks. I looked down and hurried into the next aisle.

It was quieter here, away from the busy front doors and the social land of salad. Just rows and stacks of boxes and bags and cans, rice and sauce and lentils. I felt better, the food packed away and safe instead of out in the open to be touched and breathed on. I looked at the list, past the green stuff. Pasta (bows or twirls!). Stevie had drawn a little bow next to it. I walked along the aisle, gazing up at the oranges and yellows of the boxes, the brown and white grains of rice packed tightly like tiny pearls under the lights. The pasta was at the end of the row, with people whistling past with trolleys full of fruit and bags of salad all waiting to be squashed and ruined. I stared at the shelves. Bows and twists and strings and stripes and nests and tubes and white and green and orange.

Bows. She wants bows. Just take the bows.

All the packets were crooked on the shelves, some pushed right back and some hanging their corners over the edge.

Just leave them. It doesn't matter if they're not straight. It doesn't matter.

I fought back a horrible urge that it really really did matter, that unless the bags all sat side by side and neat, the whole shop would fall down around me. My head was beginning to hurt.

Take the bows.

I reached out and took them, put them in my basket. Let out a sigh of relief, and turned to walk away.

They're not straight, they're not straight, they're not straight.

With each step I could see the packets, hanging over the edge, slipping into each other's lines, twists muddled up with tubes and all crashing down. I kept my head down and walked.

'Watch where you're going!'

The metal mesh of a trolley knocked into me, sending me smash into the magazines displayed at the end of the aisle. The trolley pushed on past, loaded up with loo roll and beer and crisps and packets of mealy-looking burgers with flecks of white fat oozing up at the plastic wrap. I rubbed my elbow and stepped back into an aisle. The next thing on the list was passata, which was what Fitz called tomatoes in a box. I felt a little pang then, right in the middle of my heart, thinking about Fitz with his pinny on and a big spoon in his hand stirring a sauce and saying, 'Here now, Saf, pass me those tomatoes in a box. That's what we need!' and me handing them to him and kissing his back through his T-shirt. I walked down the aisle of breakfast things and biscuits and went back to the pasta and rice and sauce row, trying hard not to look at anything for too long, so I wouldn't see things out of their place. I found the tomatoes in a box and picked them up before I had time to think about it, the same brand as Fitz used. It felt nice, familiar in my hand. I felt myself relaxing. Here was something I knew, something safe. I felt braver. This was not so hard. I looked at the list, crumpled now in my hand. Cheese.

That was all it said. Just 'Cheese'. Nothing else, no type of cheese, how much cheese, anything. No little picture from Stevie. As I walked down the dairy aisle, things swam in front of me. Goat's cheese, blue cheese, crumbly cheese, cubes of cheese and shreds of cheese. They swam in front of me and numbers filled my head. Calories. Grams of fat. Weights and measurements and hours and days. Half-empty boxes, a torn corner of a packet oozing liquid onto the shelf. Labels in the wrong places, things in the wrong places. People loomed past with their baskets full and their bodies wobbling, fat cheeks moving as they talked, filling their mouths with words instead of food, filling their baskets and eating with their eyes. My hands were sweating, the list wearing thin until the ink started to run on the letters, wiping away the things that were written there. I dropped the basket and pushed through the trolleys until I got to the pavement outside.

Who you are depends so much on who you are talking to. With someone you don't know, you can be anyone you want to be. With a childhood friend or enemy, you can try hard to dodge the old you without success. With Stevie I didn't know who I was. She had known me since I was small, yet she hardly knew me at all. She was family and friend and stranger all at once.

'You didn't see the money I left out?'

'No, of course I did. I just forgot to pick it up on my way out.'

'Oh. Dozy mare.'

She was still taking her shoes off, her coat sliding off the back of the sofa, her folders wobbling on the table. She lay back against the sofa and stretched. 'Don't worry, babe. Pizza it is. What time's *Top Idol* on?'

I sank into my seat, full of relief and warmth. 'Half an hour. It's only the extra show, though, all the rehearsals and stuff.'

'I know. So long as Simon's in it, I don't care.'

Just as she was reaching for the remote, the doorbell rang. She looked at me.

'Who's that now?'

I felt my heart stop. Stevie got up and opened the living-room door. I wondered if I should run, but I knew the back door didn't open and I was frozen in place. And then she called out.

'Saf! Come here!'

240

My legs had turned to stone, but somehow I managed to get up and stagger into the hall. Stevie was holding the door open. I stared into the night in terror.

The two ginger twins from across the road were standing there, grinning cheerfully.

'Hiya,' they chorused, dancing about on the step in their black Velcro-strapped trainers.

'The lads here are selling a new magazine,' Stevie said. 'They reckon it's a quid a go.'

They nodded, giggling.

I tried to smile, but my heart was still thumping in my ears. 'Oh, right. A pound's a bit pricey isn't it? Is it any good?'

'Yeah,' Stevie chimed in. 'Let's have a look then.'

The twin on the left produced a clump of glossy paper from behind his back, and Stevie and I leant forward to peer at it in the lamplight. It was a load of old takeaway leaflets stapled together. The boys were vibrating with laughter now, elbowing each other and shuffling from foot to foot.

'Cheeky little …' Stevie said. 'A quid! Jog on.' But she gave them a wink and 20p she found in her pocket, which sent them running off down the road in fits of joy.

'Sweet, really,' she said, as we went back into the warmth of the lounge. 'But proper little shits. Right, Simon-time, baby.'

I was still smiling as she turned the telly on, and not about her pervy love for Simon Cowell, but because suddenly I felt newly still; like I could be calm, in one place, even if it was just for a while.

The news was on before *Top Idol*. The opening music was just finishing as the picture clicked on. A big picture of Fate Jones was being projected behind the newsreaders, the same one of her with her hair brushed over one shoulder, grinning at the camera and at us behind it. Stevie got up to open a bottle of wine.

'The news that Fate Jones has been found alive and
well rocked the nation today, after police tracked
her to a private resort in Ibiza.'

A blurry camera-phone photo of her on a sunbed, blonde hair
blonder against Balearic tan. Fate Jones only existed in blurry
images, whether she was alive or presumed dead.

'A police spokesman said today that they had been
alerted by an anonymous member of the public, and
confirmed that the presumed abduction had been staged.
Though exact details are not yet known, there is
growing speculation that the disappearance had been
planned with the intention of a friend posing as a
private investigator to extract funds from Fate's
father, well-known businessman Lowen Jones. Miss
Jones was arrested this afternoon, along with her
former university tutor and rumoured lover, Kevin
Kitaki. We'll keep you updated with information as
and when we receive it – turn over to our twenty-
four-hour news channel for full coverage.'

'Fucking hell …' Stevie said from the doorway. She was leaning
against the frame, bottle of wine and corkscrew in opposite
hands. The TV was playing out the timeline of the case, showing
how simply the evidence had been put together, how easily we
had all fallen for it.

I said nothing. I had no idea what to feel. Something I was so
jealous of, so angry about, had been snatched away from me. It
was like having the world swirled around while you were blind-
folded – everything was the same, but I had no idea where it all
fitted any more.

The piece played on, experts drafted in to explain the details,
the image of the same red front door made tiny in the top right

corner, still shut tight, no sign of the sadness or the fury closed in tight behind it. I heard the pop of the cork, the glug of the wine. I felt the glass in my hand, but I didn't drink. I just looked at the pretty pink of it, the blue sheen it caught in the shaded light.

'That is fucked up,' Stevie said, sitting down next to me again. 'Imagine it. All the people's been looking for her. All the money people've paid. Little fucking bitch.'

'The posters ...' I said, looking at the pretty newsreader's unreadable face as she read her autocue.

Stevie took a swig of her wine. 'There's a girl on my course'll be gutted. Swear she's got a bet on her being dead. Always checking on her phone to see if she'd been found yet. Seriously, what are people gonna do now? What's gonna be on the news?'

I didn't know. '*Top Idol*?'

She laughed. 'Suits me. Woah, though. Never seen that coming.'

No. Who does?

She clinked her glass against mine. 'Cheers, babe.'

Cheers.

The news was regional after that. A new ward at the hospital, a new John Lennon statue. A child genius selling paintings to Americans for hundreds of thousands of millions.

'Eh, Saf,' Stevie said. 'If he can do it, you can. Little knob.'

I laughed. I wanted to hold her hand but I didn't know why. The weather came on. Rain and grey. It felt nice in its way, a weird comfort. Where I'd been exposed, shone on, now I was cuddled, protected – hidden in the fug and the drizzle. The constant cold was worth that.

I looked at Stevie's almost empty glass and tried to drink some of mine. I tried to tell myself that I could get rid of it later, but as the liquid sank down I felt it seeping through me, creeping through gaps in my cells and bedding down, making new little fat round rosy-pink cells, which seemed to turn bluish when they caught the light. Stevie got up to refill her glass, not noticing or ignoring mine. When she came back, *Top Idol* was starting and she snuggled up closer to me.

'Right,' she said. 'Drink every time someone says they're giving it a hundred and ten per cent or Simon undoes another shirt button.'

In life, you have to have balance. Stopping eating made me feel free, in charge, but being drunk or high made me free too. It was all give and take; knowing what you had to give up to have the other. Though I usually stuck with vodka, which was clear and safe, I would have wine or beer if there was nothing else around. It wasn't a big deal, at least not at the start, when I still had plenty of other things to deny myself. But sitting there, on Stevie's sofa, I couldn't bring myself to drink it. Because I didn't want to be free any more. I just wanted to be gone.

We used to play drinking games sometimes. We used to play games all the time, board games and drinking games and made-up games. Sometimes we played drinking games with cups of tea or glasses of milk. Because everything was fun with him. Everything everyday could be magical and silly and fun.

When the programme finished, the second bottle of wine was halfway empty and Stevie's cheeks were rosy pink too. She smiled at me.

'I've had a great idea,' she said. 'Wait here.'

She skipped out of the room. I poured some of my glass down the sink and went back to my place. She came bounding back just as I was changing the channel, a heavy book bound in leather tucked in her arms.

'Look,' she said, and she was smiling at me in a way that took me right back to dens made of bed sheets and handbags made of old cereal boxes. 'This is going to be funny.' She opened to the first page, and my own face stared back at me. 'It's our family album,' she said, giggling and leaning into me as we stared at our tiny selves, stuffed into crushed velvet and taffeta and kneeling in a sea of presents under a plastic tree. 'Mam gave it to me. She doesn't look at it any more, you know.' We turned the page so we didn't have to think about why that might be.

'There's no baby ones,' she said. 'Dad took a box of them by accident. Left his box of porn behind instead.' It wasn't as if they could have asked him for them back. He hadn't left an address or a phone number. I couldn't even remember what he looked like.

Our mothers were looking back at us now, backcombed and hairsprayed within an inch of their lives, in matching sparkly sweatshirts and ski leggings. Peggy was a blonde; Mum had lightened her red hair to a nuclear kind of orange.

'They look alike,' I said.

Stevie nodded, ran a finger across the picture. 'Like us.'

Jelli was waiting for us next, cake smeared across her face, hair teased up into two demonic pigtails. 'Here, I heard about your neighbour,' Stevie said. 'She don't change, does she?' I had no idea what she was talking about, but I realised I was smiling.

Ella was sitting on Granny's lap, reading to her, concentration on her pale little face. Stevie and I touched our heads together, just for a second. Granny had died two years before.

The Christmas dinner, the toys unwrapped. A birthday – Stevie's, with Pin the Tail on the Donkey and Pass the Parcel and tiger masks and lion masks and paper trees hanging in the corners. Granny and Grandpa's ruby wedding anniversary, with Jelli dancing on my dad's toes and Stevie and me charging people 5p to look after their coats. Another Christmas, a later one, with Barbie's dreamhouse and Etch-a-Sketch and hair-braiding kits. A birthday, Ella's, no party games, just karaoke and a sleepover, films and pyjamas and popcorn. Jelli in panto, stealing the show.

A summer holiday we took together. Stevie and I must have been eleven. My mother was pregnant with Lulu, big flowery smock and her hair cropped short. It was a cottage near the coast, a whole week of running along the beach and through fields, reading books on the battered old sofa and eating around the big wooden table in the kitchen, all of us.

We were staring at ourselves again, gap-toothed and freckled. Bundled up in woollen jumpers against the salty wind that blew our sun-blonde hair about. We were spinning around, holding hands, laughing our little heads off with the sun just starting to peek out from behind a cloud beyond us. Stevie stopped turning the pages.

'You could be this happy again, Saf.'

I felt the blood stop in my veins. I laughed, but it came out shaky. 'As when I was eleven? Is anyone that?'

She shut the book softly and turned to look at me. 'I'm serious. Let me help you.'

'You are helping. I'm really grateful, Vee. You've been a star.'

'I don't mean with that.' She put a hand on my knee. 'You're not well, Saf.'

I pulled my knee away. 'Not you too. I'm fine. For fuck's sake.'

I tried to look away, but she wouldn't let me. 'You're not fine, Saffy. You're ill. Please, let me help you. I love you. I'm sorry I haven't been around. I am now. I'm here. Let me help.'

I stared at her for a moment, and saw the tears filling her eyes. When I felt them start to fill mine to match, I stood up.

'I don't have to listen to this. You don't *know* me, Stevie. I'm fine. And if you don't want me around, I'll just go.'

She put the book down and stood up too. 'Okay, okay, I'm sorry. I'm sorry, hun. If you say you're fine, I do believe you.'

I was silent for a minute, staring at her. 'Yeah?'

'Yeah. I'm sorry. I was being stupid.'

'Okay.'

'Hug?'

I hugged her tighter than I meant to. I wasn't letting anything else be taken away from me that day.

*We see it on the news together before he knows she's there. He has the morning off and he comes round to the flat to see me. We don't live together then. We haven't even known each other long. We drink coffee even though he doesn't like it – he doesn't tell me this until he has moved in. We're watching* This Morning *and suddenly they interrupt it for a newsflash. Until then, I didn't even think those happened except in bad crime novels and worse films. We watch the footage, the taped-off station and the flashing lights and the crowds of police coats. We are quiet. We put our cups down and we stop drinking.*

In those moments, when something has happened in the world and the information is flooding through, when people are desperate to talk and tell the story before it's over, the confusion and the assumptions all bubbling up through the screen, you wonder how it relates to you. How it's connected to you. How you would feel if it were happening to you. You project and picture and you feel something different from sympathy. You feel involved, affected. You want to hear the story faster than they can tell it. You want to know who was responsible for the bomb, who has been hurt, why police were already on high alert. You want to know how the disappearance was staged, how she felt, whether she did it for love or for money. You want to be a part of the story, yet you can be infinitely glad that you aren't.

An hour later, while I was washing up the cups, he got the call to tell him his sister had been on the train. You are always a part of the story, whether you realise it or not.

Stevie shifted in her sleep above me. I was cosy in a nest of duvets and pillows and fluffy cushions from the sofa, but I couldn't sleep. Things that had seemed solid were being taken away from me, dependable walls falling down and leaving me exposed and alone. I felt as though I was just waiting for the floor to disappear from beneath me.

I didn't understand why I was so upset that Fate Jones was a liar. We had all created her story, pieced together the parts she had left us and filled in the rest. We'd all made her into this person, this perfect girl, and now we were left to wonder why she hadn't turned out the way we wanted. People didn't understand that nothing is ever true; that the things you hang your hopes on and build your life around can turn to dust in a second.

As long as I had Stevie, I felt I was safe.

There was a rift in the clouds. An icy blue puncture in the grey fug that had surrounded me; a tear in the trust and the softness that had kept me briefly still. I heard her on the phone that morning.

I'd slept in, kept up late by thoughts and feelings all cut loose. I'd slept in until the sun was shining through the clouds and through the window. I got up slowly, hearing Stevie moving about downstairs. I needed to shower away the night, clean away the thoughts, so I went to the bathroom and turned on the hot water. There were no towels hanging on the rail so I went back out onto the landing, to the pile of clean washing on the chair at the top of the stairs. And I heard her.

I stepped down onto the first stair at the sound of her voice. Something stopped me. Something made me crouch there and listen very carefully.

'No,' she was saying. 'No, that's fine. I can do something nice with her today, keep her busy. She wants to take pictures, I think.'

There was a silence as she listened. Through the gap in the banisters I could see her winding the plastic flex around her finger.

'Yes,' she said. 'Seven is fine. How far is the place? Will they be able to admit her that late?'

More silence.

'Okay,' she said. 'Great. You can text me if you're going to be late. We'll be here. A what? … Oh, okay. Where can I get those?

And how will I get her to take it? … No, no, I understand. I'll try and keep her calm.'

She listened a minute longer. 'Right. I'll be ready for you at seven … No, there's just the front door. The back one's always bolted … Okay, Pippa. See you then. Safe journey.'

And she put down the phone.

Everything hung silent and still in the air after the click of the receiver going down. I felt as if I was breaking into a million pieces, disappearing into dust. Then time snapped back and the blood rushed to my face and I was up and making for the bedroom as quickly as I could.

Soon after that she came up the stairs. I was sitting on the bed, already running in my mind. When I heard her steps on the landing, I reached for the file and pretended that all there was to fix was a broken nail.

'Morning, lazybones.'

'Morning.'

'Brought you a cup of tea.'

She came and sat next to me on the bed, setting the mug on the little table. 'You sleep okay?'

'Yes, thanks. Really cosy.'

'Good. Look, I'm sorry about last night. I was drunk. I know you've had enough grief from your parents. I just wanted you to know that I'm here for you but I went and made a hash of it as usual.'

I handed her the nail file and smiled. 'It's all right. I'm used to it. Don't worry about it, it's forgotten.'

She put an arm round me and kissed me on the cheek. 'Good. Right, I'm taking you out today. Something fun. What d'you want to do?'

I thought, trying to get some words to surface in the sea of noise that filled my head. 'I don't mind. I'd quite like to go down to the water.'

'Yeah? The docks? Or the beach?'

As if it mattered. 'The docks, I think.'

'That's a brilliant idea. There's some lovely places round there to eat or drink as well. We could stay on for a bit.'

'That'd be nice.'

'You could take some pictures? For your art?'

'I don't have my camera.'

'That's okay, you can use mine.' She stood up and opened a drawer in the little desk. 'Here y'are.'

'Thank you. I'd like that.'

'Me too. Okay, so me landlord's coming round in a bit – or so he says. They're doing something to the alarms. Spiders keep setting them off. So once he's gone we can go out, yeah?'

I made myself smile. 'Yeah.' Behind her, tucked in a corner, I saw Lulu's backpack waiting for me.

The steam filled the room and curled upwards towards the light. I stood watching, feeling the spray from the shower catch my face, and wished I could follow it. After a minute, which seemed to go on for days, I stepped over the edge of the bath and pulled the curtain shut behind me as I let the water rain down.

It was over. I had no place to go and no place to belong. All the dreams I had were gone away. I felt as if there was an end coming, as if I was standing on the beach watching all the footprints be washed away, waiting to walk into the water and walk and walk until the waves closed over my head.

What's the point in living? Beauty is like a tiny golden butterfly, always flickering just out of reach. If you catch it in your fist and trap it to you, it's crushed. Everywhere you look there is sadness disguised as happiness, or happiness waiting to be sadness, and it made me so tired. All I wanted was to be with him, for everyday to be sunny parks and doodled shoulders, always to see the world through heart-shaped sunglasses and always to have his laughter in my ear. And everything was nothing without that.

I didn't know where I could run. I didn't know how it would ever stop. I looked down and I saw the silver blades of a razor gleaming back at me.

I could never have done it. Perhaps I cared too deeply about Stevie to leave such a smudge on her clean life. Perhaps I was just too afraid, when it came down to it, too weak.

The landlord left just as the sun had reached its highest point and was beginning slowly to sink down towards the opposite terrace far below. I heard him speaking to Stevie and then I heard the front door shut. I went downstairs and tried to hold my face in its place. When I opened the door to the living room, Stevie was putting a folder into her bag. Her coat was on.

'All right, bird? Sorry about that. He likes to natter on.'

'It's okay.' I pulled my jumper round me and sat down. 'Are you going out?'

'Yeah, got to drop an essay at uni. You wanna come? Then we can go straight down the docks and you can get snapping. Or I can just come and pick you up on the way back. Up to you.'

'Just charging your camera. Okay to get me on the way back?'

She zipped up her bag and hung it on the crook of her arm while she fiddled with her hair in the mirror. 'Course it is. Won't be long. Put something warm on, gets nippy down there, even in the sun.'

As she left, I felt as if something very important was leaving with her. I had to stop myself calling out after her. But when the door closed behind her, I turned and ran. I ran up the stairs and into the bedroom, and I knew then that I would always be running.

My bag felt empty, even with all of my things stuffed back inside. Everything was empty now. I put the razor in last. There was a blister pack of painkillers on the bedside table. I took those as well and zipped the bag up. I had one last look around at what my life could have been, and then I put the bag over my shoulder and ran down the stairs two at a time. The front door opened in a blaze of bright light. And there he was.

The sun was shining down between the shingle roofs, and the grubby trainers hanging on the wires were dancing in the breeze. The car door was still gaping open as he loped across the road and onto the pavement and up to the gate and it seemed as though it only took him one step to reach me. The car radio was still playing, the engine still running; I looked over to the gang on the corner but even they were standing watching, all of them and their dogs as well, all watching with their heads cocked on one side. He took my hands awkwardly and looked into my eyes. He was trying to say something, his bottom lip moving and Al Green winding down on the stereo. But there were no words left. I looked into his eyes, all framed with fluffy eyelashes and the faint dent from his pound-shop Aviators and suddenly the gate was flung open and my arms were round his neck and we were spinning, spinning round in circles among the cobbles and the dog shit and the chip wrappers.

'It's me and you, Saf,' he whispered in my ear, and it is. It always is.

My feet touched the ground and we stood, my arms still wrapped around his neck, and his tight round my waist. We were laughing, even though nothing was funny, and my eyes were filled with hot and happy tears and my heart was racing against his. Marvin Gaye started to play from the car radio and we started to dance, just like in the kitchen that day, as though nothing had changed and it had all been one horrible dream.

I leant back in his arms and looked up at the sky through the web of wires and washing, antennae and trailing laces and lolling tongues, and for the first time since I'd arrived, there was not a cloud in sight. There was nowhere left to run.

## A LITTLE EPILOGUE

### (BECAUSE ALL ENDS ARE REALLY BEGINNINGS)

We pulled up to the place and I looked at Saffy sat next to me, and I remembered what it was like, looking at that empty seat all the way around the world and back again to get to Liverpool and picturing her sat there, and how that was what had kept me going, and now she was going to be gone again and I was going to let her be gone, and then I wanted to turn the car around and keep driving and driving for ever. And it already seemed like her actually really officially being sat next to me was a dream, even though it wasn't, and if I wanted to I could reach out and touch her, which I actually did then, as I parked the car, just reached out and touched some of the blonde hair that was lying on her shoulders with their freckles, and it felt soft and magic, like angel hair lying on clouds. I turned off the engine and we both sat quietly and watched the double doors opening and closing with a little *sssh* as people went in and nurses came out and stood outside and smoked cigs. Over in the corner a girl was being bundled out of a car by two big blokes in girly pink uniforms and she was trying to bite them and all her hair was in her face and her little parents were following along behind looking around a bit embarrassed to see who was watching.

I could feel Saffy breathing next to me in slow, calm breaths, so quiet you wouldn't hear them if you weren't me, but I heard every sound she made and saw everything she did because when Saffy was around she was everything, she was the whole world.

257

I reached out and touched her again just to know she was real, and then I said, 'You okay? You sure you want to do this? You don't have to, Saf, I won't make you, we can go home and be just the two of us and I'll look after you I'll keep you safe I promise.' I was touching her shoulder, touching each of her freckles one by one to make sure they were all there and that I would remember exactly where each one lived, and she laid her cheek against my hand and we could both feel my fingers shaking against her lovely soft skin.

'Yes,' she said, looking at the double doors through the windscreen. 'I'm sure.' She turned her head for a second so that her face was resting on my hand and closed her eyes, and her lovely long lashes kissed my fingers just once, and then she sat up and unclipped her seat belt. 'I want to do this,' she said. 'I'm going to do it for you.' And she looked at me with her eyes dry, even though mine were all shiny and blurry, and then she opened the door and got out of the car. She stood outside for a second with the door open and I could just see her little legs and her tiny waist in the open space and then she leant back down and kissed her fingers and reached in and pressed them against my face. 'Thank you,' she said. 'For coming to find me.' And then she shut the door and she walked across the car park and into the building without looking back and the doors slid shut behind her *sssh*.

## THANKS AND LOVE TO:

Lisa Baker, who was my very first reader and whose unwavering belief in the story carried it all the way through. Jo Unwin, genuinely the best agent ever, whose unfailing ability to make you feel enthusiastic about 'one more draft' should be bottled and sold in shops. Clare Reihill, who really, truly just 'got it' right from the start. The dream team: Claire Lewzey, Hilary Fawcett, Hayley Richardson and Sasia Lee, who I'd be lost without. Archana Rao, the consummate flatmate, for her wisdom, wine and company. Lee Brackstone, who has seen the book change in a hundred different ways, but who never lost sight of the story at its heart. And to everyone else who has offered support, advice or alcohol along the way: Ian Ellard, Lizzie Bishop, Emma Jamison, David Sanger, Jason Cooper, Richard Milward, Jenny Forrest, Liz Woabank, Jonny Bradford, Sam Richards and Katie Lee. And lastly, to my lovely family whom I love to bits – thank you.